Memoirs of a Dipper

In which . . . you get to learn shitloads
about me and I learn fuck all about you.
It's a memoir. It ain't a youmoir.

NELL LEYSHON

FIG TREE
an imprint of
PENGUIN BOOKS

For Gary, whose life this ain't.

FIG TREE

UK | USA | Canada | Ireland | Australia
India | New Zealand | South Africa

Fig Tree is part of the Penguin Random House group of companies
whose addresses can be found at global.penguinrandomhouse.com.

Penguin
Random House
UK

First published 2015
001

Copyright © Nell Leyshon, 2015

The moral right of the author has been asserted

All characters in this publication are fictitious and any resemblance
to real persons, living or dead, is a load of old bollocks.

Set in 13.5/16 pt Dante MT Std
Typeset by Jouve (UK), Milton Keynes
Printed in Great Britain by Clays Ltd, St Ives plc

A CIP catalogue record for this book is available from the British Library

ISBN: 978-0-241-18424-0

Me Then

All right, roll up, roll up. Come in this way, that's it. Take your seat. Pick up your book. You all right? Sitting comfortably? Good. So let's begin the Gary show.

We got a lot to get through, a lot of evidence, you could say, to sift. But I don't wanna just start with the beginning cos it'll take too long to get to know me. Let's start with a scene from the scum years, then you can get a taste of how I was once upon a time.

It's 1988, autumn. It's late evening, dark, in Camden, North London.

I'm out in the street in the pissing rain. But this ain't normal rain; this is rain what's hammering down hard enough to dilute your blood. There's cars going by and taxis with their yellow lights on. Buses with misted-up windows what the passengers have tried to clear, leaving dripping smears. Traffic lights go red, green, amber, red again. A car drives through a puddle by the kerbside where the drain's blocked with dead leaves. The water splashes up but it don't get me cos I dodge it. The truth is, nothing ever gets me.

I push open the double doors of a pub. It's all dark wood and frosted-glass windows. It's all beer stink and thick fugged air of fags. I take in a deep breath, let it out. This, I think, is my London. And my London, I think, is my playground.

I go straight to the bar, swap a few words with the barman: yeah mate it's a filthy old night all right, and yeah a drink's needed cos it's the only thing can cure a night like this and yeah may as well make it a pint. He hands the drink over: it's quivering at the rim, about to spill. I down half in one go. There's a couple next to me and I'm watching them though they'd never know it. They ain't in the first flush of youth, and I'm reckoning they're having a bit on the side cos of the way they are with each other. They ain't got no interest in anyone else. The world could be a burning ball and they wouldn't know it. The sea could come up the Thames and wash through the bar and they wouldn't know it.

I take off my jacket, put it over my arm. I stand for a bit, turn my pint glass on the beer mat, line it up perfect. I look into the distance, dreaming. I'm the worker nipping in for a pint, winding down, standing at the bar. Nothing more than that. Then, after a few minutes, I move towards them a fraction, relax my arm a bit and my jacket slips, falls down to the floor, right on to her handbag. I leave it there. They don't see nothing. I wait. No one else in the pub sees nothing. It's all unfolded at normal pace; my movements are designed to fit in and not to alert anyone to the unexpected; nothing's happened to make the hairs on our bodies stand. I lift my pint, drink the rest of it. Then I put the glass down, make sure it clunks on the wooden bar. Make sure it makes a statement. This is what it says: I, Gary, have come in from the rain to shelter. I have had a pint which I've drunk and now it's my intention to depart.

I bend down, gather my jacket (what a clumsy git am I for dropping it) and lift it up. I look towards the main pub door, see the curtain of rain falling, then look back at the toilets. I turn, go to them. It ain't far: a few steps across a crowded room. I check there ain't no one else in there, go into the only cubicle. I lock the door behind me, and unfold my coat. Pull out the woman's handbag.

It's red leather, good quality (the more expensive the outside, the better the contents). I unbuckle it, lift the flap. There's two compartments inside. In one there's a purse which I take out and unzip. I remove the folded money and the plastic cards, and slip it all in my pocket. I don't take the coins. In the other compartment there's a small make-up bag. Inside: a mirror, comb, lipstick, pencil. And under them a plastic bag. The top of it's tied and I open it up. Inside: white powder. I stick my finger in, rub it on my gums. Feel the hit. I take some out, chop it on the cistern with one of the credit cards, roll up one of the tenners, snort it up this nostril, that nostril. I feel it rush in my blood and I have to put my hand out to touch the toilet wall. Steady, lad. Steady. I feel it all through me. I close my eyes, and behind the lids there's a vision. It's me at the bar, leaning down slightly so the weight of the jacket slips down my arm, glides on to the handbag. I think of the way I waited, the way I knew not to move for a bit, the way I stayed cool, calm, collected, then the way I bent down and gathered up the fabric, felt the mass of the handbag in it. I think of the way I knew what I was doing. And that cos I knew what I was doing, no one else in the whole pub knew what I was doing.

And it occurs to me, Christ, this ain't no common or garden thieving. It's more complicated than that. I mean there's a lot involved here. There's the human self – the chatting shit to the barman, the knowing how to settle people, make them at ease. And then there's the deeper self, the animal self – the knowing everything that's happening in a room, the opening of yourself to knowing what people are thinking, what they're doing. To see things others don't. And to do that you got to get your instinct back and that ain't something we use much. Without it we're nothing. And then once you got it back you got to hone it. You got to tune in. You got to extend your vision. You got to think of a falcon. She don't swivel her head to see a sparrow fly by. She *knows* it's there.

And then as I'm sat there on the toilet, it occurs to me it ain't something just any bastard can do. This is something extraordinary. In fact, it's a bit like a ballet. It's a bit like theatre.

You know what it is? It's a fucking art form.

I shove the half-empty bag of magic dust in my pocket and ram the red leather handbag behind the cistern, put my coat on and unlock the cubicle. I catch sight of myself in the mirror. Wink. You done well, son. You done well.

Back out in the bar the woman's standing by a table, looking around. The boyfriend has his hand on her back, comforting her. The barman's checking under another table. I go over to them.

– You all right? I ask.

The woman don't even look up at me. – I lost my bag, she goes.

– Let me help you, I go.

And that's what I do. I help. Join in the goose chase. I look all along the bar, by the stools they was sat on. I look around by the doors to the toilets. I look under chairs and I even kneel down and look under tables, get my trousers dirty. I'm that helpful. That considerate.

I can't find nothing. I stand up, brush myself off. – Someone must have taken it, I go.

The woman starts to cry. – My money, she goes.

– I know, I say.

– All my stuff.

– I know, I say. – There's bastards out there. They're low life. Scum.

– I'll kill him, the boyfriend goes.

I shake my head solemnly. – He'll be well gone from here by now. You know what they're like. Grab and run. Grab and bloody run.

The woman nods. – What am I gonna do?

I put my hand on her arm. – Tell you what, let me buy you both a drink, I go. – Make up for it.

5

And I pull out from my back pocket the note I used to snort the magic dust up my nostrils into my brain. I hand it over to the barman and tell him to get out a bottle of their best fizzing liquid. Tell him to have one for his self and all. He takes the cork out, pours for us all. The woman raises her glass to me.

– Thanks to you, she says, – my faith in humanity is restored.

And she tips up her glass, drinks the bubbles what was paid for with her own sweet money.

Me Now

So that was me then, but listen, I ain't that same person now. See, I've changed.

No, honest I have.

People can change. They change all the time. We all do. But I ain't talking about the changes in what jobs we got, families we got, where we live. The changes I'm on about are way deeper than that. They go to the core of us. Cos the thing is, you're changing right now as you're reading this. I'm changing as you're reading this. Every cell in your body is gonna die and grow again. Every cell'll be replaced by another cell what's crept a few inches further towards the old grim reaper. In a few years every bit of you sat there now will be gone. Every bit of your skin will have floated off you on to the floor, and be swept up in a corner with the household dust. Your kidneys will have bled their cells into your piss. Your lungs will have breathed out their cells into the fetid air. And your brain: all them cauliflower curls will shrink back like it's winter then bloom again like it's spring. And your heart? Ha, the heart. The old blood pumper, the flutterer, the love maker. The cells of the ventricles and the chambers, they'll all dry up and weep heartbreak. It ain't no wonder love's so hard to keep hold of when your heart's in flux.

So yeah, in seven years there'll be a whole new you. A whole new me. We're changing all the time and if you ask me it's a miracle we even know who we are.

So no, I ain't the same person. I'm a different Gary now. New cells, new me. And with that a whole new life.

And to prove it I'll give you a glimpse, a peek, of what I am now. Not then. Now.

We ain't in Camden no more. We're in England-by-the-sea, my new adopted home town. I'm living on the clifftop in what was once an eight-bed hotel and is now flats. The hall carpets've got more swirls than a row of Catherine wheels on bonfire night. My flat's ground floor, doors into the garden. The only noise at night is from the foxes tipping over bins. This is an easy place to live. This is the graveyard of ambition.

It's early morning and the sun forces its way through the curtains and hits my face, wakes me before the alarm. I'm a light-bulb head nowadays; it's on or off. There ain't no in-between states and I'm up and standing before my eyelids are fully open. It's pull on clothes, empty the bladder, have a quick breakfast, then I'm out in the street, walking towards the yard.

The lorry's loaded up and I check I ain't forgot nothing. Scaffold tubes, boards, clasps, swivels. All there. I climb in, start the engine and leave the yard. I drive to the clifftop, pull over in the lay-by, stop the engine.

I move over into the passenger seat. The fresh air comes in and I breathe deeply, suck it down into every nook and cranny of the lungs. I light a fag and breathe that in. The smoke rises up in curled tongues. The sun's out and shines into the cab. I roll up my shirt-sleeves, enjoy the moment of sitting there, listen to the in and out of the tide. I see the tax disc on the lorry and it hits me, this new life I got. It's a bloody tax disc what I queued for in the post office. What I *paid for*.

And it's then I see him out the front windscreen. He's walking along the clifftop towards me and he lifts his hand as he sees the lorry; it ain't a wave, more of an *I know you're there*. He comes closer, walks towards the passenger seat. When he sees me sat in there instead of in the driver's, he stops, confused. I can see the look in his eyes, the slack of his bottom jaw, where he's working it out. I point at the empty driver's seat and he looks at it, looks back at me. The penny drops and his face changes. The slack muscles tighten into a grin. He walks round to the driver's door, climbs up in.

He don't say nothing and nor do I. He parks his arse, settles in, then reaches for the belt, puts it on.

He fiddles with the gearstick, checks it's in neutral. Puts the key in the ignition and turns it. The engine fires. He nods, grins to his self. I grin and all. It ain't every day someone's eighteen. Happy birthday, son, I say.

That's when he turns to look at me and I look at

9

him, and all I can think is it's like looking at myself. He's got the same thick near-black hair. The same eyes, the blue the colour of the ink of a freshly printed fiver.

I feel my heart swell up. My eyes fill with water.

I'm a soft fucker.

He's a chip off the old block. An apple from the same tree. A fish what swims the same sea. A fox from the same lair. A bird with the same feathers. A pea from the same pod. He's a son from the father.

A Nuclear Family

So this is a memoir, ain't it, and now we got to go back to the beginning to understand. Cos you ain't born into nothing in this world. You're born into something which is already there which has got its own rules. It's like you're born into a metal cage what's gonna form you as you grow, gonna change the shape of your body, gonna make you the person you later are.

You're born into a family.

If I close my eyes I can smell burnt toast and a bit of mould from the rubber round the kitchen taps. I can still feel the woodchip wallpaper rough under my fingers. Can still hear the lawnmower outside (not ours as we ain't exactly the family to cut grass), the passing cars, the screw top of a bottle being undone and the yap yap yap of the telly. I can taste the sugary tea what's creamy with the top of the milk. And if I close my eyes it's like it's all more real than this room I'm in now. It's like I got it all inside me waiting, laid down. If I close my eyes it's like there ain't no such thing as past and present. It's one of the miracles of being human, that we can be in two places and times at once. I can be me then. I can be me now.

I'm standing in the doorway of the lounge. I'm standing, looking. My brother Alan's on his dirty scabbed knees, pushing a tin can, making engine noises. Baby Sharon's in her pram in the hallway spinning plastic birds what are stretched out on an elastic in front of her.

And Mum? She's on the settee watching telly: she can't keep her eyes off it. In front of her, on the screen, there's a black-and-white man talking to a black-and-white woman. The man drops to his knees; he opens a box and a diamond ring glints. The woman gasps and a tear rolls down her cheek. He pulls the ring out of its velvet slit and takes her left hand in his and he shoves it over her knuckle.

Mum unwinds bog paper, dabs it to her eyes then chucks it on the floor. She lifts up her glass of sherry, puts it to her lips, takes a long drink. She sighs, loud enough to lift the ceiling.

In her head she's stepped right through the telly's glass screen. She's inside it. It's her kissing the man. It's her with the ring on her finger.

From where she's sat on the settee, from where her head's gone, she don't have a clue what's going on in the real world around her. She can't hear Baby Sharon who's started crying. She don't see Alan on the floor, looking up at her, telling her he's hungry. She don't see me in the doorway where I'm stood watching everything. Everything.

– Mum, I say.

She sighs again, her whole chest moving near enough to crack a rib.

– *Mum?*

She turns. Her eyes see me but they don't. She blinks, slow, like there's curtains over her eyes and she's trying to draw them aside. She shakes her head, looks harder. She stares at this kid what's standing there: short near-black hair sticking straight up, blue shorts he's been wearing all summer. Food on his face. And them blue eyes. She looks around the room. There's another kid on the floor, pushing a tin along, making noises. And another in the hallway; she can see plastic birds spinning on their elastic, like they're trying to fly off but their feet are caught up. She looks at us all like she ain't never seen these small people before and she don't know what it is we're doing in her house.

She blinks again, even slower, looks back at the telly. The man and woman are mouth to mouth. French kissing. Ahh, she thinks, French kissing.

– *Mum.*

I say it loud enough to cut through but she don't look at me, don't spin round with clear eyes. No. She stays looking at the telly and pats the empty spot on the settee; anything to shut me up so she can watch the end of the black-and-white story behind the glass screen. I go over, climb next to her. Pull my legs up and lean on her. Her skin's warm.

She lifts her glass to her mouth and I can smell the sharp caramel of the sherry.

Behind her, on the side table at the end of the settee, I can see the only photo what exists of her big day. Mum's in tight black trousers, short on the leg. Her black jumper's tucked in and there's a black band round her dark brown hair, eyeliner on her lids. She's got lashes bigger than any woman's ever been born with. The Old Man's got black hair, cropped short, and he's wearing turned-up jeans, cherry red Docs, a black jacket with tartan lining. She's looking up at him. He's looking at the floor, half-smoked fag in hand.

When you look close you see her belly sticks out and if you had an X-ray machine what could see into photos, you'd see me deep inside there, all curled up. A little picture of unborn innocence about to be propelled out into the world.

The words come up on the telly screen: THE END. Mum wipes her eyes again. Chucks the bog paper down. She finishes her sherry.

– Mum? I go.

– I'm watching the titles, she goes.

I watch the words go up and up till they're gone off the telly screen. When they're done I try again.

– Mum, I go, – where's Dad?

She stands, spins the channel dial, and the screen's full of crackle. She keeps going till she's found a new channel, another story she can dream her way into, and she settles back down.

I try again. – Where is he?

The music starts. The titles begin. The drama is under way.

She pats my leg. – You ask too many questions, Gary. If you keep on like that, one day you'll get answers you don't wanna hear.

Growing Pains

It's always summer when you're a kid. It ought to be called summerhood not childhood. Every day's hot. No rain never falls. There ain't no one to tell you what to do and every day's double the length. As the weeks pass, you get lines on your arms where your T-shirts stop. You get grime build-up round your ankles where you been in the dust.

It's late August and they're saying it's gonna break by the end of the day. It'll rain, they say. Thunder'll clap over us and lightning'll strike. They're talking bollocks.

It's morning. Early and the sun's up before me. I leap out of bed cos I'm a light-bulb head and there ain't no in-between, just on or off. I leave Alan in the bottom bunk to dribble into his pillow and I take my clothes outside, get dressed on the landing.

Downstairs I take a piece of bread, stick some jam on it. Slap another slice on top. I reach up, drink water straight out the kitchen tap. Then I'm gone.

Out the back of the estate is the wasteland. I'm the first out there and go straight for the big concrete pipe. I climb inside and prop my feet up on the opposite wall, watch through the circle at the end;

as the sun rises I shift myself till it's right in the middle.

I'm sat there for a bit. The concrete's cold on my back but it ain't gonna stay like it cos as the sun gets higher it'll heat up.

And then as I'm sat there I get these feelings. I get this lifting of every hair on my arm, up my spine. The air changes. It's like it's got a charge in it. I'm still, coiled. My heart slows in my chest. There ain't a part of me that moves.

There's someone out there. I can't tell you how I know but I just know. And I know who it is.

– You're dead, I call out.

And even though I can't see him from where I am, I know what happens. He sags with disappointment, and his belly slumps to the ground. The wooden gun falls out his fingers.

It's happened again.

Ginger gets to his feet and comes round and when he bends down I see the look on his face.

– I'll get you one day, he goes.

But he won't. He ain't never gonna come close to getting me. No one does and there's a reason for that. See, I ain't a normal kid. I never have been. I always had something others ain't got. I know what's going on: I read people. I watch their faces and from that I know what's going on inside their heads. And I can work out other stuff cos I hear things other people don't. Like a dog hears a special whistle, I hear sounds others don't even know are being made. I can hear the twist and crack of a dead leaf breaking from the stem and falling to the ground. If a foot stands on a piece of grass, I hear the blades fold and crumple. I can hear an eye open, the rustle of the lashes and the pleating of the flesh on the lid.

I know stuff others don't and it's just how I am.

I am an animal.

Skinny arrives after us and squeezes in the pipe. His hand's clutching a metal cap gun and some new strips of dotted red bullet paper what he's nicked off a kid from the other side of the estate. He holds the gun up, pulls the trigger. There's a bang and a stink. It sounds loud enough to make ears bleed. It's time to fight.

We run over the mounds of earth and jump from wall to wall. My heart's going, battering away. Skinny's breathless; his stomachs wobble as he runs. Then I hear Alan's voice calling for me. – Gary. Gary.

I hide behind a mound of earth, watch him running around looking for me. He moves like a penguin. His fat legs flap flap. I rest my fingers, aim at his head, imagine it snap backwards and break into pieces like a rotted apple.

Alan starts to cry and I know it's cos he's been told if he don't find me and bring me back, he'll get a clip. Skinny runs past and shoulders him over.

– They're coming, Skinny shouts. – Duck, quick, they got the planes out.

Alan staggers to his feet, calls out for me. – Gary.

I weigh it up. The longer I leave it, the more he's in trouble for not finding me. But if I leave it too long, it'll be me what gets the belting. He's about to turn back for home and I run out, stand up on the mound. – *Alan*, I go, like I'm angry with him. – Where you been? I been looking for you everywhere.

He rubs his eyes, confused again. – It's been me looking for you.

I clip him round the ear. – You wasn't looking hard enough.

Mum's in the kitchen. She's standing over Sharon who's lying on the floor, on a flattened cardboard box. Mum ain't been near the black trousers and eyeliner for a bit now. Her hair's scraped back and there's bites on her ankles. Her ring finger's got a pale band of skin on it where the ring's sat in the pawn shop, and there's only two days left on the ticket before it's gonna be melted down.

She kneels down with Baby Sharon. I know what she's thinking from how she's looking. She's lost. I don't mean she don't know where the kitchen is. I'm talking about how she ain't got no films running through her head for what's in front of her now. She don't know this story she's stuck in: she don't know how it ends, or even if there is an ending.

She looks up. – Where you been? she says to me.

– Ain't been nowhere, I go.

– I sent Alan for you.

– He never come.

Before Alan can open his sloppy lips to speak, her hand comes out and he gets it hard. She turns to me. But I can see a thought written on someone's face before they even know they got it. I back away quick and duck. Her hand meets air and I laugh.

– Come here, she shouts.

But I'm gone. Straight up the stairs (two at a time till the top when I jump three) and into my room. I slam the door shut and climb up my watchtower. I hear her feet race up the stairs and I aim my arrows at the door. Close one eye.

The door opens. In she comes. I fire but she don't go down. Fire again. Bloody die. Fire. Draw. Fire.

– Gary, you little shit, get down.

But I don't. She starts up the ladder and I fire again. Hear the arrow cut clean through the air. – Die, I go.

– You ain't funny, she goes.

I stop. Put the arrows down, lay the bow on the bed. I grin at her. – You know I am funny, I go.

And that's when I see her turn her head away to hide the smile. But she can't hide nothing from me. – See, I go, – you find it funny.

– I don't.

– You're laughing.

And she is. – You little bastard.

She grabs my arm. I kick out but her grip's tight. She pulls me hard and I crash into her; we fall to the floor in a laughing ball of arms and legs, like we're a cartoon pair. We lie there, our stomachs up and down with laughter. Then she stops, rolls over, sees the book what fell down with us. Picks it up. – What's this?

– They give me it at school before we broke up.

She flips through the pages. – What for?

– What you reckon? I go. – To hang on the wall?

She hits me over the head with it, chucks it into the corner of the room. – Cheeky little sod.

Downstairs, the kitchen stinks. Sharon's had a shit on the cardboard and she's wiped her hand in it.

I pull my shirt up over my nose while Mum cleans up. I'm sat on the stool watching and she turns and stares at me. – Bloody sit still. Stop that bloody jiggling.

It's then I see my leg's tapping away, banging against the leg of the stool. My other foot's going and my fingers are drumming on my lap.

– There's somethink wrong with you, Gary, she goes.

– Ain't nothing wrong with me, I go.

– Then stop it.

– I can't.

– You got too much energy.

And she's right. It's like it runs through me, starts in the legs. I get this popping coming up from the ankles, travelling up the bones. It's like the light-bulb head. It ain't gonna stop. And the whole of me's like it. It feels like if I don't move something's gonna break out through my skin. Something's gonna come out of me. It's always been like that. I spec when I was inside her belly in that photo, I was spinning round.

She's still staring at me. – No wonder, she says, – you're always in trouble at school.

I pick up the sandwich she's made me. White bread, margarine, sugar. – The teachers say they wanna talk to you when I go back, I go.

She sighs. – Oh Jesus. What you done now?

– They want me to do some extra work cos I can do it easy. That book they sent home. They want me to read it with you.

She lights a fag. – Oh do they?

I nod. – They do, yeah.

She shakes out the match and chucks it on the floor, blows smoke out. – All that money they get, she goes, – all them holidays. And they're asking me to do their job. Tell them to do it themselves. I ain't doing it for them.

She picks up Sharon, jams her into her hip. Carries her out.

We spend the whole afternoon on the wasteland and it still don't rain. See, I said they was talking bollocks; I'd've known anyway, wouldn't I, if it was gonna rain cos I'd have heard the drops gathering. We stay out till the light starts to go and my belly says I got to eat. I go home the long way round, through the yellow grass, back along the estate. People are still sat outside their front doors. Kids still swarm in the street.

I can see Mum standing in our front doorway. She's got a fag going and she's looking up at the sky. As I get close I see her skin's gold red from the light of the late sun. I know from the look of her, from how she stands, what mood she's in. I know she ain't seeing nothing of what's in front of her. The inside of her head's full of old dreams, scraps of stories and memories. It's full of the shadows of what she thought she was gonna get in her life.

I walk up to her. She don't say nothing. I stand by her and then, her head still tipped up to the sun, she slumps down to sit on the step. I sit down as well and we watch the sun as it sinks.

We're both painted gold. Neither of us speaks for a bit then, – Where you been? she asks.

– Here and there.

And she turns and looks at me. Smiles. – Nothing worse, she goes, – than a bleeding adult asking where you been, specially on a day like this.

She puts her hand out and I'm surprised, I am, when she touches my leg. – Look at that, she goes.

She's pointing at the scab on my knee, yellow with pus, crisscrossed with filth. The edges are crisping and I reach out to slip my nail under and pick it. She slaps me. – You'll make it worse.

So I stop. She puts out her fag. Gets another out. Plays with it, don't light it.

– Sharon in bed? I ask.

– Yep.

– Alan?

– He was tired.

– He's always tired.

– Don't be hard on him.

– Someone has to be, I go.

The sun's slipped behind the trees. She watches a cloud as it changes shape, and she wishes she could change shape, change anything and everything around her. I watch it too as it moves from cotton wool to an animal to a country then finally settles down into a line of pink. The sun's gone and the line of pink goes grey then black. Everyone's gone inside. The air's changed. Cooler.

– You going on in? I ask.

– Hmmm?

– Mum, I go. – You got to go in.

– Yeah.

I touch her shoulder to wake her out of it. – It's late, you got to get some sleep.

And then she looks at me and laughs.

– Fine thing, ain't it? she goes. – When your own son's telling you to go to bed.

But she still don't move. I look at her. If I could I'd climb over the trees, drag the sun back up in the sky. Anything for this evening not to end.

Next day it does rain. Heavy, wet. I hide in the concrete pipe till it stops. The ground stinks of wet dust and grass seeds and I run home, climb over the broken fence, go up the path. Back door's open and I go through the kitchen, into the hallway.

The front door's open and Mum's outside, looking up the road. I run out, see what she's watching.

And that's when I see him.

Rolled-up jeans, fag in his mouth, bag slung across the shoulder. He's got the lag's walk, the fresh-out-of-nick walk. It's like if a walk could speak, it'd say this: I don't step aside for no one. It'd say this: Don't mess with me cos you only got one life and you'll shorten it if you do.

He reaches Mum, kisses her. She's weak in his arms; any backbone she had dissolves inside her. Then he senses me watching. Breaks off, turns round. He clips me round the head.

– What's that for? I go.

– Breathing.

And he's gone into the house, pulling Mum along with him. By the time I follow they're halfway up the stairs and he looks back, tells me to stay where I am.

Alan comes in and asks where they're gone. He wants to see his dad, he says. I tell him he can't and he starts to cry. I watch him and wonder: If I pinched him hard enough, would he bleed?

Dad comes down later, sends me for some cans of beer. I bring them back from the shop, put the change on the table. I open a beer, and the fizz comes out the gash. I take it in the lounge where he's on the settee watching telly. He don't look at me, just puts his hand out for it. He drinks, swallows, lights up. Alan's next to him. Alan's on the settee with him.

I'm standing there, not moving.

– What you doing? he goes.

– Nothing.

He flicks his hand at me. – Piss off then.

I go back in the kitchen. Mum's sat at the table. Sharon's grizzling. Mum scoops out a spoon of sugar, gives it to her to shut her up.

I go to the back door what's stood open. A wind's picked up and the broken fence panel's blowing. The back wheel of a bike's spinning. I kick the door.

– What is it?

– Nuffink, I snap.

She stares at me. – What's wrong?

And then she looks towards the lounge, looks back at me. And it ain't like her but she has this moment when she works out what's going on. When she knows. Her eyes contract. She moves her head; it ain't a nod but an acknowledgement. An understanding. I turn back, look out at the garden. At the broken push-chair, the old chest freezer.

– Thing is, Gary, she says, – you remind him of himself.

I turn back to look at her. – It ain't my fault.

She shrugs. – I know. He says you're trouble.

– He don't know what I am, I go. – He ain't even been here.

– He says you're just like he was.

– Then maybe it's cos I'm his son.

She looks at me. – Sometimes you're too smart for your own good.

– I know I am, I go. – And I wish I weren't. I wish I was thick.

And then I feel this prickling in my eyes, feel myself start to lose it. I walk out quick and on my way I pass the kitchen table and shove the money all over the floor. She shouts but I carry on, out the door, up the stairs to my room. I shut myself in, get a hold of myself, but then I hear her calling me back down. I go out, hang over the banisters. – What?

– Come here.

– No.

– I said come here.

I drag my feet down the stairs. Go in the kitchen. She shows me the money in her fist. – How much change you bring back?

I tell her: The beers cost this. You give me this. That's how much there was left.

– There's a quid missing, she says.

– Ain't nothing to do with me, I go.

– Where is it? Empty your pockets.

I shake my head.

– You gonna tell me? she goes. – Or am I gonna tell him?

She nods towards the lounge where he's there with the rubbery-lipped snitch. – Well, Gary, she shouts. – You gonna tell me?

Only she shouts too loud and too sudden and Baby Sharon starts screaming. – Now see what you done, she goes.

– I never done nothing, I go. – It was you shouted.

27

– Where's the money?

– I ain't got it.

She grips my upper arm. Tight. Hard. Stares at me. – Look at me.

So I do. I look straight at her.

– Don't you lie to me, she says.

– I ain't lying, I go. – You know I ain't gonna lie to you.

Our eyes are staring. Pupil to pupil. Neither of us'll drop it.

Her voice starts to fall. Doubt's crept in. – Well, where can it have gone? she goes.

– I don't know, I say. – That ain't got nothing to do with me.

She puts her hand on my head and messes my hair. – No. No. Course not. Why don't you piss off and play, she says.

And so I do.

And while I play I feel down inside my pocket and there, in the deepest corner, is the tightly folded-up one-pound note.

Bless Me, Father

For this bit I need to know how old I was. No, that ain't right. Think again, Gary.

For this bit *I* don't need to know how old I was cos it's my life and it just is the way it is but *you* need to know. I got a few clues: I know I wasn't in secondary school or the last two years of juniors. So it had to be before that. It had to be when I was around eight or nine.

It must be after midnight and I'm in bed. The street light's on and there's a yellow rim round the curtain. I'm lying there in the top bunk. I can touch the ceiling above my head if I stand up even though I ain't tall for my age. I'm small, they say. Everyone says it. When you gonna grow then? they go.

The room's pitch dark apart from that yellow light round the edges of the window. I ought to be asleep, but I ain't. I'm lying as still as if I was in a coffin. The animal inside me knows something's going on. I sense the shifting and settling of air. Hear lungs expand and fall in. Then the click of a toe on the lino.

– Who is it? I ask.

– Get dressed, a voice goes. – Come downstairs.

I pull on my shorts and a T-shirt and go down. He's

waiting by the door and tells me to put on the crêpe-soled shoes. Then he leads me out to a car I ain't seen before. I open my mouth to ask where we're going but he puts his finger to his lips. He fires up the car and drives off.

And that's when it sinks in it's just the two of us. The Old Man and me. Not him and Alan.

I wanna dance in my seat. I wanna run back in the bedroom and stick two fingers up to Alan and dance and sing and tell the little sod what he's missing out on. What I *ain't* missing out on.

But I don't do none of that. I hold my legs still. Don't move. Don't do nothing that'll get under the Old Man's skin and cause him to stop the car and chuck me out.

We drive out to the main road then after a while turn off on to the new trading estate. He kills the lights and we carry on in the dark. At the end he turns the car round and pulls over. He gets out, beckons for me to climb over and get out his side, then shows me how to shut the door without making no noise. He lifts the handle, pushes the door closed, lets the handle go. He opens the boot, takes out a bag and shuts the boot the same way. Silent. He walks off, and I follow: the two of us creeping in our crêpe-soled shoes. We turn into a gate, go down a path to a building.

We stand at the front door for a bit. Listen out. There's traffic in the distance. And there's rustling in the hedge. It stops. The quiet comes down on us.

He gets closer to me, points up at the dark sky, the

thin white crescent. He whispers in my ear. – The moon's your enemy.

And then he crouches down and moves along the wall of the building. I copy. We go right round the back, and my heart's jumping behind my ribs. Everything else I ever done in my life has disappeared and it's like the whole world has become the point of a pin. There's only this moment. Here. Now. At the back door he grabs me, puts his finger to my mouth to tell me not to say nothing. But he don't need to cos I know what I'm doing. I know what this is.

He reaches into his bag and gets out gloves and a piece of bent metal. Puts it in the lock, takes out another tool. Puts pressure on and the door gives. We step over the threshold and he pushes the door shut and the already dark night gets darker still.

The torchlight circle ain't very big and he keeps it tipped down. I follow close to him. We're in a corridor. There's an open door on our right and he flashes the light in. There's machines in a row, all asleep, all silent. He opens the next door and it's a toilet. Closes it. The next one is locked. We stop, listen. All I can hear is my heart and his heart and our breathing. He gets his tool out and forces it open.

The torch looks in first and sees a big desk and a chair with a leather back. The office. We go in and the torch looks around the walls, sees the files on the shelves, the painting above the desk. It carries on round and settles on the safe in the corner.

The safe stands taller than us. The Old Man shines

31

the torch at the keyhole and I wait for him to get his tool out and make a start but he don't. He knows no tool he's got'll touch this.

He goes over to the desk, feels around all the papers, pats his hands on them. He goes round the other side and opens the drawers underneath. Pulls out some packages and rips them open, checks them with the torch. Throws it all across the room. He chucks papers everywhere. He's unstoppable.

– Where is it? he goes.

– What? I ask.

– The key. What you reckon I'm looking for, you idiot?

He moves to the shelves. Pulls files off. Looks behind.

I watch, listen to the racket of it all landing on the floor. It's time to move. Time to do something. I feel my way to the desk and go round it. Sit in the big leather chair. Me, in the big chair. I put my hand out, tap ash off my cigar. Spin the chair. I'm the big man in the big office. And then it hits me. I *am* the big man. I really have become him. I know what he thinks, what he does. I know it all. I look over at the Old Man scrabbling around and searching. And I know. I just know.

I pull the top drawer right out and put it on top of the desk. I put my hand under and feel the two runners it rested on. Run my hand down one runner. Then the other. My fingers bump into something. A lump, taped on. I feel for the edge and pick it, then peel it off. A metal object falls into my hand. I grip it tight.

– Dad, I go. – Look what I got.

I offer it up for the glare of the torch.

– Shut up, he goes. – I told you stay quiet.

And he carries on searching through papers and books. So I stand up, feel my way round the desk, go up to the safe. I feel for the keyhole, put the key in and turn, and though it's stiff and hard, I hear the locks inside the chamber start to slide against each other. And the Old Man hears it too. He stops the frantic hunt, looks round.

– What the hell you doing?

The key turns the final bit as if it's answering his question. The door swings open, the metal hinge creaking, and I hear the air come out the Old Man's lungs. He moves the torch and its beam of light sees the wads of cash and the envelopes all stacked up.

He don't do nothing. Don't say nothing. It's like everything's stopped.

He shakes his self out of it, moves closer, shines the torch right inside. He turns back to me, swinging the light round, putting me in the spotlight. I can't see him and the light is there in both my eyes. He steps closer and I feel his hand on my hair. Feel it rub me, pat me.

– That's my son, he goes.

I grow tall under his hand. I'm his son and he's my father. And this is the first time I can remember him touching me without hitting me.

★

We work together, check all the envelopes for cash. Put any notes in the bag with his tools. Then we leave the office and creep back out to the car. We drive off quick but not quick enough to squeal the tyres. When he hits the main road he puts the lights on and we drive back towards home.

He don't say nothing for a bit, then puts his hand in his pocket, passes me some notes.

I feel them in my hand. I can smell them. The used paper, the ink. My own money, earned by me.

He stops outside the house, but we don't get out the car. We sit there then he turns and looks at me.

– How did you know? he asks. – How the hell d'you know where it was?

But I don't know how to answer. See, the thing is, I just knew.

Dog Days

I caught myself doing something the other day what shocked me to the centre of my bones, and as you'll know by now, being shocked by my own self ain't my normal state.

It went like this: I'm walking along the High Street with my son, breathing in the fresh sea air, thinking how the bloody hell did we end up living here by the sea, health intact, all well with the world, when the dog – a dark brown mongrel from the dog rescue prison, thin, too much energy, even I know how like his owner he is – pulls on his lead to the left, takes us in the pet shop where he's spotted the pigs' ears. And I buy him a special dog ball and we take him and his new ball down the beach. We spend a merry hour chucking the ball what's covered in stinking spit, watching him run for it, in and out the waves. Me and my son, watching him.

I know, I know. It don't seem a shocking thing to you but believe me, for me it is. It's so bloody normal. It's like dull ordinary life. It's like a dull miracle.

Where were we? Oh yeah, I know. The Old Man's got a new hobby, an interest in life. He's taken to fiddling with motors. He lifts the bonnet and the hours disappear. There's engine bits in the lounge and Mum says they're in the way and they make everything filthy. The Old Man says what you reckon carpets are for if they ain't there to soak up oil.

I've got my arm in plaster cos I broke it jumping out my window. Day we get back from the hospital, there's no point in going to school cos it's dinner time and the day's nearly done. I go out to the wasteland and hang around. I go to the park and get on a swing. And when I reckon it's time for everyone to be out of school I start back over the grass towards home and it's then I see the puppy. It's black with a white mark on its chest and I pick it up and it licks my face and hands. There ain't no one about and I can't leave it so I take it back home. When I turn into the street the Old Man's there under the bonnet and I stuff the puppy under my jumper. I'm walking by and he knows something's going on (he knows stuff but not like I know stuff) and he asks me what I'm doing.

– Nothing, I go. Then I lean forward as if I'm peering under the bonnet. – Where you get that car? I ask.

– What are you? he goes. – A frigging cop?

The front door of the house's open and I go straight up the stairs to my room. Alan's lying on the bottom bunk and I tell him to get out. He don't and we fight and my jumper falls open and the package falls out like I give birth to it and it looks up at me then runs around the room.

– Where d'you get that? Alan asks.

– What are you? I go. – A frigging cop?

The pup needs food so I go downstairs to find something. The Old Man's finished with the car and is in the hallway looking in the mirror by the front door. I stop halfway down and watch. He combs his hair with two hands, one hand to shape the hair, the other to comb. He wipes the excess oil from the comb on his jeans, slips it in his pocket. Checks his collar. Brushes off his shoulders. He stares at his image full-on. He's charmed, bowled over.

He opens the front door to leave and Mum comes out the kitchen, Sharon in her arms. – Where you going? she asks.

The Old Man don't answer. He walks out. She follows. I follow them both, get a full view of them in the street. She screams after him. – I said, where you going?

Curtains start to move. Heads turn. It don't put her off: nothing's gonna do that. He opens the car door, puts one foot into the well, keeps one on the road, and he turns to her. Yells. – It ain't nothing to do with you.

– You gonna tell me when you're coming back?

He points his finger at her, jabs with each word. – I ain't got to answer to you.

And he's in the car and the door's slammed and the engine started and he's gone and driven off.

She stands in the road, watches him till she can't see him no more. Her body sags, like she's slipping down inside her own skin. She turns to see me watching her. – What you looking at?

I drop my eyes. – Nothing.

But that ain't the truth.

I'm looking at her, I'm looking at Baby Sharon, at him. I'm looking at everyone and everything. I see too much. Hear too much. Know too much.

She sits on the back doorstep, and I sit down next to her. We look at the broken fence panel, the broken pushchair, the broken bike. The pup squeezes past and goes out into the garden. I know Mum sees him but she don't say nothing. It's like she can't take nothing in.

Sharon calls out from the lounge but Mum don't move. I jump up, go and get her the toy she can't reach. Come back and sit down again. The pup comes running over, jumping the long blades of grass. It bounces right up to Mum so she ain't got no choice but to say something.

– It's a dog, she goes.

– That's right, I go.

– It really is a dog.

I laugh. – You ought to be on telly, I go. – On them quizzes, Mum. You'd make a mint.

And then I jump up and act it out for her. I'm the quizmaster. – And who's this little fella? Furry body, wet nose. Got four legs. Any guesses anyone?

And then I'm Mum. – Could it be a dog?

– The corrrrrecccct answer.

Mum smiles. – I'd love to be on telly.

Her face is dreamy, eyes looking off towards the end of the garden where she can't see no broken fence but a studio, a chair in front of a mirror, a make-up lady with a brush.

I get the question in quick. – Can I keep it?

She snaps back into the world. – Keep it?

I hold him up in her face.

– Poor little bleeder, I go, – he ain't got nowhere to live.

– Very funny. What's his name?

– He ain't got one yet. C'I keep him?

– You know you can't ask me that.

– Cos you can't say no?

She stares at me. – Is that it? Can't I say no?

She takes the pup off me, holds him up in the air. He tries to lick her even though he can't reach, and his tongue curls round the air. Mum looks at the white mark on his chest, rubs it as if it'll come off. – Looks like a flying bird, she goes. – Let's call him Birdy. Lucky bugger, having wings.

That evening I'm upstairs. Alan's in bed turning the pages of a book the school sent me home with. Birdy's asleep at the foot of the top bunk where I put him.

The telly chats downstairs. Sharon sleeps. Then a car turns into the street, I hear the gears change and it pulls up by the house. The engine stops. Car door slams. Then the front door opens and slams shut. I go out on the landing, start down the stairs. Alan ain't far behind.

The Old Man goes into the lounge with Mum and shuts the door behind. We go down the last steps, stand outside. We can hear them through the door. There's one high voice. There's one low voice.

High voice begins: – I know where you been.

– And?

– She's a filthy bitch.

– And you're a nun in a laundry, are you? What you got to offer me? Huh? Look at you.

– I been stuck here looking after your snotty kids.

– They ain't my kids.

– They are. They're as ugly as you.

The sound of a chair falling over, wood on the carpet. A dull thump. A cry.

Then it's the turn of the low voice: – You wind me up. Your fault.

– I only said it to get at you.

We hear feet walk towards the door and we know we've got to run. But we can't move.

– Where you going? the high voice asks. – Don't go. Don't. Don't go. Please.

The door's yanked open. He sees me there and I know what's gonna happen. I know, but I can't move. I'm stuck, pinned against the wall. He gathers his right fist. Pulls his arm back and lets fly. He gets me right in the face and my head bangs back against the plaster. Taste of blood's in my mouth, a pool of it.

Alan's there and the Old Man's seen him but he don't touch him. He goes straight out the front door and leaves it open and we can see him walk down the path and out of sight.

I stand there. Can't move. My head's ringing and there's blood down my T-shirt. I feel it in my mouth. Pool of it.

She comes out the lounge. I know she sees me cos her eyes meet mine. I know she sees me and she knows I know she sees me.

She goes to the front door. She stands there. Sees he's gone, sees there ain't no trace of him.

She sinks down to her knees.

It's later and Mum's on the settee. I'm sat with her. Leaning on her and her leg's warm. Her arm's over me. Sharon and Alan's in bed and it's the two of us and the dog's at our feet.

Under the sound of the telly I hear the car pull up. I hear the car door open and close and we both stiffen. We hear the front door, then the lounge door. He comes in the room and stands in the doorway watching us. I don't look at him. She don't look at him. We stare at the telly, our glass friend.

He sits down on the other chair. Lights up. He offers one to Mum but she don't take it.

The programme ends and the Old Man stands up, switches it off. Mum don't move. I don't move. I know he can see us but he don't mention my swollen lip and he don't mention the mark on her face. Birdy stretches and stands up and becomes the centre of the room, becomes the thing what soaks up all the attention. The Old Man points at him with his fag.

– What's that? he goes.

– A dog, I go.

– Very funny, he goes.

– It's Gary's, Mum says. – And it's staying.

The Old Man thinks a moment then looks over at us and he must see then. He must. The swollen flesh. The bruised purple. He looks away, taps his fag into the ashtray even though there ain't no spare ash yet.

– What's it eat? he asks.

– Grass, Mum goes.

He puts his hand deep into his pocket, draws out some notes. He screws them up and throws them at me. They land in my lap. – Get him some real food. But if he shits in the house I'll wring his neck.

I unwrap the notes, smooth them out on my leg and fold them. I look up at Dad. I grin. – He ain't gonna do that, I say.

And he ain't. He ain't never gonna do that.

Move Along, Now

We meet every day and play tin can. The game is you have to creep up and kick the tin without the guard knowing you're there. Alan cheats. He slips the blindfold up over the bottom of his eye so he can see feet. I don't need to cheat. I can get to anyone and kick it from them before they know I'm there. And when I'm the guard I can hear everyone, know everything that's going on. No one's ever kicked it away from me. No one ever will.

It's me, Skinny, Ginger, Alan. We even let the blond kid with the crusty eyelashes play. Alan's guard and I see him pushing at the blindfold so he can see and I'm about to say when I spot a van coming down the street, a police car following. They park right outside ours. Turn off the engine.

I run and stand on the front path. A big bloke and a thin bloke get out the van.

– Get your dad, sonny, the big bloke goes.

– He ain't here, I go.

The big bloke looks at the thin bloke and grins.
– We know where he is. He'll be in the nick. Nowhere else'd have him.

– He ain't, I go.

Big Bloke laughs. – Course he ain't. Somethink tells

me we shouldn't believe a word you say. You'll be with your dad in prison before long. Won't he?

Thin Bloke laughs. – No doubt.

And then the Old Man comes out the house. He stands by me. Birdy too. The three of us all in a row. – What you want? he says.

– The rent, Thin Bloke says, – ain't been paid since the day you moved in.

– Rent? the Old Man says. – Never knew I had to pay rent.

– Who did you think was gonna pay it, you prat?

The Old Man squares up. – What you call me?

The coppers open the car doors, get out. Watch.

Big Bloke waves a paper. – Sir, we have the weight of the court behind us.

The Old Man laughs. – You can have the weight of the Queen and Princess bloody Margaret behind you, he goes, – but you ain't coming in.

– I'm afraid we are, sir.

The coppers come closer and the Old Man looks at the two blokes, looks at the two coppers. He weighs it up, knows what the odds are. He knows what it's like inside. Knows what a cell is. He stands aside.

They sort our stuff into two piles. One what's worth something, one what ain't worth nothing. Valuables go in the van, rest is left on the pavement. The front door of the house is nailed up and they drive off. We're left standing.

– I hated that house anyway, the Old Man says.

– It was my house, Mum says.

Sharon starts to whine and pulls at Mum's leg.

– I'm hungry. Hun-gry.

Alan picks up a leg of a doll from the pile of stuff on the pavement. He looks at it then throws it back down.

I don't say nothing.

– Dave, Mum says. – What we gonna do now?

He pulls out a fag, taps it on the packet, lights it, breathes smoke in then out. He opens his mouth to speak then sees the woman from the end of the street walking towards us, having a gawp. She sees him look at her and crosses over.

He calls after her. – Think you're any better? Do you? Eh? Do you?

He walks a few steps in time with her and she speeds up. He laughs. She goes in her house, shuts her door quick. He comes back, takes folded notes from his pocket, shows Mum he's minted.

– Where you get that? she asks. – You said you wasn't gonna.

– You want somewhere to live?

– Course I do, she says, and points at us. – I got these three, ain't I?

– Then you and Sharon get in the car. We'll come back for them.

I sit on the wall of the front garden. The daylight sees the rips in the sofa and the beer-can rings burned into the varnish of the coffee table. It's like the house has been turned inside out and we're spilt on to the pavement. The neighbour's looking out his window and I turn and give him the V. The curtain falls.

The crusty-eyelash kid walks up to us, tells Alan he's got something he wants to show him and they go off. Alan don't even look back at the stuff there in the street. He don't care. That's how easy it is for him. His skin's thick and he never looks back.

But I can't do that. I just ain't like that.

They pick us up later, and we only got time to take what we need. We'll buy new, the Old Man says, and we drive off leaving most of our stuff on the road.

The new flat's up two flights of piss-stink concrete stairs, four doors along, painted red with scratch marks and bars over the glass. No garden. No wasteland. There's a walkway and some railings to stop us falling down into the courtyard.

First night we're there and me and the dog're hanging over the railings, looking down. Mum asks me what I'm doing.

I tell her. – Nothing.

– You'll get used to it.

I turn and look at her. – You just say that to shut me up. That's all you ever do. Talk shit to shut me up.

– I don't. I like it. It's a good flat.

– That ain't you who says that, I go. – That's him says that. You ain't even got your own views. You never stand up to him. He goes off with her and when

46

she's had enough she kicks him out and you take him back.

Her eyes twitch, narrow. She lashes out but I duck and her hand swings through the air.

– It's just the truth, ain't it? I go. – But no one ever wants to hear it when I speak it. And I get blamed for it even though it ain't nothing to do with me. I'm just the one saying it.

Birdy sleeps at the end of my bed that night. Hangs around the walkway all day while I'm at school. First day I get back the old woman next door calls me over. She points. – Look.

There's a pile of turds, freshly laid. – There's no pets allowed here, she goes.

I shrug.

– I said there's no pets.

– I ain't deaf, I go. – I heard you.

I kick the pile of shit off the walkway down into the courtyard.

– Can't see nothing, I go.

– You kids get ruder each day. My day we was polite to people.

– Your day people lived in caves, cooked on fires, I say.

Every day it's the same. Moan. Moan. Then one day they come round the flat. The old woman and the black man from the other side. When they leave the Old Man calls me into the lounge where he's roll-ing a pile of fags. He looks up at me standing there. – You told the black geezer to fuck off, he goes.

He lights up, takes a drag. – There's times, he says, – when it's good to tell people to fuck off. Times when it ain't so clever.

– He was going on about the dog shitting.

– And now he's gonna tell them we got a dog here and we could be kicked out.

– I don't care.

He shakes his head slowly. Too slowly. He stands, steps forward. He gets my arm and pulls me towards him. He stinks of fag. – We ain't moving, he goes. – Your mother don't wanna.

– You don't care what she wants. You're always off with some bird and leaving her here crying.

He tightens the grip on my arm, shakes me, tells me to shut up.

– You don't wanna hear it, do you? I go. – You don't wanna hear in case it stops you doing what you want.

– You little shit.

I leap backwards out of his grip and turn to run and he gives me the chase. I run down the hallway and into my room and dive behind the bed. He leans over and grabs me, hauls me out. Punches me in the chest till I feel the air leave.

Mum comes in and screams and pulls him off. – You'll kill him. And then you'll be locked up.

And that's when he sees sense, cos that would affect him. He drops me to the ground. Looks down at me. Walks off.

★

Next morning he says I got to go with him in the van. Me and Birdy. The dog sits on my lap and we drive through the High Street, past the trading estate, on to the main road, right out to where there's grass and trees. He drives down a lane then pulls up but he don't turn off the engine.

He opens his door and comes round to mine. I ain't moving cos I know something's going on but I don't know what.

He takes Birdy by the scruff of the neck and pulls him off my lap out of the van. I shout out. – What you doing?

He pulls him to the side of the road and on to the grass. He pushes his arse down so he's sat down and I'm getting out the van and the Old Man pushes me back in. He slams the door. I open it again. He punches me on the arm. Pushes the door shut. He gets round and gets in.

Birdy's sat there on the grass and his head's tipped to the side like he's working out what's going on and the Old Man puts the van into gear and by now I'm screaming at him and he drives off and I'm grabbing his arm and hitting him and he lets go the wheel with his left hand and swings round and gets me in the belly.

And when the air comes back into me enough to speak, I'm gulping and crying. – What you done? I go. – What you done?

He don't say nothing. Drives. Lights a fag. Stares straight ahead.

And as the van moves, I feel something start to shift inside me.

I look down at my hands what're in my lap. There's engrained dirt in my skin and under my nails. I turn them over. It's all in the palms of my hands. Lincs of it. And as I'm sat there and he drives back home, it's like all that dirt, all them lines, it's all getting tighter and harder. It's all becoming solid. I can feel myself transforming as we're driving. Can feel it thicken. Can feel the dirt contract and become like the pattern of a shell, become like the hardness of a shell. Can feel it all go tight round me, round my lungs and liver and stomach. Round my heart.

Eleven Minus

It's all getting a bit serious, ain't it? A bit dark. See, I know what you think when you read this. Don't forget, I know everything.

But it's all right. It ain't all like that. And anyway, I'm all right. I'm here, ain't I?

Life carries on cos that's what life does. My broken arm mends. The flat gets some more bits of furniture. Sharon gets a new doll. Alan reads the books he's brought home from school.

And then the Old Man gets caught. He's taken away and put inside on remand, and the best thing is that summer Mum don't come and look for me and I go back home later than ever. And she don't ask where I been or what I been doing. I go in and see her in the lounge where she's sat with her telly friend, let her know I'm in. And the thing is, whatever time I go to bed, I'm still up at dawn. Still got the light-bulb head. I'm still me.

And then September comes and all over the estate kids are trying on their uniforms. They got white shirts with creases from where they been unpacked. New shoes what're a bit loose so there's room to grow into. They got new socks what fit tight round their ankles. Fresh satchels.

It's time for the move. Big school. Secondary school. Everyone looks at me and says I'm too small to go. They go: Look at you, pint pot, you'll be drowned there. They say: Tom Thumb, where's your fingers? They say: Tiny Tim, whose pocket you going in?

I wake early and go down, see what there is to eat. The bread's gone; there's an open bag of crisps; there's five tins, one of them already attacked with a hammer, mouldy holes in the top. In the fridge there's half a pack of butter with toast crumbs stuck in and three milk bottles, only when I try and pour some into a cup it's solid. It's cheese in a bottle.

I find some money and go out to the shops. Pick up a box of eggs and some milk and bread. The shop bloke watches every move, always does. He has ideas I wanna nick his stuff, don't realize I got more money in my pocket than he has in his poxy till. I give him a quid, tell him to keep the change. He don't thank me for it.

Back home I cook up the eggs in the butter for me and Alan, and slap them between slices of bread. While Alan's eating I go into Mum's room.

There's bottles of tablets on her bedside table and empty cans on the floor. She's flat out in bed. I touch her skin and shake her and she feels clammy. Her eyes are closed and I can see the thin skin on the lids, one tiny blue vein. There's a pulse at her neck so I know she ain't dead, and anyway if she was I'd've heard her heart stop.

I sit on the chair in the room and wait. Alan comes in. – We're gonna be late for school, he goes.

– I know, I go.

– What you gonna do?

I shrug. Stay on the chair. He stands in the doorway. Neither of us looks at each other and neither of us looks at her. We stare at the floor. Thing is, the rug's got patterns and the lino underneath's got swirls and so there's a lot to study. There's a whole world there to look at.

I hear the buzz of a fly. It's on the windowsill. It flies up against the glass, falls down on the sill, crawls again.

I give up. Stand and leave the room. Alan follows. Sharon comes out her bedroom with her thumb in her mouth. We put her in front of the telly with some milk and bread.

I drop Alan off at the old school then go round the corner, cross the main road. I stop, watch. There's people going in the gates and I can see they all got navy jumpers on. I take my grey one off. My white shirt's filthy round the cuffs and there's old blood on the elbow.

I'm stopped at the gate. She points at my jumper what's held behind my back. – What's that?

– A jumper, I go.

– Very amusing. Where's your uniform?

– I ain't got one.

She grabs my arm, takes me through the play-ground. Into the red-brick building, into an office. The bloke behind the desk looks up and I see his eyes move up and down, take me in. I know what he thinks.

When he speaks, his voice is slow and careful, like he's speaking specially for me cos I'm that thick.
– Has no one thought to dress you for school?

– Nope.

– No, sir, he barks. He gets up and walks round his desk, stands in front of me.

– Day one, he goes. – Day one and this is your beginning. I think I know how this one's going to play out.

He looks at the woman who dragged me in. – Take this sewer rat over to lost property and find him a clean shirt and a sweater. A navy one.

My first lesson. I sit at the back and when the teacher comes in the room, the other boys stand. The teacher stares at me. – When did I ask you to sit down? Stand up, boy.

– It's a chair, I go. – Thought you was sposed to sit in chairs.

– How dare you answer back.

I see him look at the other boys, see they're watch-ing to see what he's gonna do cos he'd better make a stand now cos if he don't he'll have lost control for the whole year. He opens his desk and gets out a ruler.

He walks towards me and I jink out his way. He walks after me but I'm quicker and smaller. I go quicker and he goes quicker. I weave between the chairs and can hear the boys trying not to laugh. They stifle it, hold hands over faces, but it don't work. And the more they laugh, the faster I go. The faster I go, the faster he goes. And the faster he goes, the louder they all laugh. He rages and knocks over a desk which traps me. He grabs me, hits me on the upper arm with the ruler, and drags me outside into the corridor.

– If you think you will continue in this vein, you are very much mistaken, he says.

And he lowers the ruler on to my shoulders and gets the back of my legs. He's breathing heavily from chasing me and he's losing it and he swipes and swipes. But he knows not to touch my face.

After dinner they put us all in the hall and our names are called out and we leave in groups. Ginger goes off. Skinny goes off. There's just a few of us left: the boy who dribbles, the boy with leg braces, the boy who never speaks. Me. We're led off to the wood-working room. A man in a brown coat, Mr Janes, lets us in. His hair's razor cut and he's got an ex-army moustache, pale reddy blond.

When we're all sat down, he gives his speech. – All I ask is that you do what I say and we won't have no trouble. Right?

And that's it. That's all he says. And then we make coat hooks till it's time to go home.

*

The front door's open and Mum's in the kitchen. She looks up when I come in but don't say nothing. I get some bread and make a jam sandwich.

– You all right? I ask.

– No, she says. She takes a sip from a can of beer on the table in front of her. – Your dad's been sent down, she goes. – They chucked away the key this time. A bloke come in and disturbed him and he hit him. Was lucky he never died.

– What would've happened if he had? I ask.

– He'd never come out.

– Then I wish he had died, I go.

– Don't say that, Gary. It's your dad you're talking about.

– I know. That's why I'm saying it.

She picks up the can and drinks.

– What we gonna do now then? I ask.

She shrugs, asks for another beer. I get one out and open it. Take a sip and pass it over.

– Mum, I say. – What's the eleven plus?

– Why you ask?

– They say some of them passed it. They've gone to the other school.

– It's a test, she goes.

– What for?

She shrugs. – See what school you go to.

– I never took no test, I go. – Why didn't I?

– I dunno, Gary. Spose cos they knew you wasn't gonna pass.

She gets a small bottle of tablets from her pocket

and swallows two with some of the drink. She looks at the bottle, turns it to read the label.

– Did you take the eleven plus? I ask.

She laughs. – Course I never. You got to be clever to take it. Like really clever.

– I am clever, I say.

– Course you are, she says. She smiles.

We sit for a minute. Then I say, – It was my first day at school today.

– I hated school, she says.

– And me, I go. – I ain't gonna go no more. Gonna stay at home with you now he's gone.

– You can't. Truant people'll be after me. Don't need that as well. Dunno how we're gonna eat.

I put my hand in my pocket, bring out a pile of notes. She takes the money, fingers it, and I know what she's thinking. She ain't stupid. She knows she shouldn't take it. She should drag me to the boys in blue. Cos she knows there's only one way I could've got it and it ain't legal. She looks at the notes in her hand, the freshly minted pile of them. She folds them up. Slips them in her pocket. Pats my hand with hers.

She smiles. – Dunno what I'd do without you.

Girl Next Door

A year must've gone by cos it's summer again and I'm on my way back from school on a Friday afternoon. The sun's shining, and it's gonna be like it all week-end. All summer. It's gonna be like this for ever.

I got a spring in my step, got a feeling of all this energy, all this popping in my legs. I got the holidays coming up; long days with no one telling me what to do.

I jump up the piss-stink concrete steps two at a time, turn on to the walkway. There's cushions on the floor outside the flat door. A bottle and glasses. Mum's sat with another woman, a blonde with black roots, legs stretched out, short green skirt. Sharon's there naked, ice-cream trails down her front. Alan's playing cards with the kid from along. The ice-cream van's singing in the street. It's a beautiful summer scene. It's paradise.

Mum smiles at me and lifts up her glass. – Gary, she says, – say hello to Bernadette. She's moved in next door.

Bernadette raises her glass. – Hello, Gary.

She looks at me, hard. – Your mum was right about your eyes.

I shrug. – They don't see no better than no one else's.

She laughs. – You won't be so blasé about them when the girls come flocking.

She offers me her packet of fags. There's one sticking out. Tempting me. I look at Mum who shrugs, so I take it.

Bernadette lights it for me. – So how was school today?

– Shit.

She laughs. – That's what it was for me every day.

– And me, Mum says. She stands and goes inside to get another bottle.

Bernadette stands up as well, leans on the railing to look over into the courtyard. There's a bruise on the back of her thigh and I can see where her legs go right up under her skirt. I can see a shadow, a dark world. She flicks her fag into the courtyard, turns and sees me watching.

I go round later, take some money Mum owes her. She opens the door and takes the cash then stands aside. – You coming in?

It's the same layout as ours only the mirror image. I follow her down into the kitchen and she gets me a can of beer. My payment, she says, for being the errand boy. She asks me what my dad's like, says she's heard lots from Mum. Just when I'm about to tell her, the doorbell goes. She tells me to stay where I am and I watch her walk down the hall. I sip at my beer, hear the door open and a man's voice. I hear the brushing of a coat against the door frame, footsteps coming inside, the door closing. She comes back down the hall and the bloke follows. He carries a small suitcase and when he sees me, he stops short of the doorway.

– This is my friend Gary, Bernadette says. – He lives next door.

The man nods, don't look at me. He says he'll wait in the bedroom. And he goes.

Bernadette picks up her beer. Drinks.

– You got to go? I ask.

She shrugs, lights a fag, blows smoke slowly out.
– There's no hurry.

She smiles, a missing bottom tooth. – Seems like a lifetime since I was your age, she says. – You had a girlfriend yet?

I look out the window. – No.

– They'll all be after you. Looking at your eyes is like looking at the sky. You get lost.

She walks across the room. Opens a box what's on the shelf, takes something out. She presses it into my hand. – Take this, she goes. – Get yourself some fags or a drink or a woman even. Whatever you want, darling. Whatever you want.

I look at it even though I already know what it is. A tenner. I think of the tenners I got in my pocket, the tenners under my bed. But I don't tell her nothing of them. I thank her, put it in my pocket.

She winks at me. – Right, she goes. – I better go and see to him. Hope he's quicker this time than last. Let yourself out.

As we walk to the front door I see him, sat on the bed, limp hands in his lap. He's looking up at her like he ain't been fed for months.

Later I'm mending a bike in the lounge and Mum's moaning I'm like the Old Man with his engines. There's a knock on the door and Bernadette lets herself in. She's wearing a yellow dress and blue coat. Her lips are pink.

– He's taking me away for the weekend, she says.

Mum swallows. – Bern, she goes, – you look beautiful.

– Thanks, Jan.

– You look . . . you look . . .

Mum trails off. Shakes her head. Tries again. – You look like you've stepped out of a film. You look so different. Maybe –

She hesitates.

– What? Bernadette says. – Go on.

– Maybe you'll fall in love and go and get married?

Bernadette laughs. – I spec he's already married, she says. – And I ain't never gonna marry anyway cos I know men too well, that's the problem with my job. You see the underbelly of them. The bits you don't never wanna see.

Mum looks at Bernadette sharply, nods towards me, as if to say that's enough, he's listening and he might be old enough to smoke a fag, but not to know there's horizontal dances men and women do.

– Where's he taking you? Mum asks.

– He's booked a hotel. I told him, I said I ain't got nothing to wear. But he'd brought all this with him.

– He bought you all that?

– That's what he said. It's probably his wife's.

– A hotel, Mum says, – a *hotel*. You gonna eat in a restaurant?

– Dunno where else we'd eat.

Mum walks to the window then turns and looks back at Bernadette. She's got the old look in her eye, the dream look. She's thinking of all the restaurants she's seen in films, the way the waiter spreads the napkin on the woman's lap, the way the wine waiter pours with one arm tucked behind his back.

Mum sighs and every scrap of air comes out of her. – I've had my arms in the kitchen sink for thirteen years, she says. – What I'd give to go to a restaurant. But no one ever takes me.

Bernadette smiles. – That's cos your old man's banged up.

– He never did take me.

– Janet, there's men who'd queue up to take you away. Believe me. You get in my game and you wouldn't believe what they'd do for you in exchange for a how's-your-father.

Mum puts her finger to her mouth and nods towards me again.

– He's all right, Bernadette says, and she turns towards me like she's only just seen me. She flips open her coat so I can see her dress.

– Gar? What d'you reckon? Would you be ashamed of being seen with me?

I look at her lips with the pink and her bare legs in the new shoes, her toenails sticking out, pink same as her lips.

I shake my head. – No, I go. – No, I wouldn't.

Bernadette nods. – Good.

She picks up her small bag and does up her coat. – Right, she says. – Well, think of me.

And she leaves. Her perfume stays behind and Mum sits on the settee and cries.

Alan's in bed asleep. The room's full of his dead breath. I've tossed and turned. The pink of her lips and toes is in my head and I get up out of the bed. I pull on some clothes and I got no idea of where I'm going but I let myself out the flat and on to the walkway. I lean on the railings and look at the windows of the flats opposite. See who's up, who's not. I turn round, lean back. There's no moon. No shadows. Our front door is open. There's no one around and her windows are black.

I don't ask myself what I'm doing. I just do it. I get the small crowbar and use it on her door, lever it against the jamb. It don't take much to spring it.

It's dark inside and I turn on the torch, hold the light down just in front of where my feet go. Down the hallway, into the bedroom. Floor's covered in stuff: twisted sheets, bottles, towels. Her pants and a dress. Stockings rolled up.

I bend down, touch the dress. Rub it between fingers. Lift my fingers to my nose, smell. I stroke one of the stockings as if it'll come to life.

In the kitchen there's some flowers and a card what reads: To my weekend girlfriend.

The torch moves through the room till it settles on the box on the shelf. I use a cloth from the kitchen to get it down. Lift the lid.

There's a bundle of notes: tens, fives, ones. I look at them for a long time, then dip in, take them all. I throw the box down, throw the card and the flowers on the floor. Tip a chair over, get the ornaments from where the box was, chuck them down, then go in the other room and throw more stuff around in there.

And then I leave.

Next morning, Bernadette comes back. She stops in at ours first and Mum answers the door. Bernadette launches into her story of how the man never paid her right and took the clothes back. And the food in the restaurant was shit. And the hotel bed was lumpy. And all men are bastards. And when she's finished Mum breaks the news. There was a burglary. Stuff chucked about. Stuff taken. It was Gary who found out, Mum says. And it was Gary, she tells her, what made good the door.

Bernadette smiles at me. – Thanks, Gary.

They go next door to see the damage. I follow. They stand in the doorway, look at the mess. I watch over their shoulders, express shock. I'm pretending to look at the mess, but really I'm watching them.

I'm watching. I'm learning.

Bernadette goes into the kitchen, finds the box and opens it. She shakes her head.

– All gone? Mum asks.

Bernadette holds the box by the lid, dangles it from her hand, so we can see the empty cavity. She speaks:
– People are shits, ain't they?

Then she looks at me. – Thank God for you, Gary. Thank God for you.

Finishing School

I know what you think. But I'm trying to be straight with you and I don't wanna pretend to feel things I don't.

See, it just ain't that straightforward. There's this feeling I got when I was doing that, when I was in her room and walking through the stuff. It was like I stood out. I was different. The world's full of people who obey the unwritten rules of life, store away things they call their own, put them behind flimsy doors with holes in them with these things called keys. Each of them carries one on him, this little metal stick, and he believes it means he can stash stuff away. People spend their lives gathering stuff and then locking it up so other people can't touch it.

And when I go in and see their belongings and it's my torch shining on it all, then I'm the one in power. I'm the one who knows how fragile it all is. Cos if we all woke one day and decided not to obey the unwritten rules, it'd all fall apart. We'd just reach in and take whatever we wanted. We'd be dipping in and helping ourselves.

But there's more: there's how all this makes me feel when I do it. Me the animal. Cos it ain't like nothing else. It's the challenge, the thrill. It's being on the edge. It's that moment when I could walk away with something, or I could end up in a small room like the Old Man, with a high window and a hard bed. Only I know I ain't gonna go to that small room cos I'm smarter than him, quicker than him.

In that minute when you're somewhere you oughtn't to be, when your fingers are touching someone else's stuff, when you know a key could go in the lock, a door be opened, a footstep come into the room, in that minute you feel it all over your body. You're alive. The hairs on the inside of your nose are raised. Your ears are moving to help detect any sound. Bits of your body you didn't know existed are switched on.

It's like going back in time, crossing lines, being free. It's like all of this new world don't exist and we're back to where we come from. It's me against everything.

It's Wednesday morning, a school day, and the others are locked up in the red-brick building. Me and Ginger are at the amusement arcade in Soho where they got a new game with a screen where we move bats around and hit balls.

When we finish feeding it, we go to the penny drop. We watch carefully to time it right and drop our last coins in. The slider pushes them but none fall down. There's a geezer watching us, leaning on the wall.

– It's fixed, he goes. – You're not going to win anything.

– I know, Ginger goes.

– Everyone knows that, I go.

The bloke bangs the machine and rocks it but the coins don't dislodge. He points at the tray where the coins are hanging over the edge. They tilt up the metal underneath, he says, – so the coins gather and can't fall off. They probably glue the bottom ones on.

Ginger kicks the machine. – Bastards.

The bloke laughs. – They're clever the people who run these arcades.

He looks at his watch. – You hungry, lads?

I say nothing but Ginger nods. – We ain't eaten since breakfast, he goes. – We're spent up and we can't nick nothing cos they'll call the truant officers in. They all know us.

The bloke takes out a pack of fags. Good ones. Gives us one each. Tells us to keep the packet.

Ginger grins and puts the pack in his pocket.

I turn to go.

– Hang on, the bloke says. – There's a new burger place round the corner. They got sauces and pickles. Melted cheese. Bacon. Chips. I'll stand you to a burger or two.

Ginger turns to me. – I'm starving.

I stare at the bloke. – Why you wanna do that? I go.

– Why not? I got money.

I shake my head. – There's always a reason to offer somethink. We ain't coming.

I make a start towards the door.

Ginger hesitates. – I'm really hungry, Gary, he goes.
– Don't be thick, I go. – Come on, we're going.
– I ain't always got to do what you say, he goes.
– I never said you did.

I stare at him. He don't move. – Suit yourself then, but I ain't gonna eat with him.

And I walk towards the door. Leave. Don't look back. But by the time I get to the river, I know I made a mistake. I know it. I turn back. Walk up towards Soho again, break into a run. I feel beads of sweat between the blades of my shoulders. Along my hairline on my forehead. My lungs ache. I barge people out the way. I get to the arcade but there's no one there. I run through the streets but I don't know where I'm going. I stop, lean against a window and catch my breath. I tell myself to go home, tell myself he'll be sat on the train, ketchup at the corners of his mouth.

By evening the rain's falling. It's hitting the windows and I'm inside watching telly. There's knocking on the door and Alan gets up and goes out the room. I turn off the telly. Follow him out.

It's Ginger's dad at the door and the second I see him I know everything.

– Where is he? he asks. – He was sposed to be back early.

I stare at him.

– Please, he goes. – You must know something.

★

69

There's two of them and we're in the lounge. The older copper asks me about when I last saw Ginger. I don't say nothing. I don't talk to the filth.

– Sonny, he goes, – you better start singing otherwise I'll take you down the nick for that robbery yesterday in the corner shop.

I stare at him. – I ain't done no robbery.

– Your word against mine. Think about it. Who's a judge gonna believe? There's you, skinny little thing looks like he's been on the streets for years. And there's me, uniform neatly pressed, hat in hand. Your honour, I'll say, I found the juvenile running from the shop with arms full of cigarettes.

I stare at him.

– So you got one minute to sing or we're out of here. Shall I get my tuning fork?

I don't go to school next day. I stay at home with Mum. In the afternoon they come to the door and Mum talks to them then we go in the kitchen and I know what she's gonna say.

– Gary, she goes.

The air is still. Every molecule's like treacle. She opens her mouth to speak and nothing'll be the same again. I know what she's gonna say. I know. I always know.

– They found Ginger. They found his body.

The funeral's in the church by the school and we all go. We piss about, push each other, line up and go in.

The coffin comes in on the shoulders of his dad and brother and uncles. It's heavy. Weighs them down.

We stop pushing each other. Our eyes drop to the stone floor of the church.

When we come out no one talks about what happened.

No one says what the word on the streets says, which is he was found in a flat, no clothes on, rope in his mouth and round his hands.

They don't say what was done to him but I know. I know.

Day after the funeral, I have a fight. There's blood on my collar. Grazed knuckles. I go straight into a shop, lift stuff what I don't need. Another shop. More stuff.

I chuck it all in the corner of the bedroom: food, bread, milk, clothes, sweets.

I nick a bottle of ink.

I nick a compass and burn the point till it's black. Poke down into my skin till I bleed. Put the ink into the wound, keep doing it till I've written out numbers to spell the date when Ginger went missing. When I'm done I close the lid of the ink and chuck it in the bin. I sleep with my arm on top of the covers.

In the morning the first scabs are there.

That day I go out again, nicking. Bags of it. Stuff I don't even like. It's as if I got to clear the shelves of it all. I don't care if I get seen. And because of that I do get seen. A bloke grabs me, pushes me into a room behind the counter and locks me in. He calls the filth and the copper comes, lets his self into the room with me. And it's the same older copper who came after Ginger went missing.

He takes a chair and pulls it up by me where I'm crouched on the floor.

– So, he goes.

He waits.

– So, he goes again. – Haven't you learned from what happened to your friend?

I don't look at him: the floor, keep my eyes on the floor.

– This is your chance, son. You could change now, sort yourself out. He's not got a chance to do that but you have.

– Piss off, I say. I get up, go to the door and try to open it.

– It's locked, he goes. – Sorry.

I sit back down.

– So what do you say? he asks. – About what I said?

– Nothing, I go.

He sighs. – Thing is with you young lads, you think you know everything there is to know about life. Well let me tell you, you don't. You know nothing.

I yawn, don't cover my mouth. – Yeah, yeah, I go.

– I'll tell you one thing. This conversation'll come back to haunt you. It'll be one of those moments when your life could have changed.

For two weeks I don't pinch nothing, don't fight. I go to school every day then Mr Janes asks to speak to me.

– You been doing well, son, he goes. – Any chance of a word with your parents?

I get home. I'm gonna tell Mum she has to go to see him. I rush up the concrete stairs, and see her sat on the walkway, bottle tipped over next to her. Her head rests on her knees. I kneel down to wake her, to tell her, and I hear footsteps behind me on the concrete walkway. It's him. He's let out into the bright fresh air. His hair's cut short, he's got a small bag over his shoulder. He's got the fresh-out-of-nick walk, the don't-fuck-with-me walk.

He stops, asks me for a fag and I give him one. – I never knew you was coming out, I go.

– I never told no one.

– You come out early? I go. – Mum said they chucked the key.

– Good behaviour. Suckers.

He laughs. Taps Mum and says her name. She looks up, sees him. She rubs her eyes, can hardly make him out: she must be dreaming. He holds his hand out and pulls her up. She leans on him and he takes her in the flat, shuts the front door behind him.

That evening he's on his throne in front of the telly. Can in hand. Fag in hand. I ask him for a smoke.

– Get your own.

– You had one of mine out there, I go.

– That's different.

– In what way's that different?

Before he can say nothing he sees my arm. Spots the tattoo. He points at it with the burning fag.

– What's that?

I look down. Shrug.

– Who done it?

– Me.

He puts his fag in the ashtray, stands up. He grabs my arm tight, turns it to see the tattoo better. – What's it mean?

– It's Ginger, I go.

– That faggot.

He lifts both his hands up, grabs my face, holds it like I'm in a vice.

– If you still got that tomorrow morning I'll give you a hiding till your eyes bleed. Understand?

That night I take the knife from the kitchen and I start to cut down, through the scabs, through all the layers of skin, to the flesh beneath. I cut across each number till all there is is blood.

It does hurt but it's all right, you know. It's all right.

This is how I see it: it's a rite of bleeding passage. It's an ancient tradition.

I see it as me going back to what we human beings once was. Me going back to my animal.

Pleasuring Her Majesty

I'm out in the street. There's no moon and it's been raining all day: water's pooled by the kerb. I'm between two lamp posts, waiting in the shadows.

A car pulls up and the back door opens. I jump in with Skinny who's losing his fat so fast we might have to change his name or people'll think we got no sense of humour. It's Beak who drives. This is the first time we've met and I know the way he pulls away from the kerb he ain't the brightest. He slams the gears into first and leaves half the tyres on the road. We might as well put a flag up, announce to the world: Here we are, dirty little carful about to break the law.

We park up in a street. There's trees, front gardens, cars in driveways. It's a *nice* street. A *respectable* street. A street good for pickings.

Beak eyes me in the mirror. – Skinny says you're handy.

I don't bother to answer. He'll know soon enough.

We get out and walk till we find a house. It's easier than you'd know to spot the ones with no one in. No car outside. No light on. Open curtains. Bins not taken in. And anyway, I just know: it's the quiet, undisturbed molecules around it.

Skinny stands in the street on watch, while Beak crowbars the door. As the wood splits I raise my hand to signal and Skinny has a coughing fit loud enough to smother any noise. Me and Beak go in silent, close the door behind. Beak goes straight into the lounge. I don't. I stand in the dark hall. My heart races. That feeling again: I am alive.

I take the time to look around, see what kind of house it is. Who its people are. I get into their heads, climb right inside.

I go up the stairs, into the bedroom. Shine the torch around, see there's floorboards round the outside of the rug. I lift up the sides of the rug, see one board's got some fresh marks where it's been cut. I lever it up, lie down and put my arm in the hole, feel around. My fingers touch something and I grab it. A velvet pouch.

Downstairs Beak's empty-handed. I shine my torch on the contents of the pouch, show him gold, silver.

At home I put my share of the jewellery in the box under the bed. It's late but I can't sleep. There's blood pounding in my ears, rushing round me. I go in the kitchen and get some cans of beer, take them outside and sit on the walkway where I stay till the dark starts to get light. Till there's more fags on the floor than in the packet. More ring pulls on the floor than on the cans.

I watch lights go on in the flats opposite as people wake. They're animals like I am, only they're domesticated. They're in hutches, what they come out of to go to work. They got timetables, routines, all handed down to them by their owners.

None of that's ever gonna happen to me. I ain't never gonna be in a trap. I don't want none of it.

Next day the Old Man bangs on the bedroom door.
– They're here, he shouts.
– Who?
– The filth, he goes. – You brought the filth to my door.

He ain't finished the sentence and I'm up and pulled my clothes on. I look towards the door, towards the window, towards the back. The Old Man shakes his head. I feel like a rat cornered by dogs.
– You've shat on your own doorstep, he goes.

And he don't wait for them to knock the door down. He drags me out the bedroom and into the hallway. He opens the front door and hurls me at them. – This what you're looking for?

And he goes back in the flat and the door slams shut.

I got hands gripped round both my arms and they start to drag me off. And I'm moving along the walk-way when the front door opens again and I look round and see Mum come and stand on the doorstep and she watches me being dragged away.

The custody sergeant leads us along the station corridor and stops at a door. He unlocks it. There's a bloke sat on the bench, his head in his hands. Bare feet.

– Is this him? the sergeant asks.

The bloke lifts his head and looks at me. Beak. He looks away quick. Nods. – Yeah, it's him.

The sergeant laughs. – Choose a brighter spark next time, he tells me. – Someone we're not watching. Someone who can't sing.

– You stupid wanker, I go. I try to launch myself at Beak but the coppers each side of me grab my arms and pull them behind my back. Custody sergeant bunches his hand into a fist, pulls back his arm and lets rip at my belly. The air leaves me and I fold over. Once I'm on the floor and can't breathe, they carry me into a cell.

In court the judge is a woman and I turn the blue eyes on her and smile but she don't smile back. – What you need, young fellow, she says, – is a short sharp shock. In six weeks, you won't recognize yourself.

I think: What a stupid thing to say. In six weeks I'll know exactly who I am. They take me out and put me in a bus where I sit next to a prison officer.

– You know where you're going? he asks.

I shake my head.

– I'll give you a tip. Keep your head down and your mouth shut. They're gonna learn you a lesson for life.

I laugh. – Maybe I'll give them a lesson.

The officer shakes his head really slowly. – Oh dear, he goes. – Dear, oh dear.

★

The uniformed screw with a shaved head and long yellow teeth gives me a number: 657432.

– Understand? That's your number and you only answer to that and you better answer bloody quick. What is it?

– 65 somethink, I go.

– I said what's your number?

And he brings his bunch of keys down on my head. – 657432, he goes. – 6 fucking 5 fucking 7 fucking 4 fucking 3 fucking 2.

My fingertips is held to the ink pad then pushed on the paper where they leave prints.

– Piss off out of here, the screw goes, – but don't get ink on nothing.

I try to leave but the door's shut. I grab the knob to turn it.

– You got ink on it, you little stream of shit. What did I say?

The screw brings the keys down on my head. I put my hand up, feel it's wet. I'm taken to another room and they sit me down, put the clippers to my head, cut right through the blood and down near to the scalp. They tell me to get my kit off and I do, down to my pants. They point at them, tell me I can get them off or they will.

When I'm naked, they point at the bath, tell me to get in.

Six inches of cold water and hair floating on the top. When I get out, I put on blue trousers and a shirt what are too big. I'm told to run down the corridor and have to hold them up to stop them falling. In the room at the end there's eight of us. They slam the door behind.

Eight of us with our hair razored off. Eight bands of white round ears and neck where the sun ain't been. Eight beds with no pillows and just one blanket each.

In the night there's crying.

But not me. No, not me.

It's still dark when the door opens and slams hard back against the wall. Two of them rush in, shouting: Get up, scum. Get up. They hit metal batons against the sides of the metal beds.

Showers are long metal pipes hung off the ceiling with holes in where water dribbles through. We have to strip off and go through in front of the men with their batons. I got more hairs up my nose than on my legs and my dick's a white worm in a bed of bald flesh. The main screw puts the baton out in front to stop me. He looks me up and down and I cup myself with my hands.

– Look at this, he says to the other screw. – He don't belong here. You wanna get back to the nursery, lad. This is a place for men.

Breakfast is bread and porridge with water and salt. Then it's the gym for circuits. We run and drop to the floor when told. Jump the pommel horse when told. Sit when told. Stand when told. Breathe when told. And all the time, in our faces, shouting: Chest out, chin in. Start being a man. You done the acts of a man. Now be a man.

For a couple of weeks it works. We're all scared. They keep us on edge all the time, never knowing what's coming. They burst in rooms, disturb us. They shout. Scream.

Then one morning I'm in the blacked-out room and the mattress is hard under me and I'm lying there awake and I realize why. I'm getting ready for them. I know what's coming. The feet in the corridor. The metal door. The baton. I'm prepared, braced. Cos the thing about patterns is you get used to it, and you know what to expect. Your body learns the rhythm and can get its defences ready. It's almost wanting it to come. We're less than two weeks into the sentence and there's no shock to the short sharp shock. There's only short and sharp.

And the next weeks pass easy. It's become like everything else. It's become a game. Them. Me.

And when they chuck me out in the street after six weeks, I'm fitter, harder, more brutalized.

Homecoming Parade

I walk out the prison's front gates, breathe in the fresh air. The Old Man's sat there in a new van, and he leans over and opens the passenger door for me to get in. He hands me a pack of fags and I light us one each then try and give them back but he won't take them. He pushes the pack back at me. – They're all yours, he goes.

I stare at him, make sure he is my Old Man, not someone who just looks like him and dresses like him.

He turns the key in the ignition, shakes his head. – You were an idiot to get caught, he says.

Thanks. As if I didn't know. As if I couldn't work that out on my own.

He drives off and we smoke and I watch the world go by out the window. It's bright and everything moves quick and it's like while I was inside there was only black and white; out here it's colour. I can feel my head trying to keep up.

He pulls up outside a pub. Takes a comb out his pocket, looks in the rear-view mirror. Turns his head this way, that, combs his hair, and as he combs, looks up his nose. Then he checks he ain't got food stuck in his teeth. He puts the comb away and gets out the van. Brushes down his jacket, straightens his collar, reties the laces on his Docs.

The barmaid's young with dark hair thick enough to hide in, and a tight red top. She smiles as we come in, is about to say something to the Old Man when he gestures to me. – My son, he goes quickly.

– Oh.

He points at a table, tells me to sit down. As I walk over I look back and see him touch her hand across the bar.

He brings two pints over, says one's for me, but if the filth come in I'm to hide it.

– Who is she? I ask.

His eyebrows go up. – Who?

I nod towards the bar.

He looks round. – Oh. Her. She's always here.

He downs an inch of pint and swallows, takes a drag on his fag. – So, he goes. – Learn much in there?

Yeah, I think. Yeah, I did. I learned more about the human frigging race than I ever wanted to, and what's more none of them disappoint me as much as you do. But then he offers me another fag and he picks up his glass, and he says, good to have you back, son, and our glasses touch and clink and I feel the chunks of ice start to melt.

Alan opens the door. He's leant against the frame. School uniform. Tie, clean shoes. – You're a chip off the old block, aren't you? he goes. – Great pair, you are.

I stare at him. Yawn in his face. – Yeah, yeah. You gonna let me in?

He shrugs. – Ain't got much choice, have I?

I go on through and put my bag down on my bed. He follows. – So you going straight this time?

I keep my back to him. Unzip the bag and take out my stuff.

– Or d'you not know how to go straight?

I turn to look at him and it's then I see. I ain't been away that long but it's like everything's changed. I see he's shot up and his flab's turned to muscle. – You know what the best solution is? I say. – You ignore me and I'll ignore you.

I put the bag under the bed and go out into the hallway just as Sharon comes through the front door, only it ain't the same Sharon. This one's moved up schools and wears a grey skirt rolled up near short enough to see her pants.

– Don't do that with your skirt, I go.

– What makes you think you can come home and tell me what to do? she goes. – You got any money?

– That's a nice way to welcome your brother home.

– Yeah, well I'm broke.

I put my hand in my pocket, pull out some change. – Only got this.

She takes it all. – That'll do.

And she opens the door wide, goes to step out. I ask where she's going in that short skirt.

– Mind your own fucking business.

– Oi, I go. – Wash your fucking mouth out.

She laughs. – Fuck off, Gaz.

And she slams the door and runs off.

Mum comes out the kitchen into the hallway. Sees me. She focuses to make sure it really is me. Puts an arm out to steady herself on the wall. –It's you, she goes. – Welcome home, Gary.

That night I don't go out. The Old Man goes for a drink, which is his word for whatever he's doing: a job, a shag, sometimes even a drink. I watch telly with Mum, who looks over at me and smiles every time the adverts come on, like she can't believe her eldest is back and is staying in, being a normal person. I go to bed at a normal time and lie there. Alan's sat up reading.

I listen to his breathing, listen to the pages turning, the scrape of them on the sheets. He sighs and pulls the pillow up behind him. Grabs a pen and writes a note on his book. The pen scrapes on the paper. The paper scrapes on the sheet. It's like the two of us are locked into this thing. No talking. One bed each. It could be the cell only there ain't many cellmates what study all night. He shuts the book and I think here we go but he picks up another one, opens it.

– You gonna do that all night? I go.

He closes his book. – Thing is, Gary, I had this room to myself. You got to understand that.

– Don't speak to me like I'm thick, I go.

– Then don't act like you're thick.

I sit up. – Don't speak to me like that.

– I can speak however I want. I can say what I think. You're an idiot and you ought to go to school, get some education.

I curl up my fists under the covers. Count to five. It ain't worth spilling words or blood. I get out the bed and pull on jeans and T-shirt. Walk towards the door.

He asks where I'm going. I don't answer.

– Gary, he goes. – You'll get in trouble. You know you will.

But I won't. I know I won't. You know I won't.

It's the quiet hour. The hour between people going to their beds and the first of them getting up for the early shifts. It's the hour when only a few sleepless are awake. The baby feeders. The floor pacers. The ill.

I'm walking without reason, I ain't going nowhere. It's walking for the joy. It's walking cos I can, cos there's no steel door between me and the world. It's walking to see the world.

There's enough moon to throw my shadow on the ground and I watch my own walk. I know how it looks. Like inside each leg there's a coiled spring, like I'll never run out of energy. I'm thin, wiry. Every muscle defined, like they're drawn on. I look young but I move like someone who's lived a thousand lives. I move like I know things.

I know all these streets. Know the shapes of the blocks of flats, the houses. I know every tree, every dropped kerb. I turn down into the road with two cars every house. This is the border, the line between us on the estate and them in their tightly locked prisons with their locks and keys.

I clock each house as I pass. It don't take much to work out which ones are empty, but wherever they are, the owners can sleep safe. I ain't gonna do nothing. It's too light cos my enemy's out in the sky. The planets are moving in the wrong circles.

And anyway, you know what, I don't want anything. I just want this, the pavement beneath my feet. The air parting to let me through.

I stop in the High Street on the way back. There's a new supermarket, twice the size of any other shop. And in the shiny new doorway there's an old boy slumped, brown paper bag in his hand, rim of a glass bottle sticking out of it. His eyes are shut and he don't know nothing. I bend down, take a fiver from my pocket, sneak it into his hand and imagine the moment he wakes, when he realizes what he's clutching. I keep imagining it, playing it over and over, and I like the idea of it, this little scene I'll never see yet I know everything about.

I sit down on the bench. I can't even hear a car. This side of the planet's all asleep. It's just me knows what's going on. It's just me in the secret world. A sheet of newspaper blows along the street, stops against a lamp post. Leaves in the trees above rustle and I hear the stems groaning. A pigeon in the eaves of a roof stands and stretches its wings, resettles, and I hear every feather rustle. The neon light of the sign above the supermarket fizzes.

And then I see a fox. He enters the precinct, weaves along, his nose to the ground, reading the smells. He knows everything that's happened that day, what everyone's eaten and chucked away. What everyone's trod in. He stops at a wrapping, noses it open, eats some fish in batter. He ignores the chips. He looks up, and though he don't look at me directly, he takes me in. I know cos as he carries on, nose to the ground, his head moves a fraction as he checks I ain't too close, as he keeps his eye on me. He knows where I am and what I am and my position in his world. He stops again, excited now cos he's found a bit of old cake. Before he eats it he looks up at me and I look at him and he don't move nor nothing and I don't know who's the stillest of the two of us.

And then he eats quickly, like he ain't eaten for a thousand years. His eyes are still fixed on me, cos while he's eating, I'm moving to the edge of the bench and I'm getting nearer to him. But he knows me. Knows all my games. Knows every game I could ever play. I'm fixed with that eye. I get too close and he scoops up the rest of the cake in his mouth and he's gone.

Cherry Pop

Time's moving on and I'm getting older. The clock hand turns and it's unstoppable cos whatever you do, you ain't never gonna get younger. There's only one way to go in life, down that slippery slope to the hell pit. But before you reckon I'm being too bleak, remember that before you get to that hell pit, there's some good things to find on the way, and you better seize them cos this is your one and only chance.

That's what I always told my son and it's what I'm telling you.

It's a Friday night and the pub's rammed cos there's live music on. The air's heavy with smoke and it's six people thick all the way to the bar. I look about for Skinny cos he said he was coming early, and spot him at the table in the corner. Round the table there's four chairs. And in one of the chairs there's a bird.

I sit down and Skinny pushes a pint my way. The bird smiles and I nod at her. She's got skin as white as eggshell, pale red hair.

I lift up my pint. Touch my glass on his, then on hers. – Our friend didn't introduce us, I say.

– I'm Samanfa, she goes. – You don't have to tell me who you are. Everyone knows you.

The very next day I'm in the park and I got a can of beer in my hand and the sun on my face. I'm on the bench by the main path where people're walking. I got my eyes closed and everyone reckons I can't see them, but they're wrong, they couldn't be more wrong. I know exactly what's going on. I hear everything: the grass growing and the worms under the earth turning. The leaves creaking on their autumn stems. The water in the boating lake rippling against the stone walls. The feet of every single person who passes, if they're men or women, the type of shoes, the way they're walking, what size their feet are.

A pair approach, hesitate as they go by. It's a young woman. Heels, no rubber tips. She pauses, turns round, comes back towards me. I open my eyes. She's there. Standing in front of me. Her mouth's slightly open, hand raised up to it, as though she's surprised. As though she's just realized who I am. – Oh, Gary, she goes. – It is you, ain't it?

And I laugh out loud. – You know it's me, Samanfa. She laughs too.

– How long did it take you to find me? I ask.

– Not long.

She's wearing a short skirt, shorter than last night, and I can taste her perfume. She fiddles with her hair and I offer her my can. She takes it and our hands touch.

– Where is he? I go.

– Who?

I stare at her. – Come on.

– Oh, him. Skinny. We split up. Last night after the pub.

She closes the bedroom door and slides a chest of drawers in front of it. She switches on the radio and it sings tinny songs at us. We drink vodka from the bottle and sit on the bed so close our thighs touch.

She's got a vest on, tight as skin. I put my arm round her waist and feel the weight of her tit on my hand. We don't speak. She leans in and I lean in. It's tongues in mouths and I've got my hand on her tit and it's heavy and the way it fits my hand it's like it's been waiting for me. Like it's grown specially to fit me, like my hand was the mould it was poured into. I slip my hand down between her legs and she opens her legs and then she stops me. She stands and takes off her vest.

Skinny's in my head and I know I should stop. But it's too late. The weight's tipped too far towards this happening. I can't stop. It'd be like putting lava back in a volcano.

And after, I'm lying there thinking so this is what we was made for, what all the fuss is about, and I'm thinking it's a bloody miracle and what's more it didn't cost nothing and I'm wondering how long I can leave it till we do it again.

– Gary, she goes.

I shake my head, re-enter the world. – What?

She don't say nothing for a bit, and she's looking up at the ceiling, not at me. I know she's about to drop something on me. And she does. – I ain't split up from him.

I snatch my arm away, pull back towards the wall. – What you say?

She starts to cry. – I don't know why I said it, she says. – I'm sorry, Gary.

I pull up my pants what're twisted round my ankles. Climb over her, pull on my jeans, grab my cherry red Doc Martens.

– Don't go, she goes.

– You lied, I go. – He's my mate. You know what that means?

I move the chest of drawers out the way and I'm down the stairs three at a time.

I stay away from the normal places. Every night I go out from dark till near light. I go to bed in the days. But one night I'm at the station to catch the train and it's pissing down and I'm hunched under the shelter. And I'm watching the rain hit the glass walls and the people who come towards it are blurred and then before I know it he's come in the shelter and there's nowhere for me to go. And I can't deny I'm me.

– Gary?

I turn round. – You all right, Skinny?

– Yeah, I'm all right, mate. Where you been? Been looking out for you.

– Escaping cops, I go. – You know, on the run a bit.

He sucks air in through his teeth. – It's a fascist state.

Not quite, I think, but I let it go.

– I'm going into town, he goes. – Looking for something to do. You coming?

The train tracks start to hum as the train approaches the station. The rain's coming down in buckets. I shrug. – Don't think so.

– We could go into Soho, play the machines. Old times, Gary.

The train gets closer and we see the front of the engine. – It'd be good, I say, – but I forgot somethink. I better go back for it.

He nods, fails to hide the disappointment. Then a fresh thought comes to him. – You seen Samanfa?

I shake my head. – Not for days.

– She finished it. Won't say why.

– Shame, I go.

The train pulls up alongside. – Pity you can't come, he goes.

– Next time, I say.

He nods. – Yeah. Next time.

That night I put the small crowbar and torch in my pocket, go out.

That night there ain't no moon and I walk and walk

till I find a house I know's empty. I lever the door, put my weight on it, and it gives. The hallway's dark and I go in the lounge first. There's no telly, just a record player and rows and rows of LPs. I pull one out, take out the inner sleeve, then the black disc from inside that. I lift the lid, slip the hole in the centre of the record over the button. I turn on the dial on the front and a row of lights comes on. Lift the needle and the disc starts to turn. There's a hiss as the needle touches the vinyl. I can't hear no music at first then it grows louder and the sound builds. I sit down on the chair, listen. The sound's growing. Violins. Classical stuff. The street light comes through the lace curtains and makes patterns on the walls.

I'm sat in a leather chair and I can feel everything about this house. The people and the way they sit here listening. And I stay for longer than I reckoned I would. I'm not me. I'm not in my own skin but in some other skin. And when I'm sitting there I'm thinking so this is it, this is how different we can all be. This is how many different ways of being a person there are. And there's something about sitting there I like. I'm not breaking and entering and rushing to get out before someone comes home and catches me. I'm just being there. Doing exactly what I want.

Robbin Hood

The woman comes up the road from the factory, bag over her shoulder. It's Thursday and she's in a hurry. I start to follow, walk on the opposite side of the street. She goes to the precinct and then into the bank. From where I'm hid in the doorway opposite I see her come out and spot she's walking differently. Her weight's tipped to one side, and her hand's tight on the handle of the bag. I follow her back down the same way she came and she weaves through a couple of streets, turns down to the factory at the end, goes in the front door.

I clock her, clock what she done. The next Thursday I'm waiting for her. Out she comes again. Same pattern. Same routine. Same weight in the bag.

This time when I follow her back I wait and watch the workers come out. On the dot of five they're out the gates. Shoulders up, heads down. Collars against the wind.

I go back the following day, Friday. They come out at four thirty but they ain't the same people. They're laughing, saying: See you next week. Saying: See you later for a pint? They're alive again. And it don't take a genius to know what all this means. The wages come in every Thursday, are given out every Friday.

I wait till a Thursday night when there's no moon. I creep round the back of the factory to the frosted-glass window and put tape over so the glass don't fall out, then cushion it with my coat before hitting it with a stone. I peel off the tape and reach through to unlock it. The window swings open and it's big enough for me and the torch to climb through.

The corridor's long and my heart's at it. All of me listening, watching.

I go into the office where there's two desks and a safe and I do the old trick, wait till I'm the person what works there, till I'm the person what knows everything. I feel around me, look in the normal key-hiding spots. Under the desk and chair, behind the books, under the rug. Nothing. I sit back down, think of myself imagining hiding it, think where it could go where no one would ever get it. I stand up. Go into the next room, a small toilet what's got a sign on the door MANAGEMENT ONLY, and I feel up in the cistern, dip down into the cold water and find it wrapped in plastic. Management only. That'll teach them.

The pay packets are all made up. Names and jobs and amounts on the outside. I imagine taking out all the notes and stuffing my pockets. But then I put them all on the desk and lay them out in order of pay. Management one side. Workers on the other. I undo the envelope of the highest paid and take out the money, put it in the workers' envelopes. I do it till all the management ain't got enough for a pint and all the workers have doubled their wages. I seal the envelopes and put them back, lock the safe and put the key back in the cistern.

While I'm doing all this there's a soundtrack playing in my head. It's me laughing. I know what the reaction'll be and I can play it out. The workers'll get to the pub on the Friday afternoon, open their envelopes. They'll hesitate at the size of the wad of notes, then they'll count it, then they'll call out to the barman for a bigger round. Slap each other on the back. Drain their pints.

I'm still laughing inside thinking what a hero I am and for once I ain't using my instincts, I ain't listening. I go back down the dark corridor, feeling the walls so I don't have to use the torch, and I climb out the same window and as I do I'm picturing the pay packets being opened in the pub, and as I land I find myself in the arms of a security guard and his dog who gets hold of my trousers. The guard tells me if I move an inch his dog's gonna sink his fangs in and feast on my bollocks.

The old blue light illuminates the scene and I'm taken to the station and banged up. Next morning it's court. It's serious this time, they say. It's remand this time, they say. And we know what happens after remand when you're caught with hands as red as mine. Prison.

The cells are bigger, the doors heavier. The men what hang around the landings are bigger, louder. A group of them stop me on day one, ask me what I done, who I am. I tell them about the Old Man and one knows him. He slaps my back, says I got nothing to worry about, says it's gonna be a doddle, says I just gotta keep my nose clean and time'll pass cos time does. And they talk to me, tell me stories, out-talk each other. It's: Yeah and I broke in and nicked the lot. It's: I hit him till his own muvver wouldn't know who he was. It's: I never meant to stab him, sonny, but what did he expect, jumping my old woman's bones?

I'm in with a cellmate whose arms are black with ink. He sits on the side of his bed and rolls up fags and tells me the story of every law he broke and every nose he broke and every heart he broke.

Days pass and if I stand on the bed I can see a small square of sky which is mostly grey but sometimes blue. My legs pop with energy and I just wanna get out and walk. I just wanna be free and that's the one thing I can't be. I tell myself there's no choice: I just gotta shut up and do my time. I just gotta kill my time. I spend my days on the landings talking, listening. I spend my days learning. By the time I go I've done an apprenticeship. I know every lock there's ever been made and how to spring them. I know ten different ways to hide a body, from the acid bath to driving it up to a Scottish island and weighing it down, then lowering it into the black loch water till there's only the smallest ripple on the surface.

*

Time does pass and they let me out, send me home. I step out into the street where there's no one to meet me. It's a walk to the bus (a fresh-out-of-nick walk) then it's the train. I walk from the station to the estate and up the concrete piss stairs. I still got the key to the door so I open it, shut the door quiet behind me. I can hear faint singing from the kitchen and go down to see.

Mum's at the sink, her back to me. She's looking out the window. I know from the shape of her back what her head's full of. The old dreams, the how did it come to this dreams. Her singing stops. She sighs. Her shoulders dip down. She wipes her hair off her face with the back of her hand. And then she dries her hands on a cloth, puts it down and turns round, ready to get a drink and go and turn on the telly, see if she can lose herself in the moving pictures.

She sees me standing there looking at her. She jumps, her hand to her throat.

– You scared me, she says.

– Sorry.

– You never told me you was coming out, she says, then she leans back against the sink. I hear her voice catch. – I would've cooked you somethink if I'd known.

– It's fine, I go. – I ain't hungry.

– I could've done liver and bacon. I could've done mash.

– It's all right. I had a sandwich.

And then the tears build up and spill over.

– Where've I gone wrong?

– Don't, I go. – It's nothing to do with you.

– Course it is. It's got to be, ain't it?

I shake my head. – You're all right. It ain't nothing you done.

She don't speak for a bit. She wipes her eyes but the tears don't stop. I don't move. I stand there and she cries. My hands are hanging by my sides like my fists are too heavy to move. I can't do nothing. And she can't do nothing. There's only five feet between us but it might as well be a football-pitch length.

Mum mops the tears. Speaks: – Your father's moved out.

– He'll come back, I say.

She shakes her head. – He says he ain't never gonna.

– And where's Alan?

– He's left home. It's only me and Sharon now.

– Well I'm back now, ain't I?

– But you ain't gonna be here long. You'll be locked up again soon.

– Not this time.

– But you will cos the pattern's set, ain't it? You're just like him.

– I ain't, I go.

– But you are. Look at you, Gary.

She points at the window. – There's all that out there and you ain't seen none of it. All you seen is the inside of police vans and the inside of cells.

And with that she shakes her head and walks past me, goes down the hallway. I stand there, and you know what? Something she's said has stopped me short. It's making me think. She's found a chink in the armour, the soft bit under the shell.

I stand in the doorway and this voice speaks to me. It ain't a voice from outside; it's my voice and it says this: Maybe, son, it's time to do something else. Maybe, son, it's time to use what you got and what you know. Maybe, son, it's time to stop the lock-up, four-wall shit.

Maybe, son, it's time to end this chapter.

Fool's Gold

That morning, when we was in the kitchen, when my fists was heavy, my hands by my side, that moment wouldn't happen with my son. I'd be the one to step forward, put an arm on him. I'd be the one.

Camden, London. I stand outside the address I got on my scrap of paper. There's rows of bells and I find the one I'm looking for, press it. Press it again.

He opens the door. His hair's cut shorter, rockabilly style, and he wears a red checked shirt, sleeves rolled up; a new tattoo crawls out from under his shirtsleeve.

He stares at me. – Well, bloody hell. They let you out.

– They never, I go. – I broke out. Escaped.

– Escaped, he goes. – Wait till they all know what kind of son I got. How d'you do that?

– I nicked a uniform, I go. – Pushed out the dirty sheets.

– How d'you get the keys?

– I hit the bloke over the back of the head, stunned him. Chucked him in a cell and locked the door. Let myself out. When I got to the main door the

Governor was there and then I hit him and knocked him out. There was blood everywhere.

He looks at me. A cold fish's eye. – Very funny. What you come here for?

– That's a nice way for a father to speak to his son, I go. – Shouldn't you say come in, good to see you?

He sighs and slowly stands aside. I follow him up to his room. There are two beds and he sees me clock them. – No, he goes.

– Just till I'm sorted, I go, and I put my bag on the spare bed.

He shakes his head. – I was trying to get away from everyone.

– Well, you ain't doing very well. You can't get rid of your kids. You can't unfather yourself.

– All right. So what you want? What you doing up here?

– I come to see if the streets are paved with gold.

– There's so much gold, he goes, – that they're panning for it in the Thames.

– Then I better get a sieve. I need some money. I need some work.

He looks at me, has a bright idea. – You can come and work with me.

– I ain't going out nicking.

– You ain't gonna have to.

– I've gone straight.

He grins. – I've gone straight and all.

I start to laugh. – You?

– Ain't funny. I'm doing scaffolding. Got loads of work. Might as well be printing the notes cos they're building everywhere. London's on a boom, son. There's no stopping it.

He goes to the window, looks out, shows me. – See, sky's full of cranes. When they're all there you know there's folding stuff to be made. When they migrate to other places, you know the money's on the down.

The early morning air's cold enough to freeze my hand to the door handle of the lorry. I climb in first, get the middle seat. The Old Man follows. Tony's in the driving seat: he's not much taller than me, got bleached blond hair and a trilby. He lights up, starts up, and we drive into the City, stop outside some offices what've got scaffolding up to the second floor. Tony jumps out, climbs straight up the corner scaffold tube like he's in the ape house, starts undoing the metal clips. He moves quick, never stops, undoes each and chucks them down to the Old Man, who puts them in a wheelbarrow. I follow Tony up, copy him. When the clips are off he gets each tube on his shoulder and slides it down till it touches the ground then the Old Man takes it, adjusts how he stands as he balances its weight, carries it to the back of the lorry.

When the last bits are loaded, we drive east out of the City, and pull into a yard where there's racks of scaffolding tubes and boards. Two flatbed lorries.

– This your yard? I go.

The Old Man laughs. – No.

He gets out, and we unload the gear into their store. They hand the Old Man a wad of cash and we get back in. Drive off. Tony pulls up at a cafe and we order three full Englishes. The girl brings over plates what are nearly cracking with the weight of the food.

Tony watches her walk off. Takes a sip of his tea. – Her arse, he says, – is like two fried eggs.

The Old Man near spits out his tea. – Fried eggs is soft.

– Not the way I fry them.

– Not eggs, the Old Man says.

– I hate to interrupt, I go, – but I was wondering what gear we're gonna use now you sold all that?

The Old Man looks at me like I just been born. – Wasn't never mine to sell, he goes.

– So whose was it?

He just stares at me. – You joined the cop squad? I don't know whose frigging stuff it was. I just took it down.

– Thought you was going straight, I go.

– I'm straighter than I was. Thing is, Gary, is not to get caught. That's what's important.

We're in South London and this time we're putting up. The Old Man's having a minute's shut-eye in the lorry though it's turning out to be a long minute, and Tony's taking it on his self to teach me what he knows. We lay out base plates and secure the bottom to make sure it'll stand firm so we can build the next lifts.

We move quick without chat: we lay the boards down and start on the next lift. We build up two more and we're near the top of the house when we run out of clips. He goes down to get more, tells me to stay put. He'll chuck them up to me.

I stand waiting and he throws one up. I put my hand out to catch it and I'm expecting it to land hard, cos they're metal lumps. But it don't come like that; it comes up real slow and it's brass-coloured and the sun lights it and it arcs through the air, a lump of gold, weightless. And it's like time has slowed and slurred. I don't move my hand to get it. It just lands on me. His aim is so bleeding perfect I don't even move my hand. He chucks up the next. The next. They all land the same, all the same arc. The same perfect aim.

He climbs back up and we finish off the handrails and the toeboards, then when we're done we stand on the top lift and look out over London. The sun's broken out of some clouds and the birds are shouting. We can see out over the roofs, see right over London.

I look at him standing there. – Tony, I go, – how d'you do that? Chuck them clips and swivels like that?

He shrugs. – I always been able to. I played cricket as a kid.

– Was you good?

He nods. Don't say nothing for a bit. Then: – It's all I ever done, chuck stuff, used to play all the time and got spotted from school, played at the Oval.

He points it out in the London skyline. – There. Used to go and watch and when they bowled I'd feel it in my arm like it was me doing it.

– You still play? I ask.

He shakes his head. – No.

A plane flies high up, over the city. There's a white trail behind.

– I stopped when I was eleven, he goes. – Dad kicked me about. Broke my arm.

He bends down, tightens a clip. Stands back up and gets fags out, offers me one. We light up.

– Some things, Gary, ain't for the likes of us. That ain't the lives that was chosen for us.

– You reckon they're chosen?

He nods. – Your cards is all marked the day you're born.

I shake my head. – Not mine, I go. That ain't gonna happen to me.

The Old Man shouts up, asks if we're coming down but we don't say nothing and he climbs up to join us, sees us standing there smoking.

– What's this, he goes, – a holiday?

– What was that, I go, – sleeping sickness?

He looks out over the view. – So, Tony, what's he like? Gonna make a scaffolder?

Tony flicks his fag end off the roof and it floats down. – Tell you the truth, he goes, – he's the quickest learner I ever known.

The Old Man nods. – Good.

And inside me there's this feeling, and I don't know

what to call it or if it's even got a name, but I feel it. Cos this is something I know I can do. I get it.

I look over the view, see all of London there, and I got this swelling in my chest and I think: Look at it all, son, spread out there in front of you. And I think: Look at me, here I am up high. I'm young, strong, I got so much. And I reckon everything's gonna turn out like I want it.

That evening, I'm showered and changed into the spare jeans and walking under the street lights. I got cash in my pocket and I'm walking like I could walk for ever. Like nothing's ever gonna stop me.

There's a pub up ahead and there's two tables with benches outside. A woman's on one of the benches, knees drawn up to her chest. Her head's leant back against the wall. Eyes closed. She's got short, dark hair. I know who it is even before I see her face properly. I stop. Watch for a while. See the lids over her eyes, hear her breathing. It's heavy, uneven.

I touch her knee. – Bernadette?

She looks up. Only she can't make me out cos her eyes ain't fixing. They're all irises, all pale blue. Pupils smaller than the head of a pin. She's got a bruise down her left cheek. Her skin's shining with sweat. I can smell it on her. It lines my nostrils.

– I'm Gary, I go. – Gary. You used to live next to us.

Her eyes roam around, try to get a fix on me. They don't have nothing in them. I can see her searching, trying to remember me.

– You were mates with my mum. Janet. Remember?

– Janet.

– In the flat on the estate.

She nods. Her brain searches through, and I see the flicker in her eyes as she recognizes the name Janet, the word estate. – Who are you? she asks.

– Gary.

She nods and I see she's got it. The flat, the walkway, the kids next door. Her friend Janet. – You're Gary, ain't you?

– I am, yeah.

She lifts her hand to her cheek as though she can rub off the bruise. As though she can hide it. She pulls herself up, tries to sit straight. Even now, even in this state, she don't wanna be seen like this. Inside her somewhere there's a scrap of being a human, of pride.

– I just nodded off, she goes.

– Yeah, course you did, I go. – We all do that.

She nods. – Yeah, we all do that.

– You okay?

– Ain't never been better, she says.

I put my hand in my pocket and pull out a small wad of notes, check there's more than I took from the tin in her flat. I hand them to her. She holds them like she ain't never seen money before.

– Put them away, I go.

But she's still staring at them and so I take them, fold them, put them in her pocket.

She puts her hand on my arm. – Thank you.

Then the eyes shift and the focus moves and I see her react to something over my shoulder. – I got to go, she says.

I look round to see what's caught her eye. There's a bloke stood there, a briefcase in his hand. He stares at her and I stare at him. His eyes shift, meet mine, but he don't look away.

Bernadette brings her legs down, stands, sways. I grab her arm.

– You all right? I ask.

– Yeah. Fine. Got to go.

She squeezes my hand where I'm holding her then pulls away. She walks towards the man, and I wish I didn't know everything, see everything. I wish I didn't know that his hand's in his pocket, round the fiver he's gonna give her for getting down on her knees. He knows what state she's in, but he's in a state too and there's something he needs her to do for him and that need is bigger than her need and he ain't gonna be put off from getting exactly what he wants.

They leave together, walk round the corner. The street is empty. I sink down on to the bench and feel my own breathing, feel the air around me settle as I lean back.

The wall's soaked up the heat of the day and the bench is warm beneath me. I sit for a bit. Think. And this is what I decide: Let that, son, be a warning to yourself. Not that you need one cos there ain't no flies on you and you're the one person what knows what he's doing. Don't forget this, son. Don't forget it.

And I won't. It's one of them moments you know you ain't never gonna forget. Whatever happens in your life you'll have it in your head.

The King's Cross

I move out from the Old Man's bedshit, and get a flat off a bloke who rents it off a bird who's on the council rent book. It's in a block round a courtyard and it's on the third floor. The windows have gaps and cold draughts. The floorboards are rotten and where they're soft your foot goes through. There's a mattress on the floor. But it's mine and the Old Man ain't in it.

King's Cross is a madhouse and no one ever stands still nor sleeps nor nothing. The pavements are coated in kebab wrappers and old papers. There's windows boarded up. The newspaper sellers call out the headlines. Kids come fresh off the trains like moths fluttering down south, blinking at the bright lights. There's women selling what they got on the corners and blokes watching them.

And there's also the dealers, cos the drugrush has begun. They're selling the latest product what's arrived: smack, brown, horse, white, poppy mush, sucker crumbs, whatever you call it.

Tony and me go for a drink after work each evening, then one night he says we ain't going to the pub but we're going to see this bird he's been seeing.

We drop off the Old Man and drive down to the river, go along towards Chelsea. Cathy answers the door. She takes us in the kitchen and gets beers out the fridge. Tony's got spare clothes there and chucks me some. I go to the bathroom, dunk my head in the sink to get the dust out, pull on a shirt and trousers. When I come out, there's a new bird by the window. Tall. Slim. Dark hair.

Cathy turns to me. – Ah, here's Gary, she goes. – Gary, this is my friend Georgina.

Georgina turns slowly from the window and looks at me.

– You all right? I go.

She raises her eyebrows. – I am now, she says.

We go to her flat after the pub, the club, the walk through the park. She pours vodka and as I drink I feel it hit my blood. My head comes clear and I go in the bathroom where I eyeball myself in the mirror. I look at my hair, skin, eyes. I look good. I'm fit, hard from work. I'm in London and it's all mine. I nod to myself. You're doing good, son. You're doing good.

We stay up all night. Shag, drink, shag, drink. As dawn comes we're in the bath together and her legs is hooked over the edge.

– I've got to go to work, she goes.

– Stuff work.

– I have a good job.

– Where?

– In a gallery on Cork Street.

– What d'you do?

– Look beautiful and speak nicely if a rich client comes in. Then I take them round, tell them how much the painting will appreciate in five years, pour them a drink, tell them they have impeccable taste. I am an art prostitute.

– You're a pimp. The painting's the prostitute.

She brings her legs back in the bath and I put my foot between them, push her knees apart. She shakes her head. – I'm getting out. We need breakfast. When are you coming back?

– I ain't.

– You look good here. Your eyes go with the walls.

I look up, see the bright blue wall tiles. – Fuck off.

She laughs and gets out. I go and lie down on her bed. My head starts to go and my guts are churning. There's some vodka left in the glass by the bed and I pick it up, swig. It sorts everything, sharpens the brain and the tongue. I get dressed, go into the kitchen.

She's put food on the table but I can't eat. She laughs and pushes some toast towards me. – Is my bit of rough feeling rough? she asks.

– No, I go. – I just need a piss first.

I go to the bathroom, lock the door. I sit on the pan. I dunno what it is but there's something ain't right. It's like the room with the food in, with her in, I can't go in it.

There's a knock on the door and the handle turns.

– Gary? What's going on?

I don't say nothing. I think of the food on the table, the two chairs opposite each other. My guts churn. I stand, lift the lid, puke into the pan. She knocks on the door. The smell is acid. I got beads of sweat on my forehead. I try to open the window so I can breathe but it's locked. I pick up the bathroom scales, use them to shatter the glass. I can hear her knocking and shouting and I dunno what I'm doing. I got to get out. I smash the glass out till there's room to climb through, and I'm dropping down to the roof below, down to ground level, and I'm gone.

In the park I'm still sweating. I go to the trees, lie down underneath. The earth stinks and it's like I can smell too much. I close my eyes. I got Tony's clothes on and I dunno whose head I got on my shoulders but it ain't mine.

I open my eyes. Look up at leaves and branches. All I got to do is lie here till it all passes.

And that's what happens. I sleep and when I wake it's all different. I'm fine. I stand up, brush earth and grass off Tony's clothes. I walk out the park and through the West End to the City where I know they're working.

Tony's up on the second lift taking down. The Old Man's loading gear on to the lorry. He sees me walk towards him. – Where the hell you been? he goes.

I don't say nothing. I get some old clothes out the lorry, change, climb up to the second lift. Tony asks me if I had a good night and I say yep. Yep yep yep. A bloody good night. And it's true. It was a bloody good night.

I grab the clips and doubles and make a start.

We stop round dinner time when we're done and we get in the lorry, the three of us. The Old Man tells Tony to drive to a bank in North London. There's scaffolding right up to the roof and a couple of skips outside. I'm reckoning we're taking down the gear to flog but there's a bloke outside waiting on the door-step, and the Old Man gets out, tells me to follow. He goes up to the bloke and shakes his hand. I follow them into the bank, see the wooden panelling and the parquet floor.

– Being demolished next week, the Old Man goes.

The man nods. Looks around. – How much?

– Five hundred and we'll deliver it to your door. Soon as we rip it out.

– You're done.

– Two hundred down, the Old Man says, – so I don't sell it to no one else.

The bloke counts out his notes, hands them over. They shake hands and he leaves. – That's the tenth time I sold it, the Old Man says.

He takes the stack of notes back to the cab of the lorry and fans them under my nose. I can smell old ink, sweat, the money stink. – Easy pickings, he goes.

– You said you was going straight, I go.

– I never.

Tony turns on the engine, starts up. – Where we going?

– We got to go to the halo shop for Gary, the Old Man goes.

– Ha ha, Tony goes and he pulls out into the traffic.

– I told you, I go, – that I didn't wanna go nicking no more. I told you that.

The Old Man lays a hundred in used notes on my lap. – Think about it, son, think how long it would take you to earn that. Think what you can do with it. Take a bird somewhere decent. Buy yourself some good threads. Save somethink for later.

I look out the side window.

– Thing is, Gary, you can sweat the crack of your arse off the rest of your life to make money for someone else or you can use your noggin and earn a decent screw like me.

I turn from the window and look at him.

– You know I'm right, he says. – Go on. Put them in your pocket.

And so I do.

Antiques Roadshow

It's the Old Man who sets up the meeting; all I got to do is turn up at a pub in a backstreet of South London. The bloke I'm due to meet is sat in a corner seat, his two King Charles Spaniels on another. He ain't difficult to spot.

– Jim the Belly? I go.

– That's me.

He waves a tenner at me. – Get the drinks in, Gary, he goes. – Two pints plus chasers. And ask for the whisky up top. Not that shit in the upside-down bottle. And get some pork scratchings and if you ask nice, they'll give you a bowl of gravy for the dogs.

I bring it all back and he puts the gravy on the floor. The dogs jump down from their chair, slap their tongues in and splash it around. He smiles as he watches them. – She boils bones overnight. It's the marrow makes it tasty.

I down the chaser quick and feel it heat the inside of my belly, work its way through the blood to my head. It sharpens me, polishes my brain.

Jim the Belly pats his lap and the smaller dog jumps up, only it's a balancing act what with Jim's short legs and the belly. He raises his pint glass. – I reckon if I'd seen you in the street I'd know whose son you were. An apple don't never fall far from a tree.

He laughs and the dog falls off his lap where his belly shakes. It whines and jumps back up. – You'll be wondering why I asked to see you, he says.

– It occurred to me, I go.

– Your dad says you're a fast learner.

– He ain't wrong.

– That panelling he sold in the bank, he says. – You know why he made so much? It was walnut. That's what made them all jump for it. Walnut, mahogany, all worth a good bit. Me, mind, I like a spot of oak. Or elm. Elm has a nice grain on it, wears well.

– How d'you tell the difference?

– Colour and grain. You got to know that wood is a beautiful thing, Gary.

He strokes the table where we're sat. – This is only cheap pine, but look, not many stains is there, even though it's been in this filthy old pub for years. That's cos wood can perform miracles. I had a takeaway curry one night, spilt it on my elm table. This massive yellow mark. But after a few days it was gone. The wood just absorbs it. That's the mystery of it, Gary. That's the mystery.

He sees me feeling the wood of the table.

– Know why I wanted to see you? I been keeping my eye out for someone to work with me, and I got a feeling you're exactly what I been looking for.

★

Jim the Belly pulls up in an old Daimler what smells of wood and leather. The bigger dog climbs on me to look out the front windscreen and as Jim drives off it digs its claws in to get its balance.

– Where we going? I ask.

He don't answer. He points at the dashboard.
– What kind of wood is that?

It's dark, got a heavy varnish on it and tight swirls.
– It ain't oak, I go.

– If you'd said it was oak I'd call you a dopey cunt and chuck you out at the next lights. It's walnut. Takes a walnut tree a long time to grow and it ain't easy to cut, that's why there's a premium on it. Look, see the small dark marks, the tight grain. That's lesson number one. Walnut, son. – Got it?

– Yep. Got it.

And I have got it. Click click in the brain. Get the information in, sort it, make sure it's in the right folds of the cauliflower head. Click click.

He drives and I listen to the engine. It's deep, smooth.

– Nice car, I go.

– Nice car? he says. – Drinks more petrol than my dogs drink gravy. I wouldn't've nicked the frigging thing if I'd known the tank was empty.

He parks up and we leave the dogs in the car, walk round the corner. It's broad daylight and we stop on the pavement opposite the old courtrooms. He looks at the carved wooden sign by the door, checks how it's fixed on. He whips a small crowbar out his pocket and wrenches it off the wall. He don't run off but stands there, turning it over in his hands, checking it. He makes it look like he's got nothing to hide. Then he nods to me and we start walking back towards the car. When we get in he puts it on my lap.

I look at it. – Why we got this?

– Lesson two is don't say nothing, Gary, he goes. – Not yet. Half the art of life is knowing when not to speak so you don't make an arse of yourself.

We go to an antiques shop in North London. A woman lets us in, asks Jim how he is. They do the catch-up (yep, yep, the family's fine, weather's been terrible, you wouldn't believe it was this time of year, yeah can't wait for the election though the other lot's just as bloody bad, and what about you?), then he brings out the sign, shows her.

She looks at it for a bit, then tells us to come through to the back room where she gets out her magnifying glass, turns the sign over this way, that. She puts them both down, looks at Jim. – How much do you want for it? she asks.

– Five hundred?

– Would you take four?

And before I can say four bloody hundred, they've agreed on four fifty and shaken hands on it and she's counted it all out and Jim the Belly's slipped the wad in his pocket.

– Thank you, Patrick, the woman goes. *Patrick.* Then she looks at me. – And you are?

– This is my partner, Robert, Jim the Belly says quickly before I can open my gob. – He sourced the plaque for me.

The woman sticks her hand out and shakes mine. – Lovely to do business.

We go back to the car and Jim the Belly counts out half the money, a clean two hundred and twenty-five, and gives it me.

– I ain't done nothing, I go.

– Apprentice's wages.

He watches me thumb through the stack of cash.

– Stick with me, son. Antiques is the way forward. Antiques.

Lessons three, four, five and the rest begin the next day. We drive a van up to Hampstead in the evening and as he drives he tells me he's spotted a big old house and he reckons the owners are away. He's seen the alarm people come out to price up an installation, so he wants to act quick before it's done. He parks up the van in an unlit street and is about to open the door.

– Wait, I go.

– What is it?

– Wait.

He looks at me, surprised, but don't say nothing. We sit there a while then a bloke walks past the car with his dog. I wait till he's gone then say: – All right. Let's go.

– You knew he was coming?

I nod. – I saw him when we parked, knew he was lazy from his walk and cos he's fat, so I knew he was only gonna go far enough to find a few blades of grass for the dog to shit on.

Jim the Belly nods slowly, taking in his lesson one. – Good, he says. – Good.

The house is big, backs on to the heath. We force the back door and I stand in the hallway, get a sense of it. Jim goes into the lounge, checks a small chest, picks it up, turns it over. I watch him. This is something different from what I done before. There's no in and out, grab and run. This is slow, considered. He pulls out a small drawer in the chest and turns it round, looks at the back. He shines the torch and shows me the handmade dovetail joints, tells me how long it would take the carpenter to make, how much work went in to the back of a drawer even though it'd never be seen.

We look for handmade nails, turn over plates for marks, shine the torch behind china to see if it's cracked. Quality, Jim says. – Quality is what we're looking for.

In goes the lesson. Click click. By now the old bonehead is stirring at what I just realized there is to learn. It's all about quality, craft. I'm gonna learn about things of real worth. I think of all the houses in that same street, reckon up how many houses in how many streets got stuff like this to be hunted down. It's like a chase, and I got a scent of the quarry. Cos this is the thing. All money's the same: brown tenners, blue fivers, green oners. It's only worth what it's worth cos we all play the game, and agree that yeah this little scrap of paper's worth more than the actual paper it's printed on. But these things I'm learning about ain't like that: they're real. They're objects to be hunted down. I got a spear in my hand, I got a film of sweat on my skin. I got a purpose.

He shows me the fireplace, points out the hand-carved details on it, the fine chisel marks, then he gets his bar and we lever it off the wall and it comes off easy. We carry it out to the front and stand it by the door.

He goes off, says he'll get the van, but as he's about to head out the door I put my hand up to stop him. I stand still and listen. Even though Jim can't hear nothing, I can. A car approaches then passes. I slip out the big bolt and let him out.

I follow him out with the fireplace and I'm halfway down the front path when a soft-shoed woman approaches, taking her dog for a piss walk. She sees me and I see her hesitate.

I jump in first before she can do a 999. My voice is confident. No question that I'm in the right. – Lovely evening, I go.

– Yes it is, isn't it?

Her voice is saying more than the words. I can tell from the tone what she's thinking: she should check who I am, ask why I'm taking out that fireplace. But her problem is she's English and if she's English, she's gonna be polite. It ain't easy for her and I feel sorry for her, so I help her out.

I smile. Point at the fireplace. – Lot to restore on this one, I go. – We'll have it in the workshop for a while.

I see her facial muscles start to relax. – See here, I say. – Look, come and see.

She hesitates but she don't wanna be rude so she steps closer. I point at the mantel. – See this hole here, I go. – It's the beginning of worm. The house'll be riddled with it if I don't do somethink about it.

Her hands flutter up to her chest. – Oh dear. How dreadful.

– Don't worry, I go. – It's in safe hands now. We'll stop it getting any worse.

– That's good, she goes. – It's a beautiful fireplace.

– You're right, I go. – It's unusual for its age. I've worked with one similar which I wonder now if it was made by the same bloke. That's a nice thought, ain't it? The same pair of hands created them both. And then it's the same pair of hands, my hands, what'll restore them both. We're both craftsmen, just separated by a few centuries.

I'm getting warmed up, rising to this. I'm enjoying it.

– And look at this little touch, I say, pointing out a bit of carving. – It's a carved bee, come to get nectar from the flower.

And then the van pulls up and Jim gets out.

– Richard, he says.

– Sorry, I say, – my partner, Patrick, is calling me. We'd better get on.

– Of course, the woman goes. And she walks off. Her step is changed now. Jaunty like the dog. Little jaunty gin legs. She's not just reassured, she's thinking what a lovely man, those twinkling blue eyes, and who would have thought he'd have all that knowledge, all that sensitivity. Just shows, don't judge books by covers. She'll smile as my words come back to her. My hands touching the same fireplace as the original carpenter's hands.

We go to an all-night cafe and Jim orders the Big Man fry-up. Stirs four sugars into his tea and beckons over the waitress. He asks her to bring out some extra sausages for the dogs then, as she turns to go, reaches out and pats her arse like it's a tennis ball.

– Mr Wilson, she says, – I told you before, do not touch me.

And she marches off.

Jim winks at me. – You'd think they'd be grateful to be admired. That's the thing with the world, Gary, it's all upsidebloodydown. Just cos there's a woman in charge of the bleeding country, they think they're our equals.

He starts to butter a piece of toast then stops, looks at me. I drink my tea; he's still looking.

– You're staring at me, I go.

He nods.

– Why?

– There's something about you. You got something.

– Toast?

– No. I'm serious. The speed you're learning, what you done tonight to talk your way out of it. You got something.

I smear the butter on my toast, take a bite. – Thanks, Jim, I go.

– Just make sure you keep your nose as clean as you can. Make sure you learn all the lessons. Don't chuck away what you got.

– I won't, I go. – I won't.

Another lesson. Click click.

Visiting Time

I already said we're born into a family what's like a metal cage what forms us as we grow. But I been thinking more about this and the trouble is it's more complicated than that. Cos we can be born into the same cage and be different. Take brothers: sometimes they can be the same. Other times they can be so different they're like enemies in a family. They can hate each other's guts. They can wanna rip the skin from each other's throats.

I been thinking about this cos I been studying my son as he's been growing up. And when you got your own, you got to think about what it is you do to him, just like you got to think about what your own family've done to you.

Mum's tried. She's brushed her hair, smeared colour on her lips. When she opens the door she looks out past me as though she was expecting someone.
– Thought you might be bringing a girlfriend with you, she says.

I smile. – Ain't I enough, Mum?

– Course you are. I just thought you'd have one by now. Thought that's why you was coming to see us.

– I come to see you, not show you somethink.

– Well, that's lovely. Yeah. Lovely.

We go to the lounge what's been tidied. She goes to put the kettle on in the kitchen and while she's out I look around to see if anything's changed. Wallpaper's the same. Fireplace's still full of fag ends. Arm of the sofa's still ripped, still got grubby sponge oozing from it. I'm just thinking, Christ, ain't nothing ever gonna change when Sharon – I think it's her – comes down the stairs and walks in the room. She's got permed hair, blue above her eyes. She's wearing stretchy towelling shorts and top. All too tight, like she's been blown up with a bike pump.

– What you been eating, Shaz? I ask.

– It's puppy fat, she goes.

– Ain't never seen a puppy that size, I go.

Mum comes back in, puts a box of French Fancies on the table. – Bloody hell, look at them, Shaz goes. – We never get these when you ain't here.

– Stop fucking swearing, I go.

– Why? It's how I talk, Gaz, she says. – You wouldn't want me to speak no other way than how I speak.

She rips open the box, chucks a pink cake in her gob, carries on talking, spraying bits everywhere. – Mum said she thought you was bringing a girlfriend home. I told her you was too ugly to get one.

– Mum don't think I'm ugly, I go. – She says I'm the family looker.

– Ha ha. She always had a problem with her eyes. Getting cataracts, ain't you, Mum?

The doorbell goes and Sharon's off to answer it.

Comes back with Alan. He's double denimed, baggy jeans, thick hair flicked back off his face, blond streaks.

– Y'all right? he goes.

– Yeah, I go. – You?

– Yeah.

The three of us sit at the table. Sharon eats another cake. Mum gets the tea and milk and sugar, sits down.

– Look at this, she goes. – All of us together again. Almost like a real family, ain't it?

– We are a real family, Alan goes.

Mum waves the air. – You know what I mean. If your dad was here we'd all be together.

– If Dad was here I wouldn't be, Alan goes.

– Don't speak about him like that, Mum says.

Alan's eyes turn up to the ceiling so far they're near all whites. He drinks his tea. Puts the cup down. Turns to me. – So, Gary. What you been doing?

– This and that, I go. – Some scaffolding with the Old Man. Some work with his mate who's got a company what delivers antiques. And you? What you doing?

– Got a job in the factory.

– Smithson's?

– Yeah, that's it.

I pour some more tea. The factory where me and the Old Man went. Where we stood outside in the dark. Where the moon didn't shine.

– They've put me on management, Alan goes.

– He's doing brilliant, Mum says.

I nod. – Good. How many hours you got to work?

– Forty.

– What holiday you get?

– Twenty days. It goes up to twenty-five after five years.

Even him saying it makes me choke up, makes me feel like I can't breathe. It's like his weeks off are stuck in my throat.

Sharon's hand creeps across the table but before she can get to them, I slam my hand down on my pack of fags. – You gotta ask, I go.

– You're family, she says. – You don't have to ask family.

– You gotta ask family more than anyone else.

– Don't be tight, she goes.

– All right then, have them.

I shove the pack over towards her then start to take off my shirt. – You want this too?

– Ha bloody ha, she goes.

I stand up and pull the linings out of my pockets. – You want any of this?

– That's enough, Gary, Alan says. – You always got to take things too far.

I slam my fist down on the table. – *Shut the fuck up.*

There's a silence and Mum looks down at her tea.

– Don't be so bloody aggressive, Alan says.

– Don't tell me how to be.

Alan stares at me. – You proud you're so like the Old Man?

I jump up and I'm about to go round the table. Shaz jumps up too. Screams at me, stands between us. – Don't, Gaz, she says. – Don't.

I look at Mum, her head bowed. I manage to sit down.

Alan puts up his hands. – Sorry.

Sharon takes one of my fags and lights up and I don't say nothing. Mum stands up and goes out to the kitchen. My heart is banging and my fists are clenched. I uncurl them. We sit there, the three of us. Then as my heart slows I hear sounds from the kitchen. A cupboard door. The crack of a screw top opening. The pouring of liquid, a throated gurgle.

She walks back in clutching a glass of clear liquid. She puts it down, overly careful. Keeps her hand on the stem and plays with it. Don't take a sip instantly cos this way she reckons we'll believe she's in control.

None of us look at her. Alan stands up. – I got to get on. I only had a minute to call in.

Sharon stands up. – I got to go and all.

And they both leave and the door slams behind them.

There's one cake left, half out the box. The icing's thick and yellow. Mum picks up her glass. There's a tremble in her hand and I can see the surface of the liquid move, as though there's a wind inside the room. She lifts it to her lips, drinks. Soon as it touches her inside world, every cell in her body starts to soften. She feels herself coming back. She drinks again, again. Then puts the glass down, reaches out and grabs my hand.

– I'm so pleased you come to see me, love. So pleased.

– That's enough, Mum. Don't start.

But once she's started she can't stop. She drinks, cries. Drinks, cries. I fill up her glass then fill up a glass for me. We drink till our eyes is as glassy as the liquid we're holding.

I put her in the chair by the fireplace and switch on the telly. I tell her I got to go.

– Why?

– I got work, Mum. You don't want me to lose my job?

– Course I don't.

– So I better get going. You'll be all right. I'll come and see you soon.

– Don't leave it so long. Come back and see your old mum. Come back and have another drink with me.

– I will, I go.

And I know when I say it how much I mean it. They're written, them words, in umbilical blood.

Pension Fund

I'm inside the flat in King's Cross. There's a knock at the door. Three beats. Rat tat-tat. Then another three. Rat tat-tat, but this one's louder. Everyone's got their own knocking music just like they got their own walk, and I know whose this is.

Jim's leaning against the doorway, out of breath. – You might as well live at the top of the Eiffel frigging Tower, he goes.

– What you doing here? I ask.

He looks at me. His eyes narrow. – Got something to hide?

– Course I ain't. You just didn't say you was coming.

– You don't normally when it's a surprise visit.

I stand back and the dogs come in first. He follows. He looks around, and I see his surprise at what I done to the flat. There's an oak mantel propped up against the wall, a pair of red velvet Louis the Fifteenth chairs with gold legs and arms, a set of three eighteenth-century oil landscapes in gold frames. A hand-dyed Persian rug. A blue and white Chinese bowl on a mahogany table.

He lets air out, long and low, between his teeth. – Quality, he says. – Quality.

– I had someone to impress, I go.

– A bird?

I nod. – Yep.

– Where is she? Hiding in the bedroom?

– I opened the cage door. Didn't like the way she sang.

He grins. Picks up the Chinese bowl. – Nice. You done a nice job here.

– Thanks.

– You should've been an interior designer. Lot of money in it. Specially if you nick the stuff then charge your client for it. Where you get it all?

– Here and there. Done a couple of jobs.

– Now you done this, you better find a new bird to move in.

– I ain't gonna do that, I go. – You can get one.

– Me? These two dogs is enough for me. Gave up on women when I couldn't see my dick no more. You got anything to eat?

We go out once it's dark, drive through Kensington, out west. We park up the van and sit for a bit, let the world settle around us, then when we're ready we slip out, close the doors quietly. We creep round the corner to the white house with scaffolding. There's a skip and a delivery of sand in the drive. Jim nips down the side, round the back. I see the alarm but he wags his finger to let me know it ain't a problem. He points to the window what he's paid the builder's lad to leave open.

I get my gloves out my backpack, pull them on. My heart's beating louder to let me know I'm aware, ready for this. I pull the ladder out from behind the shrubs what he's also paid to be left there, and climb up on to the flat roof. I stop, crouched, listening: footsteps and a car approaching. I stay, still. Jim's down there, still. The feet pass by. The car goes. I make my way to the window, test it. The sash opens easily and I climb in. It's dark inside and I feel my way along the wall to the banister, feel my way with my feet to the top step. Downstairs I go along the hallway to the back door, slide the bolt and turn the key, let him in.

Everything's been crated up and covered while the work's being done. There's dustsheets over tables, chairs and sofas. Anything moveable is in crates. We look in the first crate, unwrap china and glass.

Jim pulls out a plate. – Might be quality but it's horrible. Keep looking.

We find what we're looking for in the second crate. They're tiny ivory figures, wrapped in old copies of the *Telegraph*. He takes out a few, puts them on the table.

– Japanese? I go.

– Good guess. And what you reckon they do with them?

– Ornaments?

– No. They wore kimonos what ain't got no pockets, see, so they have boxes to keep their things in. They tuck these little buggers in their sashes and the boxes dangle from them. Japan's the big thing. It's bloody boom town, son. Lot of money in these.

We take out the rest of the figures, put everything back as it was and let ourselves out the back door. I put the ladder back then stand still in the dark to make sure it's all clear before we go.

Jim starts the engine. Drives off.

– How d'you know them things were there? I ask.

He grins. – The bloke what lives here wrote a book on them. Then I see he's in America flogging the book and I put two and two together. See what happens when you do your homework, Gary.

Click click.

– These'll be our long-term investment. Pension fund, Gary, everyone needs a pension fund.

Click.

Next day Jim tells me we got a big job on next so we'll need an extra pair of hands.

I go into Paddy's pub for a pint and it's packed and I push through to the bar where there's a bloke who's got fox-red hair, so tall he near brushes the ceiling. He's pleading with the lad behind. – Just one more pint, he's going. – I'll pay you next time.

– Piss off, Tiny, the barman goes.

– A half. That's all. Go on. Go on.

– I said piss off.

I catch the barman's eye and order two pints. When they're poured, I stick one in front of the tall geezer.

He whips round. Clocks me, takes me in with these small brown eyes.

– Go on, I go. – I ain't poisoned it. You're safe to drink.

He looks at me for a second, sums me up, decides I'm to be trusted. – You're a fine bastard of a man.

I nod in agreement, hold up my glass, tell him I am indeed, and we drink.

– What's your name? he asks.

– Gary. Why ain't you got no money? I ask.

– Straight out the nick, mate, and spent what they give me. Government lock you up for years and brutalize you, then they got the cheek to chuck you out with a fiver and expect you to live on it.

– And I don't spose you done nothing wrong.

– Exactly. Mistaken identity.

– With respect, Tiny, I go, – you ain't the kind of person what's easily mistaken.

– Everyone's got a doppelgänger.

– So your doppelgänger just happens to be what, six foot four, hair the colour of a dead fox, and just happened to be caught doing what? Nicking?

– GBH.

– So he was caught doing GBH near where you happened to be?

– Not outside the bounds of possibility.

– But likely? I go.

– Possible. And, Gary, where there's an element of doubt, how can a conviction happen?

– If you're still hanging on to the old-fashioned

idea that the law obeys shit like that, my son, you're in for a shocking awakening.

He drains his pint like he's a dying man and I chuck him a fiver.

– Get two more.

As the barman's pouring the pints, Tiny looks round, takes it all in. I know how he sees it all. Fresh out of nick, it's the colours and sounds that do you in. He's trying to get his head round how the world's gone and changed while he was inside. A pint's near doubled in price. The logos on the beer mats've been redesigned. There's a new jukebox, louder, songs he ain't never heard of. The world's moving so fast he feels like he's gonna slip off it.

I ask him what he's gonna do now he's out.

He slams his forehead with his hand. – You a tossing social worker? Gonna ask if I'm going straight?

– No, you thick twat, I go. – Was gonna ask if you wanna come on a job.

– Job?

– It's all right. I ain't offering you a shift at a factory.

– What've I got to do?

– Can you carry?

– I might look like a strand of spaghetti but I can lift. And I can run. I can outrun the whole of the Met.

I know what we look like. Jim's the shape of an apple, his two dogs on leads. Tiny's taller than the circumference of Jim's belly. And there's me, wiry, moving quick, beady blue eyes watching everything.

The van's newly nicked special for this job. It's lined in Astroturf and it stinks where one of the dogs has shat on it thinking it's grass. Jim asks me to drive.

– It's automatic, I go. – Only toy cars are automatic.

– That's why I ain't driving. And you work for me so get behind the wheel.

– You nicked it, I go.

He gives me the key. – Just do it, Gary, he says. – If I get stopped I could lose my licence. If you get stopped it don't matter cos you ain't got a licence to lose.

We sit in the front, the three of us, the dogs across our laps. Jim directs me out of London and we drive till we hit Surrey. We pass through a village, out the other side, and he tells me to kill the lights, go slow. There's a sign to a country club and we go up the drive and round the back. It's a big old house, been empty for a bit – grass on the drive, paint starting to crack – and it don't take much to get the door open. The rooms've been cleared of furniture but there's fireplaces what'll fetch a good bit, and some panelling. We lever it all off the walls, get it stacked up at the door ready to go.

Jim stands in the doorway and lights up. Tiny scouts around for any last bits. I'm crouched down, the torch on the floorboards. I'm thinking: Old oak, worn, nice patina and good grain. I'm thinking it might be worth lifting it all up. I stand up and the beam of the torch catches sight of a door handle; the light bounces off the brass. It's shiny, well-used and there's grubby handmarks on the paint surrounding it. I turn the knob, but it's locked. I know there's something in there. I know.

I get the screwdriver and run it down the crack of the door, press the metal lock inwards and spring it. The door goes back and I feel the walls, find a light switch, press it: nothing.

The torch shines down the steps, round the turn of the staircase. I make out a bar, then a dance floor.

I shine the torch up high till I find the fuse box. Switch it on. The spotlight hits the glitter ball and the room explodes. Light fragments cover walls and floor. The bar's still fully stocked and there's a DJ's kit up the end, boxes of records still in covers. I rifle through them, pull out a black disc. Drop the needle. A crackle then an intro. The song starts. I turn it up high. Pet Shop Boys.

I've had enough of scheming
and messing around with jerks
My car is parked outside
I'm afraid it doesn't work
I'm looking for a partner
someone who gets things fixed
Ask yourself this question
Do you want to be rich?

I've got the brains
You've got the looks
Let's make lots of money

You've got the brawn
I've got the brains
Let's make lots of money

I can hear Jim the Belly shouting as he comes down the stairs, Tiny following. But then he sees the dance floor, the glittered light. He sees me behind the bar, the optics behind me. And for once he ain't got nothing to say.

I rub my hands together. – So, gentlemen, what's it to be?

– Stick that glass under the optic, Tiny goes, – and don't stop.

– Jim? I go. – You might wanna see this.

I go to the door behind the bar. Open it and turn on the light. The bottles are all lying down, floor to ceiling.

– Well bugger me, Jim the Belly goes, – I just found out there is a god.

We carry wine, champagne, brandy, cases of beer up to the van. Shove bottles by our feet, in every gap we can find.

We load up the fireplaces and drive off back through the village. We drive till we can see London there in front of us and we know we own it. It's boom time in the growing city, and we got the keys to it. We open a bottle of champagne and pass it mouth to mouth to mouth.

– Till yesterday, Tiny says, – I thought I was gonna have to get a job. You saved me.

– What job did you reckon you was gonna get? I ask. – You was still grey from the nick and you had one set of clothes to your name.

– Dunno. Don't spose I ever had a job anyway. Don't want one neither. You see them walking to work in the morning. Heads down. May as well stick the balls on their ankles.

– Pass me the bottle, Jim says. He drinks, chucks the empty out the window. I open another and he looks at me, out the corner of his eye. – Slow down.

– Slow down? I go. – We got a lot to get through.

– You don't have to drink it all now.

– I know, I go. I turn to Tiny. – My brother, I say, – has to ask to have a piss.

– We wasn't made for that, Tiny says.

– No, I go. – We was made to roam the earth. We was made to find what we needed to keep us alive. Made to keep a woman in our cave.

– You can't do that now, Tiny says, – keep a woman in a cave.

– We was made to sharpen weapons, I go. – And tell a story round the fire.

Tiny nods. – That's about the size of it. That's what it all boils down to.

– This shit, I go, – all this shit ain't never right. Living like this, needing money for everything we want.

– It's called evolution, Jim goes. – Progress.

I pull some coins from my pocket. – Look at them, I go. – End of a week's work you get a few of these what you then give to someone else in exchange for stuff you ought to be hunting down anyway. And some stupid idiots make the coins in factories, get paid a few of them for making loads of them. It's all too complicated. It's all gone too far.

I chuck the coins out the window. – We ought to stop using them.

– Yeah, Tiny says. – Yeah. Yeah. Bloody right.

Jim takes the champagne out my hand, chucks it out the window. – Oi, I go. – What you doing?

– I thought if it's all too complicated you won't be needing this. I'll just drop you both off in the woods and you can get on with it.

To celebrate, me and Tiny go to Paddy's. They let us in cos there's a lock-in still going on. I put my hand into my pocket and fish out notes, order drinks for the whole pub.

Tiny drinks three doubles in a row then slumps in a corner, eyes closed. A woman at the bar, long brown hair, thin at the ends, raises her glass to me.

– I'm Katherine, she goes. – I seen you about.

– Gary.

We touch glass.

I get up, put a coin in the jukebox, choose songs. Try to wake Tiny, but his eyes might as well be glued together.

Music plays and we drink. We get Paddy to turn up the jukebox.

My heart speeds up as I stand. I'm cushioned, away

from myself. Katherine laughs. I laugh. The music's louder and we dance. Feet sticking to the carpet. Hearts racing. Her pelvis sticks into me.

She takes my hand in hers. It's dry. Bony. We open the pub door and walk out into the night. We go back to her block of flats and get in the lift. She presses ten.

She takes me into her room. She moves the toys off her bed, and we fuck till it hurts.

In the morning the sunlight comes in. Plastic toys of all colours are across the floor. There's grey sheets, damp mottled wallpaper. At the centre, naked on the bed, Katherine.

I turn and see a kid in the doorway dressed in a small vest and a nappy what hangs down between his knees. He looks at me and I sit up, pull on my clothes. He stares, don't move.

I shake her shoulder and she groans and shifts in the bed. I shake her again, tell her I got to go. Tell her the kid's up. And I get off the bed, walk past the kid, through the hallway and out the door. I run down all ten flights of stairs. Get out into the air.

That night I go to see Jim. He opens the door, looks at me. Lets me in. He's got wine glasses (eighteenth-century, engraved) lined up on the table, three bottles open to breathe.

– You all right?

– Course I am, I go.

– You been drinking?

– Only a spot.

He nods. – Where's your new mate?

I shrug. – Ain't seen him today. I left him at Paddy's.

He nods again. Pours the first bit of wine.

– That was a good job we done, Gary.

– Productive, I go.

– Productive, yeah, exactly. Now you sure you wanna taste this? It's from that over-complicated world you was on about.

– That was just chat.

– I know. And that's what his company will do for you. The two of you set each other off. People can lose themselves, Gary.

– I ain't gonna lose myself. I know myself too well.

– You think you do.

– Come on, Jim. He's all right.

– Is he? Jim says. He pours more of the first bottle, turns the wine glass in his hand, tastes. – The body on this is a rare one, you know.

He passes me a glass to taste, watches me carefully. I leave it in my mouth, let it soak into my tongue, roll it around. He pours another wine then stops. He looks up at me and his eyes narrow.

– I wanna tell you something, Gary.

He don't say nothing for a bit. The smaller dog nuzzles his hand but he don't take no notice and he always notices his dogs. He puts his glass down. Looks at me.

– I want you to be careful, he says.

– Why you say that?

He points at his chest. – Something in here's moved me to say it. I'm a great believer in instinct, Gary. In feeling something and listening to it. Thing is, we're mysteries. We don't know nothing about all this. We reckon we do but we don't. We're icebergs, Gary, icebergs. There's this tiny bit of white above, but beneath the water there's massive hunks of black ice. Unknowable. And something tells me you should be careful.

– Christ, I go. – What's come over you? I know what I'm doing. I'm all right. I'm always all right.

– We all say that, he goes. – We all think that. But all this, all this out here, is much bigger than any of us.

Something from all that stuck in my head. Cos that was what you could say was a turning point.

It was the kid in the doorway. The weight of the nappy hanging down. A whole night's piss. That and the way he looked at me.

My son never looked at me like that.

Seconds Out

From outside the boxing club you can hear the dead smack of gloves into bags. The trainer counting. The thwak of the skipping rope on the concrete.

Inside there's the stink of sweat, of rubber soles, of fear and rage. At the back, pummelling the bag, there's a bloke. He has near-black hair shorn close to the scalp; every muscle of him's tight, raised, like there ain't a scrap of fat. He's got on red shorts and vest. His fists land heavily, stop. He takes a breath then picks up a skipping rope. He starts to swing it, starts to move his feet. He makes it look easy, makes it look like his body's light, weighs nothing. He makes it look like he could do this all day, all night. He could skip till dawn. Till the sun rises over the river.

And then the skipping stops and the rope hits the floor. He hangs his head down, catches his breath. Sweat stands out on his forehead, stains the back of his vest. His heart starts to slow down and he lifts his head from his chest, turns to look towards the doors. And he looks at you and you see his eyes blue as the ink on a freshly printed fiver.

The trainer wipes the sweat off me. He checks my long laced boots, tightens them. I hold out my hands and he wraps them, pushes the gloves on then does them up tight. My fists are heavy.

– You know what to do? he asks.

I nod. He slips in the mouthguard.

– Just do what I said, he says, – and you'll be all right.

I nod and he lets go. It's time. I duck down, under the rope. Dance, move. Show him I got feet what work. Show him what I got.

The bell rings and it's me lands the first punch. Then it's me lands the second. By the end of the third round he has a cut lip and bleeding nose and then I land it on his right temple and he staggers to the ground.

The countdown finishes and the trainer raises my arm. I'm handed the trophy and I slip it in my bag, take it home to the flat where I put it on the oak mantelpiece what leans against the wall.

This is the new life. Everything I done before, the listening at doors, the standing in dark hallways, the knowing where people would hide stuff, all that's been channelled into reading what way someone'll move, how they'll punch.

I flex my muscle, see how what I done has made me what I am right now. The work has built the muscle and everything goes down my arm into that hard fist. I'm reshaping myself. Making a new form what ain't been made by the cage that was put round me. And I know that if I keep doing this, I'm gonna prove Tony wrong. My story's gonna change direction from how it started out, take me to a new ending.

★

In the daylight I work with Tony, back on the scaffolding. We work quick, in step. We pull stuff off the lorry, build and tighten. He chucks me balls of metal and we don't need to tell each other what to do.

Then one morning he says there's a job he needs me to do while he goes off to price another, so he drops me at a house in North London. We unload some boards and tubes; I just got to put up an extra lift so the roofer can get to the chimney. He drives off and leaves me on my own.

I climb the ladder up on to the roof. I can see right down over the heath. It's one of them days when the clouds move fast across the blue, and I'm up high in the clean air and I can sense my muscles, feel fit. I'm putting on swivels and doubles and I'm getting that feeling again. I'm outside. Doing what I'm good at.

I'm so full of how everything is that I get distracted and my foot slips and a roof tile cracks. When I'm finished I go down to tell the woman that she's got to tell the roofer when he comes, so he can put it right. I knock. Nothing. I know she's in. I knock again. She opens the door but only as far as the chain'll let it.

I can see one rheumy eye, the edge of her grey hair.

– You want money? she asks.

– No, I go. – I just put up the scaffolding so they can get to the chimney.

Her hand's shaking. Rattling the chain. – I told him, she says, – that I didn't want it put up. They didn't have to do that.

– Who you told?

– The man. The other man. The one with a hat. I don't know how much they're going to charge me now and I told him I've got nothing left to give him.

When Tony comes by I jump in the lorry. He drives me home but when he pulls over I don't move from the cab.

He looks at me. – You getting out?

– No, I go. – What's the game, Tony?

– What game?

I turn, eyeball him. – Don't treat me like I'm thick. You only doing work for the elderly now? The ones what ain't got no one to protect them?

He shrugs. – Got an expensive girlfriend.

– The old dear was shaking like a newborn.

– Thing is, Gary, he goes, – you ain't got no grounds to speak. Look what you're like. What you done. You ain't no angel.

– We ain't talking about me.

– You got a flat full of nicked stuff.

– This is different.

– You reckon you can sit there and give me a lec-ture on what I can and can't do? I ain't gonna take it from the likes of you. Look at you, you scum.

– Is that what I am? Scum?

– Yeah, Gary. That's what you are.

I open my door. Swing my leg out. – Get out, I go.

– No.

I lean over and get the key out the ignition. I climb

out my door, run round and grab his arm. Pull him out on to the pavement.

– Tell me what I am again, I go.

– Come on, Gary, he says.

I grab his T-shirt. Shove him against the wall. I push my face up to his.

– Don't ever ever do anything like that to an old woman again, I say.

I pull my fist back, send a right-hander straight under his chin, hear his head whip back and hit the wall; he don't even make a noise, just crumples to the ground.

I'm standing there and he's bleeding and I'm waiting for him to get up. He don't. I bend down, shove him. He don't move. I put my arms under his, pull him up to sitting.

A woman passing stops. – Don't move him, love, she says. She bends down, checks his eyes. – You called an ambulance?

I shake my head. A window opens in a flat opposite. A voice calls out. – They're on their way.

And the woman takes off her coat, places it on him. We hear the siren. Tyres. An ambulance comes then the police.

They keep me in overnight then charge me. I'm let out the next day and by the evening the trainer's at the door of the flat. He stands by the mantelpiece, sees the trophy. He looks at me. – You know what I'm gonna say.

Yeah, I know what he's gonna say.

– You could've killed him.

– But I never.

– But you could have. You got to learn some things, my son, and I hope you learn them before you die.

– I ain't gonna do it again.

– Not on my patch you ain't.

– I've learned, I go.

He shakes his head. – That's it. The end of your beautiful career.

– You can't do that, I say.

– I believe I have.

– But you don't even know why I done it, I go.

– And I don't wanna know. See, the thing is, Gary, why you done it ain't the point. The world's gonna do this to you, throw up stuff you don't like. It's how you deal with it that counts.

– But you don't know why. You don't know what he done.

He shrugs. – Nothing you tell me can get you out of this. It's all over. There's absolutely no room for losing a temper, no room for lack of discipline.

– I got discipline, I go.

The trainer shakes his head. – You think you have, Gary, but you ain't. That is the one thing you ain't got.

The door slams shut and before the sound finishes echoing around the walls of the flat, I've put my boots on and got my money in my pocket. I'm out the door. Down the stairs and out into the street. I go straight to Paddy's pub, order a pint and chaser. I lift the glass, raise it to myself: Here you are, son. You're a bloke who done the right thing. You're a bloke who done something good. In fact, you know what? You're a frigging hero.

The whisky hits the throat and then it hits the blood. My head runs clear. I buy a pack of fags. I pick up the pint and drink and I remember starting it, remember the feel of the glass on my mouth, the taste of the beer, but I don't remember seeing the bottom of the glass. I don't remember nothing.

Next morning I wake in the flat. The table's turned over and a pot's smashed. The paintings are ripped. No one else is there so it must've been me what done it.

My hands is shaking and I got a pit of acid in my belly what feels like it's eating me from the inside out. I go out, get a nip of vodka to stop it, and it's fine. I'm cured. I spend the next couple of days inside, then I think, that's it, I've had enough. Anyone would, cooped up like that. So I chuck money, the trophy and some clothes in a bag and I'm out of there.

Cracks

I ain't got a clue how much time's passed but I wake up on the settee in a flat in a Georgian house (nice original fireplace, worth a good bit; original shutters, ditto) what's just south of the station. A floppy blond bloke who's got a voice full of plums and silver spoons stands over me.

– Does the offer of coffee appeal?

My eyeballs feel like there's the dust from a sheet of sandpaper under.

– I said, coffee?

I nod and my brain moves inside my skull as if it's floating in water. – Is it real coffee? I ask.

He claps his hands together. – At last, someone with taste, he goes. He holds his hand out. – Jacob. Only they all call me Cracker. Jacob's Crackers. Crack. You have beautiful eyes. Like lapis lazuli which they used round Tutankhamen's eyes. Do you like bacon?

– Don't everyone?

– I don't suppose pigs do. We'll leave your friend to sleep. Come through.

In the kitchen I watch as he cooks. He asks if I enjoyed last night.

– Ain't got a clue, I say.

– Blackout? God, what a bore. Of course there's the joy of the release from this shitty world, but then you don't remember all the fun things. Where do you live, Blue Eyes?

– I used to live round the corner but I had to leave. I'm staying with a mate.

– And your friend?

– He's on his mate's settee.

Cracker smiles. – I've got room here. Two rooms. I'm looking for some company.

We settle into a routine and time passes and it feels like I never lived nowhere else. Then one night we're in the lounge and there's an empty bottle of whisky by my feet, an overflowing ashtray on the table. Cracker's sat by me and Tiny's on his back on the floor.

The door goes. Bang bang. It ain't no one's knock we know.

– Who's that? Tiny goes.

– You won't know till you answer the door, I say.

– I can't get up, Cracker goes.

– I ain't going, I go.

Tiny moans. He rolls this way, that way, this way again till the momentum gets him on to all fours. He crawls to the door, reaches up and opens it.

I hear a voice I recognize. – Does Gary live here?

– You better come in.

Tiny crawls back in the room and behind him there's a woman. I know she's got to be Sharon cos it's her voice, but it don't look like her. She's lost weight from the right places as though she's been sculpted out of all her old fat. She looks like Mum did once. Tight jeans short of her ankles. Stiletto shoes. Make-up. Low-cut top. Hair scraped back. She looks down at me on the settee. I look up at her.

– The Old Man, she says, – sent me to the fat sod with the stinking dogs, and he sent me here. Said you'd landed on your feet with some posh git.

Cracker opens his eyes. – Posh git?

She looks at him. – Posh git, yeah. That'll be you then.

– And if I'm the posh git, who are you?

– This is my sister, Shaz, I go.

Cracker drags his self off the sofa, goes on his knees. He hobbles forward, stretches out a hand. – Delightful to meet you.

Sharon looks at his hand. – This your place? she says. – Cos I need somewhere to stay.

Cracker gets his self up to standing, staggers, makes a chivalrous half-bow as if he's found his self stepped into the pages of another time. – I wouldn't want to see you out in the streets, he says. – You can have my bed.

– You ain't coming here, I go.

– So you can shack up with him and luck out, but I can't? That what you're saying, Gaz?

– What's going on? Tiny asks.

– Who woke you up? Sharon asks.

– You, Tiny says.

157

– I ain't got no money, Shaz goes to me. – I can't stay at home. Got nowhere to go.

– You won't need money, Cracker goes. – I said, you can stay here.

– Why can't you stay at home? I ask.

– Mum's got a boyfriend. She met him at the pub and I hate him. And Alan's got a baby now. A boy, Daniel. You're an uncle.

– Uncle? I go. – Didn't even know he was with someone.

– You ain't exactly calling round on him every five minutes.

– I been busy, I go.

– Yeah, I can see that.

She picks up the whisky bottle, sees it's empty.

– We'll get you more, Cracker goes. He pulls out some notes, hands them to me, asks me to get some for him.

– You coming? I ask Shaz.

– I'm tired, Gary.

On the way to get the whisky me and Tiny call in to Paddy's. It's an old-fashioned night of pints and roll-ups, music on the jukebox. When we're spent up we go back to the flat but there's no sign of Cracker. No sign of Sharon. I check the kitchen and the bathroom then open Cracker's bedroom door. I see the bed. Two heads side by side. And then I see a pipe by the bed.

Cracker opens his eyes and looks at me. I look at him. Then I move so quick there's no thought in it, no plan. It's animal. I pull the covers back, grab him by his posh skin and drag him out the bed. Shaz wakes up and screams at me not to be so stupid and she ain't a kid no more and she can look after herself.

I drag him bollock naked into the other room. He falls against Tiny, who's slumped on the settee and wakes up to find Cracker naked on top of him. He piles in and the two of us pummel and smack him. Shaz comes in (she's bothered to dress in vest and pants to conceal the animal nature of all this) and climbs on my back. She screams and grabs my face and digs a finger into my eye. My fist connects with Cracker's nose and I know that the bone's gone, splintered under my hand. I stop.

I get my bag, any clothes I can find. I tell Shaz to get dressed.

– No.

Blood drips off Cracker's nose on to the floor in splats. He's bent double and Shaz moves towards him, puts her arm round him.

– I'm taking him to hospital.

– Please your bloody self, I say.

I put my bag on my shoulder. Open the door and go out. Slam it behind me.

Jim's got his dressing gown on. He looks me up and down. I'm in a T-shirt, shivering with cold, bag over my shoulder.

– You look a state, my lad. Where you been? I been trying to get hold of you.

– I been busy, I say. I bend down, rub the dog's head. – Where's his mate?

Jim the Belly puffs on his cigar. – He got stuck in the railings there. Had to be cut out, railings and all. He's in a cage inside, ain't allowed out till he's better.

– Them railings? I ask, pointing.

– Yep. They was round his neck.

– Fire brigade come?

– Yep.

I'm trying not to laugh and he knows it and he knows I know it. – It ain't funny, Gary. I nearly lost him.

– I know.

– So what you come for? he asks. – What do you want?

– Who says I want somethink.

– You reckon I was born yesterday? You got a bag on your shoulder.

– I found somewhere to live, I say, – only I had to leave all of a sudden.

– The answer's no.

– Just a couple of nights then I'm gonna get my own place. Gonna put a deposit down.

– Two nights?

– Two.

On the third night Jim calls me to the table and we sit in front of asparagus, broad beans, peas, a poached egg on top. On the side there's rustic white bread he made earlier. Unsalted butter. He puts his hands together. – For what we are about to eat may we thank your good friend Jim the Belly.

He opens a bottle of Muscadet and pours it into two glasses. He sees me watching. He stops.

– You got a taste for the old booze? he asks.

– Dunno what you're trying to say.

He eyeballs me. – Don't play stupid.

– I ain't. I dunno what you're saying.

He passes me a glass. I hold it. Don't drink straight away. I swill the liquid round, watch it go up and down the sides of the glass. – Jim, I go.

– What now?

– You gonna be doing any more jobs?

– Not till he's out the cage. And then I dunno. I'm getting on, Gary. My bones get sore when I stay up all night. And I keep thinking, look at all this. I mean, look.

He waves his arm round the room.

– Look at it. I got everything I need. Got my dogs, got beautiful things on the walls, got quality food with provenance, got real wine and brandy and cigars. Got a footstool. Very important that. A man needs somewhere to rest his feet. You name me one thing I ain't got what I need.

– Cash?

– But cash is only for things, ain't it? I mean it's an exchange. What do I wanna exchange my cash for?

He lifts his glass to me and I wanna ram it in his smug cunty face, but I don't. He puts the glass down. – It's gonna be three nights, Gary. You said two.

– I know, I'm working on it. I been out looking for a place. Got word there's one up at the Cross. Waiting to hear, might even hear tomorrow.

That night I get out of bed, leave the room. I stand on the landing, still. I hear Jim's snoring, wait to check it's steady. I go down, stroke the dogs, give them a biscuit each. I take the bunch of keys from where he keeps them in the bowl, and leave the house.

The stock in the store's going down where he's been selling. I find what I'm looking for in a drawer of an inlaid chest and stash them in my bag. I sneak back into Jim's house, put the keys in the bowl. Next day I make my way to Islington. Down the antiques passage.

The old queen looks up from where he's plucking his eyebrows in a mirror. He recognizes me, puts the tweezers down. – Your eyes haven't faded, darling. Lapis lazuli.

– They put that round Tutankhamen's eyes, I go.

He claps his hands together. – You're such a fount of knowledge. Now, what do you have for me?

I slip my bag off my shoulder quick and unzip it. Bring out the pouches of Japanese objects, tip them on to the desk.

The queen stares and the air in the shop changes. He gets this stillness in his body. The about to pounce quiet. That's how I know I'm on to something. He clears his throat to try for normal so that I don't know he thinks they're special.

He gets out his magnifier. Picks up each object and scrutinizes it. Turns it over. Puts it down. Flicks his eyes up, checks what I'm doing, tries to see how much I know about them. He starts again, looks at each in turn, then puts them all back in their pouches. I know what he's gonna say and he don't let me down.

His voice affects casual ignorance. – Do you know what they are?

– Do *you* know what they are? I ask.

– I'm not sure.

Like hell he ain't. Cos I know he knows exactly what they are and what they're worth.

– They're Japanese, I go.

– I thought they were, he says. – I'm not a Japanese expert.

– Then maybe I need one, I say. I put my hand on the pouches as if to take them away. He puts his hand on them as well.

– I'm sure, he says, – that I can help you.

– So what you reckon?

– Five hundred?

I laugh. – You gotta be joking?

– How much were you thinking? he asks.

– It's more a question of how much I need, I go. – I'm looking for enough for a deposit for a flat, then I need money to live off. Plus they belonged to my Auntie Annie and if I don't get enough for them, I'm gonna have that on my conscience and that's no way to live, is it?

– Let me think.

– Auntie Annie's husband worked in Japan, I go.
– He loved to collect stuff. Had a flat full of it. Lovely woman, she was. Salt of the earth, whatever that means. What does it mean? You'd know, an educated man like you.

– I'm not sure.

– Two grand, I go.

– Fifteen hundred.

– Eighteen.

– Seventeen.

– Meet me halfway.

I stick my hand out and we shake. He counts out the money, all seventeen hundred and fifty.

Next day my head's hammering where I had a skinful. I'm in the kitchen and Jim's letting the dog out the cage. He watches it run around the house then gives it half a cup of tea with extra milk and sugar. He settles down on the settee.

– Take a seat, Gary, he says.

I tell him I was just going out to see if I can pick up the keys for the new flat, but he tells me again to sit down. Opposite him. And I know something's up. He waits till I'm settled.

– Do they like dogs in Japan? he asks me.

My heart ups a beat. I tell it to calm, don't show nothing on my face. – Dunno.

– I thought you knew about Japan.

– What's this about? I ask.

He smiles: slow, wide, crafty. – Just making small talk, he says. – Chitchat. Passing time. I'm not sure about Japanese food. Leaves me hungry. Leaves me feeling like I've had the inside of my stomach stroked. Food's got to fill you up. Mind, samurai warriors, they must do it on a bit of old fish, eh? And the fat wrestlers. What are they eating to get like that?

I'm listening and I know where this is going but I can't help thinking when's the last time you looked in the mirror cos you're the fattest of all, in your house all day shovelling as much in your mouth as'll fit.

– Japanese kimonos, he goes, – they ain't got pockets, have they? Where you reckon they keep their stuff?

– Just say it, I go.

– Feeling emotional, Gary? Not like you to have an outburst.

– I ain't in the mood for this. I ain't the games type.

– Oh. The straightforward type, are you?

The ex-caged dog jumps up, licks him on the lips. He holds her face with both his hands. – My lovely girl.

He turns back to me, still holding the dog in his hands. – Thing about dogs is they're loyal, Gary. They know it ain't in their interests to do you over. They know what side their bread is buttered.

– Just say it, I go.

– You say it.

– I ain't saying nothing.

– No comment then?

– No comment. Nothing to say. Anything I say will be taken down. All that shit. You're a fat twat anyway.

– I know I'm a fat twat cos it's all here in front of you, he goes. – But at least you can see it and know it. Whereas you, what you are ain't for the human eye to see, is it? It's tucked up, hidden away. It's more dangerous. See, I may be fat, but I wouldn't rip you off. It ain't how it's done, sonny. I thought more of you. Thought you was better than that. I reckon you better ask yourself what it is you wanted to buy so bad that you ignored that voice inside you what was shouting out don't do it. Cos you have got a voice what says what's right, what's wrong, and I can see from your face you wish you hadn't done it. But it's too late, ain't it?

– This a sermon? I go. – Never knew you'd taken up ministry.

He shakes his head. – The only dog collar in this house is gonna be on pooch here. Now remember what I said to you before, Gary? I said be careful, didn't I? There's only one way you're going and it ain't upwards. Now I suggest you get your bag and you get out of here before I call in some mates to teach you how to find out where that little voice is inside you. And one more thing. If I find out you sold my pension for a pittance I think I'll remove your skin from your body with a sharp crochet hook. Okay?

Happy Families

When I wake up I ain't got a clue where I am. I put my hand out to feel. Beneath me there's wooden rails and under them concrete. My head's sore where it's rested on something hard. I can hear cars and a siren. I open my eyes. There's trees above and sky between branches. I turn my head to the side and see a kid walking with a mother. A cafe with tables under the trees. Birds rooting for something to eat.

My back's stiff and I'm slow to sit up. When I swing my legs round, my foot kicks an empty bottle and it spins, the sound of glass on stone. I pat my pocket, see I got a few notes left, open my bag what's been my pillow all night and find the boxing trophy.

But it ain't all bad. None of it's bad. I ain't in a nine to five. I ain't doing no one else's bidding. The air's fresh and I'm alive. Morning, son, I say to myself. Morning, son.

At the station commuters stream through the barriers towards me: clip, clip, suit, heels. I go the other way, fight my way through the mass of them. I jump the barrier, go down and catch a train. I'm the only passenger in my carriage. We pass through blocks and blocks of flats then the train stops and picks up a young woman. She goes to sit near me then hesitates, changes her mind, walks further past, right down the far end of the carriage. If that's what she wants she can. I know I might look a bit of a mess but the stains on my jeans ain't blood. It's ketchup.

I knock but there ain't no answer. I try again. Rap on the window. Shout through the letter box. Then I hear feet and the chain being undone. A lock turns and the door opens. A short stocky bloke answers: he's got a shaved head and a tattoo of a hand on the front of his neck, looks like it's throttling him.

    – Is Janet in? I ask.

    – Who's asking?

    – I'm her son, Gary.

    – Her son's called Alan.

    – I'm his brother.

    – You the messed up gone missing one?

    – It ain't exactly how I'd describe myself, I go.

    – She's sleeping.

    – Look, mate, I go. – You gonna let me in?

    – No need to be aggressive, son. I'll see if she wants to see you.

And he goes to close the door, only I know exactly what he's gonna do and my foot's in the doorway.

He stares at me. – You asking for somethink?

    – Yeah. I'm asking to see my own mother. Tell her I'm home.

He turns, shouts into the flat. – Jan, Jan. There's some little bloke out here says he's your son.

She comes out her bedroom wearing a dressing gown. Her hair's messy and the roots is grey. Matches her skin.

– Tell your Rottweiler, I say, – that he can let me in.

She stirs three sugars into the tea, makes bacon sandwiches. The bacon's undercooked, brown sauce dripping out. The Rottweiler has one and I have one. As he eats, he beckons her over to stand next to him. He puts his arm round her waist. – You ain't been to see her, he says. – It upset her.

– You upset? I ask her.

– I'm all right, she says. – You got work, have you, Gary?

– Yeah, I go. – Been doing this and that. Spot of scaffolding with the Old Man.

At the mention of him Rottweiler's face goes dark like he's bit his own tongue and released the blood into his face. He pushes Mum away. – Go and get dressed, he says to her. – I said I'd take you out. Said we was gonna do somethink special.

– But Gary's here.

– We arranged it. I told you.

– I don't remember, she says. – I can't go out, anyway. Not when he's just called round.

– Don't worry about me, Mum. I can come back.

– No. Don't go. Let me go and get dressed.

She goes off and he picks up our plates and takes

them through to the kitchen. Comes back and sits down. I ain't gonna speak to him and he ain't gonna speak to me. So we don't.

We sit for minutes. The only sounds are the creaking of his chair as he moves, our breathing, and time passing through the air. I know what he's thinking, how he wants me gone. And I know more than just what he's thinking: I know under the table his fists are bunched. Under his clothes his body's tense. There ain't no difference between us. We're reeking, coiled animals. There's silence. More time passes. A car goes by out the window. There's another shift of the chair.

She comes back in the room and releases us. He half stands, moves closer to her and kisses her on the lips. I look away.

– We ought to get going, he says. – Or we'll be late.

– What you gonna be late for exactly? I go.

– I'm taking her out. It's her late Mother's Day present.

– Very funny, I go.

Mum can't stay in the room. She retreats to her kitchen. I know what she's doing: a small nip of drink, a little something to pick her up, help her through the day.

The Rottweiller goes for a piss and leaves me on my own in the room. I go to the mantelpiece, take down the tin she keeps there and undo the lid. There's notes, folded. I take them out. Borrow them. Put the tin back.

He comes back in and I pick up my bag. – You going? he asks.

I don't answer. I walk to the kitchen door, catch Mum with the bottle raised to her mouth. She turns and sees me. Drops her eyes.

– I'm off, I say.

She puts the bottle down. – Come and see me again, Gary. Please.

– Yeah, I will, I go. – I will.

I walk back through the room and he watches me to the front door.

The receptionist looks through the book of numbers then makes the call. I can hear the ringing from where I stand. She keeps looking back at me.

– Hello, Alan? she says. – I have your brother in reception, she says. She listens to the voice down the other end of the phone, then looks at me. – Is it Gary?

– Yeah, I say. – Gary.

She listens again then puts the phone down. – He says can you wait here.

He don't keep me long. He rushes in, exchanges a look with the girl before he meets my eye. He's in a suit. Buttoned up to his neck, black shiny shoes. He's thinner, taller than I remembered. – Let's go outside, he says.

I'm gripped by the elbow and steered out of the main doors. We stand on the exact spot where I stood with the Old Man on the moonless night. Alan stinks of aftershave. His hair's short, combed flat. – Look at you, he says, hissing the words through his teeth as though everyone can hear. – You're filthy.

– It's just my clothes. I spilt somethink.

– You can't come here looking like that.

– I just have so it's too late.

– Look, Gary, what do you want?

– I don't *want* nothing, I go.

– So why are you here? I mean, why did you come to my work? You need money?

I laugh. – No.

– You need some clean clothes?

– Got some in my bag.

– Then what is it? You need a bed?

I laugh again. – Why'd I wanna bed? Ain't even dinner time and my feet still work.

He looks at his watch. – I'm sorry, I'm really busy. I've got lots on today.

He shifts on to one foot, as though he's gonna go back in through the doors.

– Sharon told me you had a son, I go.

He stops. Settles his weight back on his two feet. He looks at me, nods. – I have, yeah. Daniel. I got a daughter too. Laura.

– Congratulations, I go. – That's nice.

He's silent for a bit then, – Gary, are you all right?

– Yeah. Yeah. Course I am.

He looks at me. Right in the eyes. – So how long can you carry on like this?

I look away. – Look, I've seen you now and that's all I come for, make sure you're still alive.

– Don't be like that. D'you need help?

– No.

– Sure?

It's my turn to start to move away. – Yeah. Look, I got to get back, I go. – I got some work with the Old Man.

I put my bag down, unzip it. Take out the boxing trophy, hand it to him.

– Have this for Daniel, I go. – So he knows his uncle was a boxer.

Alan holds the trophy, turns it in his hands. Reads my name on the plaque. He didn't know. He knew I busted people's noses, knew I could handle myself in a fight, but he didn't know I could do this.

– Thanks, he goes. – Thanks.

He holds the trophy in the crook of his arm, cradles it. And even though I don't turn back I know he watches me as I walk off, watches till he can't see me no more.

Grime Pays

Honest Pete wants to talk to me. We're in his flat in King's Cross what's in a block on the same estate as my old one. Tiny's sat on the floor, leaning back against the wall, eyes closed. Me and Pete's on the settee.

– What you doing hanging round with him? Pete asks.

He points at Tiny who's spooling spit down his face. Tiny lifts his heavy slow hand, wipes. When he pulls his hand away, a strand stretches out then snaps, swings under his chin. His eyes contract as he fixes on me. There's a slow blinking as he takes me in, then the eyes close again.

– He's all right, I go.

– He's an idiot and you ain't stupid. Where you living?

– Here and there, I go.

– There's a squat going next door.

And he goes into the bedroom, comes back with a crowbar which he hands to me. – This'll get you in.

I lay it down on my lap. Stare at him. – What you want?

– Why you reckon I want something?

– It's called human exchange, I go. – Every human

being talking to another wants somethink. That's what life's made up of, all of us running around trying to get what we want.

– You're sharp, that's what I like. There's a lot of stupid idiots out there. And cos of that there's a lot of business. Looks like the streets of London ain't just paved with gold. Between the stones there's rolled-up notes, each of them coated in coke and snot where they been up bankers' noses. It's trickling down, right into our pockets. I need a runner.

– Runner?

– I ain't talking about a kid to drop off but someone who can sense trouble, get out the way, someone who ain't an obvious. Someone who can work with me, develop some business skills.

– I'm interested.

– You don't wanna think about it?

– I have thought about it. I'm that quick.

– Good. But you can't take that lanky twat with you.

– If I took Tiny with me there wouldn't be nothing to sell.

Pete laughs. – You know how to look after yourself?

I nod. – I know what's what. Can see people before they see me, can smell bacon when the pigs is close. No one'll know what I'm doing.

– And if there's trouble?

– How you reckon I got this nose? But I ain't gonna punch no one less I have to. Most times violence ain't about action. It's about demeanour. It's about the threat of it. All you got to do is stand right, have the right attitude and they'll back down.

He grins, nods. – You got a point.

– I always have, I say.

I start my new job the next day. I dress in paint-spattered overalls and boots; over my shoulder there's a bag with the handle of a roller sticking out. I got paint splashes on my hands, on my hair, on the roller handle, on the bag. I'm sat slumped on a seat on the tube, knackered from a day hard at it. No one looks at me: I'm dressed in the city's camouflage. I'm invisible.

At Camden station the train stops and the doors slide open. I walk along the platform and go up the escalator. Out into daylight. Turn left and walk up the road, shoulders down, the opposite to the fresh-out-of-nick walk. This is the walk what says: I done a bloody hard day's work and then reluctantly plodded back to the shit bedsit I've lived in since my wife had the affair and kicked me out.

I'm nearing the address Pete gave me when I see blue lights. I slow. There's an ambulance parked out-side, the back doors open. A police car. I go into the cafe opposite, put my bag down. I have tea and a sand-wich and watch out the window as the paramedics come out, load up a stretcher. They close the doors and leave. I order more tea, more food. The police come out and drive off.

I wait long enough to be sure it's clear, then pay up. I cross the road and knock on the door. It's answered quick: a bloke my age, tall, asks if I'm Gary. When I nod he leads me into the back room what's dark where the curtains are shut. There's two birds in the corner. The older one's got her arm round the young one who's got cropped green hair and is crying. I ask what the blue lights was.

– We had an overdose, the bloke says. – Her boyfriend.

– I'll come back.

He shakes his head. – No. It's safe, man, safe.

I kneel down in front of the low table, unzip the bag and take out the three packages. The bloke and the comforting bird come to the table, kneel down. They stare at the packages like they're gold, frankincense and myrrh. The bloke reaches out to touch them and I put my hand out to stop him. – Money first.

He takes the cash out from his pocket, hands it to me. I count it all then nod, let them at it.

While they check and test it, I take some vodka out my bag, sit back to drink. It hits the back of my throat and my head at the same time. I lean against the wall and it feels like it's moving, reshaping itself to my back.

The bloke nods. – It's good. It's very, very good.

He stands, picks up two of the packages. – Got to go and get this cut up, he says, and he's gone.

The comforting bird stands up, takes the third

177

package. She looks over at the crying bird. – Mandy, she goes, – I got to take this.

And she's gone.

And now it's the two of us in the room. I put the top back on the vodka, put it in my bag. I'm about to stand, to go, when she speaks:

– Ain't you gonna offer me some?

I look at her. She's crouched on the floor, arms round her legs. She's looking at me and her eyes don't blink. They're as green as her hair. She's got freckles across her nose. I pass her the vodka and she drinks from the bottle.

We watch each other. We don't speak.

And while we're sat watching each other, in that exact moment, up the road, the body of her boyfriend has been unloaded in the mortuary and is cooling down. His blood's thickening and pooling in the small of his back, the back of his legs. The colour of his skin's fading fast and his lungs are drenched.

She's the first to speak. – This is messed up.

I nod.

She's the first to break eye contact. She stands up and goes to the window. She's got jeans on, ripped under the arse. She's thin and there's a gap between her legs.

She turns and sees me looking. – What we gonna do now?

I pick up the bottle. – I've got to go and deliver the money.

She blinks slowly, walks over. Stands over me. I can smell her, feel how close she is.

– You ain't leaving me here, she says. – I'm coming with you.

Mandy takes one more step and her ankle is touching my leg and I reach up my hand and grab her and I don't even pull but she sinks down and I open my arms and she moves into them.

– Don't leave me, she goes. – I ain't got no one else.

We walk to King's Cross and she holds my hand all the way. She ain't letting go.

I drop the money in with Pete and he gives me my cut. I go next door to the flat. Mandy walks straight in. Tiny stands there, twice her height.

– This is Mandy, I go. – Mandy, this is Tiny.

Mandy smiles. – I'm his new girlfriend, she goes. – I'm moving in.

– Quick work, Gary, Tiny says.

Only he don't know quite how quick.

That night it's her and me on my mattress. We have sex. We have sex and when we do, it's gonna sound stupid, but it's like we was made to fit together. It feels like she's a door I go through, like she was made for me to fit in. It's like coming home.

She wakes up in the night and climbs out of bed. I listen to her move about in the flat. Hear her piss hit the bowl. Hear the flush, then a tap, then the creak of the floorboard. She turns on a light and stands in the doorway of the bedroom. The light's behind her and her legs are apart and her pubic hair's on fire with light, but it ain't green. It's the same as the hair in the pre-Raphaelite painting we nicked from a house in Chelsea. It's gold.

She turns out the light. Gets down on the mattress next to me. The street light outside is yellow and draws lines on our skin as it comes through the broken venetian blind. She smoothes out some foil, puts some powder on it, lights a flame and runs it underneath till there are fumes.

The flame light flicks and moves on her face and she looks at me as she breathes in the smoke. We're eye to eye, and I feel like I'm her and she's me and it's like the colours of our eyes is blended and I dunno what this is. And I'm the one who knows everything.

She holds the foil out towards me and the light catches the silver; it's reflected in the room and her pubes are gold and the light on her face is gold and everything's gone gold and silver. And I've forgot about the stench of death in the afternoon and the body and the blood pooling underneath.

Me Now, Again

It's time to have a break, ain't it? A breather. You feel it. I feel it.

If we was together in person and not speaking through this page then I'd take you for a walk. We'd put one foot in front of the other. We'd breathe in some fresh air, look around us. We'd look at some trees and we'd look at the sea, at the waves doing their in and out thing. We'd look at the sky and spot cloud shapes and that'd put us both in mind of me sat on the doorstep with Mum that hot night.

And while we walked and saw them things, our hearts'd start to beat more slowly and our blood pressure'd begin to plummet. Cos by looking at all this nature shit we'd come to an almighty realization. We'd realize that we ain't so frigging important. The sun don't rise just for us. The planets don't circulate just round us. We'd realize there was stuff going on before we existed and there's gonna be stuff going on after we exist.

But we ain't together in person, are we? You're there reading this. And by the time you are reading it, I dunno where I'll be. Or do I?

I already told you where I live now. By the sea. I go down every day to look at it. And when I look at the sand I think about how it was all once rocks till the sea smashed them into grains of sand, and I wonder is that what'll happen to me in time?

My son lives by me. Along the clifftop. That's how it should be cos we've lost that connection with family, ain't we? We scatter our selves over the country. We spill sperm, spawn brats, then scarper. I ain't gonna do that. Shared blood gets sticky, holds you close.

We needed that break cos we ended on a dark bit. But I'm gonna tell you a truth now. There ain't no life in the world what ain't got no dark corners. Yours has. Mine has. But we ain't gonna dwell on the dark. You and me, we got an understanding. You know it's all gonna be all right cos here I am walking along the sand, my son up the road, the water at my feet, seagulls screaming at me, shouting their greedy beaks off.

All right. Ready now? Let's get back to it. Back to London.

Cohabits

The flat's transformed. Tiny's moved out and it's all ours now. We got a bed and we got a red vinyl settee from a skip and an old cable reel for a table. Mandy's happy: brought up in care, she's dreamed of this. A place of her own. She's cut out pictures from magazines and stuck them up on the walls. She done it all one day and wouldn't stop till she was finished and she put me in mind of a bird plucking feathers from its breast and lining a nest.

We've become domesticated.

She brings me coffee in the morning and I close my eyes and pretend to be asleep even though I been listening to the whole routine. Water. Kettle click. Lid screw. Stir. Footsteps.

She puts it down by the bed and climbs on top of me, sits astride. Holds my face and pulls my eyelids open till I see her freckle-splattered fizzog. – Gary.

– What?

She smiles. – You're so lucky.

– Why's that?

– Guess.

– Cos I got a free flat from the council?

– Nope.

– Cos I'm alive?

– Nope. Come on. You know why.

– Cos I got a coffee?

– Cos you live with me.

She laughs. Pokes me in the chest. – Admit it, you're lucky. Go on. Admit it.

– You're a pain in the arse.

She lowers her head and kisses me. The old animal brain unfurls, wakes up.

I put my hands up. Surrender. – All right, I go. – I'm lucky.

She rolls down next to me on the bed. – I'm never gonna leave you, you know that? I'm your shadow.

– You're chewing gum on my shoe. A verruca on my foot.

She laughs, kisses me again.

Then I remember. – What time is it? I got a job for Pete. I got a train to catch.

– I'm coming with you. I am. He won't even know. Don't go without me. Don't leave me here.

We get a cab from the station to the address I'm given. The house is in a terrace of red-bricks and the door's answered by a big bloke, shaved head, long beard, muscles splitting his T-shirt. We go in and wait while he checks the stuff. He hands over the cash and I count.

– No reward for us, then? Mandy goes. – We brought it all this way.

The bloke stares at her. She smiles. He sighs and hands Mandy a few wraps. She grins, blows him a kiss. And we're gone.

We stop down an alley, sit on the ground to take it. When it hits me, the pieces of my brain what ain't never met before touch and join up. It's like I been dead for ever and now I'm alive. Or I've been alive, too alive, and now I'm dead. The cash is in my lap in an envelope.

Mandy's looking at it. I'm looking at it. – We come all this way, Mandy goes. – We ought to get a drink. We never go out and do stuff like that.

We get drinks in the pub and sit at a table. – Look at us, Mandy goes. – We're like a real couple, out for a drink.

We clink glass, smile. The drinks don't last long. We down the first, then another and another. There's a pool table and we put our coins on the side, get in the queue to play. The blokes who are playing finish and hand over the cues. We get another drink, make a start. I break the balls and pot one. Then it's her turn and first thing she does is pot the black. I tell her she's lost and she says I don't know what I'm talking about. And then we start rowing and she finishes her drink then grabs mine but I grab it back and the drink slops on the carpet. She climbs up on to the pool table and stands on the edge. The barman tells her to get down but she don't hear him cos she's shouting at me. He turns us out into the street.

The rain's started and the shouting's stopped. It's dark and the lights of cars reflect in the wet. I got the bag over my shoulder with the cash in and she slips her arm in mine. It's getting late and we walk towards where we reckon the station is only we got to pass the end of the street where we dropped off. We don't look at each other and neither of us says nothing. We ain't got to speak. I know what she's thinking and she knows what I am. We don't know what the difference is between us, or if there is one. We turn up the street, still don't say nothing. We knock on the door and the man with the beard and the shaved head answers. We hand over some of the cash he gave us earlier, and he gives us something for it.

Dawn finds us on the first train home. We walk from the station and she's lost her shoes and I pick her up and carry her and when we get in the flat I lay her down on the bed and her feet hang off the end and they got a coating of leaves on the soles.

I lie down next to her and she asks me to stroke her hair, back off her face. – I remember my mum doing it, she goes. – Before she left.

We lie together and it's all quiet and it's all ours.

There's a knock at the door. – Leave it, she goes. – Don't stop.

And I know what she means, that we just wanna stay like that as long as we can. I stroke her hair. The knocking, again. Then the shouting starts. – Open up before I smash the door in.

And so I do.

Pete's stood in the doorway, and he looks me up and down. – State of you, he says. – Where you been?

– Ain't been well, I go.

He smiles but he has a tight mouth and his eyes are dead. – Spec you're well enough to remember where you put my money.

I put my hand in my pocket and pull out the roll of cash. He takes it, feels the thickness of it. – And the rest?

I shrug.

And then something happens. Even though I am the person who can hear the twist and crack of a dead leaf breaking from the stem and falling to the ground, even though I can hear a foot stand on a piece of grass, even though I can see a thought as it's born in a person's head, he catches me by surprise.

His fist lands on the side of my head and I see cartoon stars. I throw one back at him but my arms are heavy and I ain't my own self. He throws another and I hit the floor. He picks up the stack of cash from where it's fallen and turns to go.

But I ain't done. I stagger to my feet, stand southpaw. Hold up fists. – Seconds out, I go. – Round two.

Pete shakes his head. He shakes it so slow I wanna knock it off his neck.

– Look at you, he goes. – Carry on like this and you two are gonna mess each other right up.

Grimm Tales

Once upon a time, humans never needed money. They ate what they found and that was nuts and fruit and grubs. And if they come across something bigger they killed it and dragged it back. They lit fires and cooked. They slept on bundles of dead grass or nests of feathers. They dried animal skins to keep warm. They gouged mud out of the earth to make bowls then cut down trees for houses.

When one of them wanted a thigh of an animal to eat, he'd swap it for a set of bone needles or a comb. But then it all started to get too complicated and they decided that instead of swapping things they'd invent these discs what you give instead. And so money was born. And this money, this meant that everyone took a step back from what mattered and what life is and that is this: birth, food, sex, birth, more food, death. In that order.

And then once money was invented, we spent our days running around trying to get as much of it as possible, whether we needed it or not.

Me included.

My hunt for money begins at Jim the Belly's. His house has scaffolding up the outside and I stop to check it, can't help myself. The boards are rough, cheap, and the base ain't been put up straight cos when I push the tubes they give more than they ought. I'm tempted to fix it. My hand's on the tube, feels the cold of the metal.

But I ain't here to scaffold his house so I shake the thought out of my head, get round to the task, which is to knock on the door. I take a breath, prepare to tell Jim I made a mistake in taking them things, that I'll make up for what I done, that we can pick up where we left off. I'm forming sentences in my head, thinking that I'll even say the sorry word, but no one's answering. I rap on the window. No dogs, nothing. I'm about to go when the neighbour comes out, sees me on the step. He tells me Jim's lucky time came to an end when his store was raided and he got put away. He tells me the two dogs are in Battersea Dogs Home looking for a new owner and if I want them I could probably have them if I hurried.

Me? Want his dogs? Do I fuck.

I walk up from South to North London. As I walk the rain starts and my shoes get damp then wet then start to leak. By the time I get where I'm headed I look like I dragged myself up the bank of a river.

The Old Man opens the front door and stares at me. – What's happened to you? he goes. – Don't even look like you, state you're in.

His hair's still quiffed and oiled, combed straight back off his head, the track marks of the comb showing pink scalp between the hairs. He's put on weight; his checked shirt's straining at the buttons and his jeans are too tight, the belt cutting his belly into two.

– You all right? I go.

– Was till I saw you.

– Just need a bath, I go.

– No bath's gonna make you look better. What you after?

I gesture inside the building. – You gonna let me in? Standing there asking what I'm after when you ain't seen me for months.

– Don't spose I got a choice.

I follow him and he walks slow. Reluctant. When he opens his door I see why: there's a woman in his room, dyed black hair, eyeliner drawn on with a shaky hand, tight black skirt and thin drinker's legs. I know what the attraction is straight off. When he looks at her he sees Janet when she was young, and that means he sees his self young.

She smiles at me. – Afternoon.

I nod. – Afternoon.

The Old Man gestures at me. – My son, Gary, he goes.

She laughs. – That's the one thing, Dave, you don't have to tell me. Look at him. Chips and old blocks and all that.

She pours me a drink, hands it over.

– So where you living now? the Old Man goes.

I tell him and while I'm talking, the woman's

watching us. She's looking at me, looking at him, and I know she's comparing. She's seeing what she fancies in the Old Man but in a younger model. And I know what she's thinking: if the Old Man wasn't in the room, would I stand a chance with the son? Have I still got it?

She ain't.

– Still working with Jim and his belly? the Old Man asks me.

– He's inside.

The Old Man looks surprised. – Ain't like him to slip up. You working with Tony?

– No, I go. – Are you?

– Had enough of working, he goes. – Takes up too much time. Cuts into what I wanna do.

– So you out doing jobs? I ask.

– Can't be arsed. I'm letting the Government keep me for a bit. I paid enough taxes.

– You ain't never paid no taxes in your life, I say.

– You know what I mean.

– I don't, Dad.

– Oh well, you know. Anyway, don't go on, it's boring.

– The truth's always boring for you, I say.

– Yeah yeah. So what you been doing then?

– This and that, I go. – I moved in with this girl.

– You should have brought her to meet us, the woman says. – Tell us what she's like. Describe her.

– She's young. Got short green hair.

– Green? the Old Man says.

– Green, yeah.

He splutters out a laugh. – She sounds like a frog, he says. – Or a pea. Or a leaf.

– Leaves change colour in the autumn, I go.

– All right. Don't be arsey.

He pulls a fag out from above his ear, lights it.

– You got one for me? I ask.

He exhales smoke, looks at the fag in his hand as though he ain't never seen one before, looks back at me. – That was my last one, he goes.

– I got some, the woman says. She rummages in her bag and brings out a pack, offers them up. The three of us smoke and the room fills.

– So? the Old Man goes. – You come for a reason, you may as well spit it out.

– The flat I'm in is a bit of a shithole and I wanna find somewhere decent for the girlfriend. I need a deposit.

The Old Man puts his hands out, like a stop sign. – Yeah yeah yeah, he says. – Heard it all before.

– Honest. I got to get her out of there.

– I ain't got no money, he goes.

The woman smiles, grinds out her fag. – You've got to be able to help him, Dave, she goes. – You know what it's like, starting out. We've all been there.

– If I give him money he'll only drink it.

– You'll get it back, I go. – I'll let you have it.

– If you reckon I believe you, you're thicker than I thought.

192

But as he's saying that, the woman fishes into her bag again and takes out a purse. He watches her, look of horror on his face as she counts out some notes and then presses them into my hand.

– What you doing? he asks.

– I just think young people deserve a chance, she says.

The Old Man stares at me. He knows he's lost, shamed into action. He shakes his head and reaches into his back pocket, brings out some notes, more than any government'll be giving him. He peels off a few, hands them to me. – Go on, then, he says. – You got what you wanted. You can piss off now.

At the flat I empty my pocket. There's five twenties from the Old Man, two tenners from the woman. We spread the notes out on the floor and kneel in front of them.

– I wanna spend some of it on some new sheets, Mandy goes.

– Sheets? I ask. – I run around and get this for you and you wanna spend it on sheets?

– I never had my own sheets. Foster carers gave me cast-offs. In the home it was any sheets what come back from the laundry. I just want my own. New. In a packet.

– All right, I go. – Just don't make me cry.

That night we press our noses to the shop windows of Oxford Street. We'll be back, I tell her. Soon as they open the shop doors in the morning we'll be standing there ready to go in.

As we walk off she slips her hand in my arm and squeezes tight. We pass down through the streets, see a pub where the crowd's spilt outside on to the pavement. We go in and get a drink each, then another. Then somehow it's chucking-out time. We start walking home but she says she ain't ready yet and we go to get something from a flat in Notting Hill and the night goes on and then we're walking home at dawn. My nose is bleeding but I don't know why and I'm looking at the red splatters on the pavement and each one's different. And then we're home and I lie down on the mattress and pinch my nose to stop the bleeding. Mandy kicks me. – You ain't sleeping, she goes.

I close my eyes and she jumps on the bed on top of me. – Get up, Gary. Talk to me.

– I wanna sleep, I go.

– I wanna talk.

I close my eyes and turn my head away but next thing she straddles me and slaps me right across my cheek, the palm of her hand slamming into me. She pulls her hand back to hit me again and I grab her wrist tight.

– Don't hit me, I go.

I grab her other wrist and she starts to fight with her legs. She hangs her head over my face and lets go a dob of spit. It falls down on to my cheek.

– You stupid bitch, I go.

In one move I spin her so she's under me and I'm on top. I get both her wrists in one of my hands. I got red flowing through me. It's behind my eyes. My heart's pushing it out. I'm about to swing for her, crack her across the face, when blood drips from my nose on to her chin. The red on her pale skin stops me, like I've seen what's about to happen, like the blood drips are telling me to stop.

And then she starts to cry. It ain't a normal cry but something else, a noise from inside, from a dark place she never knew even existed.

– What is it? I ask.

But she don't know. She don't know.

Adult Education

It's a crap afternoon. There's bird shit on the table and dog shit on the pavement. We're on a bench outside a pub in North London, and we're supping froth from two pints what I paid for with loose change we found in the flat. The pub door opens and an old geezer comes out. He lights up a fag and blows the smoke upwards, and it's the same grey as the sky.

He looks over at Mandy, stares. – Snot hair, he says.

Mandy stares back. – Tortoise skin.

The bloke laughs till he starts to wheeze. He goes red, then pale again. He raises his glass to Mandy. – You're all right, you.

Mandy points at me. – What about him?

– I wouldn't be talking to you, he goes, – if I didn't like him as well.

– Didn't take you long to decide, I go.

– It never takes me long to know who I like. It's bleeding obvious, ain't it? People've got to look right, smell right.

He puts his pint down, fishes in his pocket. – Tell you what, he goes, – I'll buy you both a drink.

– Why d'you wanna do that? I ask. – What d'you want?

His eyes narrow and he nods approval. – I like you

196

even more now you said that. Always check a person's motive then you know where you are.

– Everyone wants somethink, I go. – Every human exchange is about what someone wants or needs.

– Exactly, he goes. – So if we're gonna tell the truth, all I want is a bit of company. And I'm prepared to pay for the pleasure. All right?

He disappears, comes back out with a tin tray, hands out the drinks. He raises his glass and we touch. Clink clink.

– To London on a grey afternoon, he goes. – My lovely old London town.

He hands out fags, and we all light up. He clears his throat, gobs on to the pavement behind him. – It's all changing though, he goes. – If there's nothing but money-making, there's only one way we can go. Cos once you unleash the old greed from the box you ain't never gonna get it back in.

– There ain't no money coming my way, I go.

– Then you need to learn better. It's all a game, son.

He does a little side shuffle, a dance. – You might not have any money but you got each other. You got youth. You got beauty.

– She has, I go.

– She has indeed, he goes.

He claps his hands. – What's your name?

– Gary, I go.

He shakes my hand. – And you, snothead?

– Mandy.

He jabs at his own chest. – John, he goes. – John

197

Fingers. There's a reason for the Fingers bit. And I reckon I could teach you how to make money.

He's waiting for us at Oxford Circus tube station only we nearly walk past him. He's wearing a tweed jacket and tie, cord trousers. Perfectly polished brown brogues. He's a different person.

We set off and as he walks he swings his stick, grins at passers-by. He's excited, feels alive like he ain't for years.

Marks and Spencer is a sea of satin and shoulder pads and sweatshirts. We wade through it all, follow him to household. He passes the bed linen and Mandy stops, fingers packs of sheets. John picks up a full bed set – duvet cover, sheets, pillowcases. He takes Mandy's arm and steers us over to the customer services desk.

The woman behind the desk's got an over-tight perm like a swimming cap. – Good afternoon, sir, how can I help?

John Fingers smiles. – I hope you can, my dear. You see I'm feeling terrible cos my mum, gawd bless her, bought me these only I can't live with this maroon.

The perm takes the items. – Do you have your receipt?

– No, but let me explain. They were a present and how can I tell my mum? My son here and my daughter-in-law didn't want them neither. Their walls are blue and you know, don't you, love, you can't put blue and maroon together.

The perm sighs. – You should bring a receipt in.

– I know. I'm sorry but you can see my problem. I can't exactly ask her for it.

– All right. Just this once. But we can't give you cash, only vouchers.

– That's all right, John Fingers goes. – I wanted vouchers anyway cos I'll get some more but not today. We're painting the room, you see, but we haven't chosen the colour scheme yet.

He takes the vouchers, thanks the perm and we're off. Outside he leads us along the back of Oxford Street to a rundown pub in an alley. The barman, a tiny bloke with a bald head, looks up as the doors open. – John bloody Fingers.

John spreads his arms out: he's the big man, the conquering hero. – Get a round in for us all, he goes. – Get yourself one too.

The barman throws a glass in the air, spins it, catches it. – Ain't seen you for a bit, John.

– I ain't seen me for a bit neither.

– This your son?

John chuckles. – This is my friend Gary. And his bird, Mandy. This here's Bob.

We all shake. – So, the barman says, – what you up to, John?

John Fingers does another of his little dances, faster this time, light on his feet. – I got things to do, people to see. We're taking on the shops, the banks, the whole world cos they're taking us for a ride.

Bob hands us a drink, pushes away John Fingers's

fiver. – These are on me, he says. – You two got to be miracle workers. It's a resurrection. The old sod was on his knees last time I saw him.

John laughs, hands over the vouchers to Bob.

– Look what we got. We're hunter-gatherers us, only we ain't hunting buffalo. We're hunting bits of paper.

Bob checks the vouchers, hands over cash. John Fingers counts. – Sixty per cent?

Bob grins. – Normal's fifty but for you, John, it's sixty.

John takes a tenner off the top of the pile, hands the rest to me and Mandy.

– You can't give us all that, I go.

He shrugs. – You need it more. Anyway, there's plenty out there to be had. All you got to remember, my son, is tell them a story. It all lies in the storytelling. Get it right and include enough details and they'll believe you.

John raises his glass and we raise ours. He clears his throat. – Let's drink, he goes. – To Marks and Spencer, St Michael, patron saint of the English shoplifter.

Next day, I practise. I go to the same shop and then go to the pub and swap vouchers for cash. I go back again, into another shop this time. I'm queueing at customer services and a woman in front's arguing over whether she can bring something back and whether she can get cash for it. She starts quoting her statutory rights and I'm listening and she's quoting this act and that bit of information. And I'm taking in my lesson. Click click. The woman goes and it's my turn. I quote the same act and rights and the woman behind the counter knows what's going on but there ain't a thing she can do and we both know it. She counts out the notes and I tuck them in my pocket.

When I'm done I go back into the bedding department and pick up a pack of sheets. The best they got. I take them downstairs and pay for them. At home I give them to Mandy and she stands there with them in her hands. She just looks at them.

– Ain't you gonna open them?

She nods but she don't move. I try and take them off her but she shakes her head. She undoes the cellophane wrapping, takes them out and holds them to her face.

We invite John round to eat with us. I meet him down in the courtyard and he's wearing a dicky bow and a dinner suit. He's got glossy black shoes on and his hair's combed back off his face. He does a tap dance, shows his jazz hands.

I whistle between my teeth. – Nice.

– Nicked it a few years ago, thought I'd better get some wear from it before I snuff it.

He opens the jacket, shows me the purple silk lining, all hand stitched. – You need to get yourself some threads, he says. – You'd brush up good. Get yourself a nice pale blue shirt to go with them eyes.

– You wanna run my life for me? I ask.

– If I get to sleep with Mandy each night.

– Dirty sod.

– Listen, my son, your body may age but your eyes and your head don't. When you're my age you'll understand.

I lead him up the stairs past the graffiti and piss and the syringe in the corner with a bent needle.

– Who'd do this? he asks.

– People, John, I say.

– People are cunts.

Mandy opens the door to him and he takes her hand and kisses it, pulls a small bunch of flowers from his bag and gives them to her. She clutches them to her chest. – No one's given me flowers before.

He turns to me. – Then you ought to take note, Gary. This girl needs care, you know.

– What you reckon I'm trying to do? I go.

Mandy takes her flowers away, comes back with fish fingers and beans and buttered bread. Fish fingers is cold in the middle. – Didn't leave them in long enough, she goes.

– Rubbish, John goes. – It's perfect. Lovely company. Lovely evening. First glimpse I got of you two, he says, – I knew you'd be good.

– I ain't a good person, I go.

– I know, Gary, that's why we're here together. I know what you are and what you think and everything. See, I can read people like others can read

202

books. I know from what you say and how you say it, what's really going on inside. It's the great human mystery: we never really know what's going on inside another person. But there's a few of us can cross that line and know what someone else is thinking. And you and me, son, we're in that category. Correct me if I'm wrong.

When we meet the next day he's dressed different. His hair's messed up and he wears a tatty checked shirt and beige trousers what are rolled up at the ankles and held up with a thick belt. On his feet are brown brogues, scratched and worn down at the heels. Two different-coloured laces, frayed at the ends.

He takes us to a shop, tells us to watch him from a distance, says to observe him closely. When he leaves we're not to follow but hang about a bit then meet him at Bob's pub.

As he moves around the shop, this is what we see: an old man, brown and beige. A moocher. A pain in the arse customer who fingers the clothes but don't buy nothing. He moves slow then, almost like he's moving under water, he takes up a jacket, folds it in his arms, mooches on through the displays, mooches down to the front doors and mooches straight out the shop.

At Bob's pub he holds up the jacket. – Never been caught, he says, – and I ain't losing it now. I still got what it takes.

– He can lift anything, Bob goes. – From anywhere.

– It's all in what you project, John says. – Most people are stupid and accept certainties. Long as your story is believable and long as they think they know what they're seeing, they ain't gonna question it. Just create a story they can believe and you'll have them. Always remember, people like to be reassured. Do the work for them.

He hands me the jacket he lifted. Then pulls out a pair of trousers what I never even saw him take.

– I been working out what story you can tell, Gary. I reckon you're from the East End, went from working at Smithfield Market to a job on the floor of the City. That's where the bright lads go. The trading floor. You need to brush up, get the gear. Then when you're dressed right, always stand tall and never look back. Walk like it's all yours. Don't be approachable. Be entitled.

We go out, lift the clothes that'll tell my story: suit, shirts, tie, striped braces, black brogues. I dress up, practise my walk. Practise my talk.

I see myself. I'm a new person. I'm reinvented.

I go down to the big shop in Knightsbridge. I take stuff in the changing room, hide silk ties in a suit I say I'm trying on. I put the ties in my pockets, walk out. I go back for more and then when I'm leaving the shop a hand touches my shoulder. I turn round, see a suited security guard.

– Excuse me, sir, he says, – did you just come out of the changing room?

I say nothing. We stare at each other. Time stops. The molecules of air between us move and drift. I breathe deeply through my nose, don't let my heart speed up. This is my suit, these are my clothes. I could buy any number of them. I am entitled. I'm a man of bright eyes, I'm wearing the suit, I'm the City worker.

His eyes drop and time resumes. And I know I done it.

– So sorry to bother you, sir, he says.

And he's gone.

And as I stand there I think: I can do anything. There ain't nothing I can't do.

I find out a lot. I study the shops and know everything about them all. How the cost of things for sale's all to do with the brand. How the brands are created for us to have something to save up for. I'm the one person what can see it's a con, but the thick-arse public don't see that. They flood the shops, pay to wear logos and become walking billboards.

And now I can do anything in front of anyone and they never ask a question. I walk into a department store, take a bag from the luggage department then go up to the men's floor, find the designer men's clothes collection. I take each thing from the hanger, fold it with tissue, put it in my bag. I do it in full sight of customers and staff. No one questions me cos I've told a story. Today's story is I'm a posh shop assistant folding up the old collection, making space for the new one. Then I'm on my way towards the doors with my bag of clothes when I see the window display. I go right into the window and put my bag down. Unbutton the jacket and trousers, take the suit off the mannequin then fold it up and put it in the bag. Shoppers watch me from outside on the street and I know what they think: lovely young man, smartly turned out. Must be so sensitive to dress the windows so beautifully, must have such refined taste. Look at the leather soles of his shoes as he kneels. The stitching and the gold scroll of the writing of the brand's logo. He's so *English*, they all think, such a *gentleman*.

Game Over

I'm an expert now. I stand in the shop in front of the changing-room mirror. The light comes in from the side window, shines slant. I got the suit on, the shirt and tie. I got my brogues on my feet and their black leather gleams. I've got it all. I'm a blue-eyed cocky little shit.

I go out on to the floor, walk around. I'm looking through the clothes trying to see which'll look best while I'm at my desk on the trading floor. There's a stand of leather jackets and I take one from its hanger. I don't hide it, know there's no need to. I just fold it over and hold it close to my chest then stride through to the down escalator. I'm halfway down and I stand tall cos I'm the big man, the City man, the money maker. A security guard's gliding up the other escalator, and he passes me. I see him clock me and stare him down. He ain't gonna touch me cos I know who I am. But he don't look away. Then I hear the crackle of his radio and my knees start to shake. A drop of sweat runs down next to my spine, a ball of mercury sliding down skin. The escalator ends and I have to walk from there in a straight line to the doors. Through no man's land. I hold myself straight, play the part, and as I get to the doors, I'm thinking ahead, working out which way to go once I'm out the door cos I need to know whether to go left or right and how far I have to walk before I can break into a run. And it's the one thing gives it away, that moment of indecision. Two of them leap forward and the big one gets my arm, twists it up behind my back.

– Game's over, sonny, he goes.

They charge me down the nick then send me home. Mandy lets me in and leads me to the mirror in the bedroom. She stands me in front of it. – Look, she goes. – Look at yourself.

– I'm all right.

– Your trousers.

She bends down, shows me the rip at the knee.

– It ain't nothing, I go. – Just a little tear.

– And this?

She opens my suit jacket and shows me where there's a brown stain down the shirt.

– Only an accident, I go. And anyway you can't see it cos the jacket's always shut.

– You can't see it, she says. – You can't see what you look like.

– Course I can, I go. – And there ain't nothing wrong with me.

And I eyeball myself. Nothing wrong with me. No, sir.

That night we go to Paddy's for a pint. I lift up the glass, down most of it in one mouthful. It hits the blood in my body and I want more. Mandy keeps up with me, drink for drink. We stay till the end then stop off on the way home and buy something and when we get in the flat we smoke it and it ain't nothing I've had before and I have ice in my head and it feels like my brain's gonna split in two.

Mandy shakes my arm and I open my mouth only I can't speak. I put my hand out. All I'm gonna do is touch her and I don't know what happens next but I fall down like I've tripped over only there ain't nothing to trip on.

She puts me to bed and curls up by me and I try and sleep. My head's going at it like a battering ram and all I want's a blackout. I curl up tighter. Stick my head right under the covers. My body's shaking and she nudges me. – Stop that. You're making me seasick.

And then my teeth start clacking against each other and she gets extra covers but then I'm too hot and I'm sweating and she washes me down with a wet flannel. And I can't sleep all night and in the morning she brings me some brandy and whisks raw egg into it. I drink it.

– What we gonna do with you? she asks. – You been crying all night.

– Dunno what you're talking about, I go. – You're talking shit.

And then I reach over the edge of the bed, throw up. She looks at the blood what's in it.

– Jesus, Gary, Mandy says.

– Jesus never bled through his mouth, I go. – It was through his hands and feet.

John Fingers comes round that night. When I answer the door he's dressed up, moustache points waxed so hard you could clean your nails with them. He's wearing his tweed jacket and a green hat with a feather in it.

He looks around the flat, looks at Mandy sat on the settee. He shakes his head. – What are you two doing? he asks.

– We're all right, I go.

– I thought you said you knew everything, Gary, could see everything.

– I do. I can.

He twiddles the ends of his moustache, waxed and knife sharp. I push stuff off the settee, make a space. I take stuff off the table. – Just needs a quick tidy, I go.

– There ain't no quick tidy's gonna put this right, he says. Then, – Sit down, Gary.

I'm caught by surprise and do what he says. I park myself on the settee and he stands over me.

– You might have good intentions, my son. But intentions don't add up to nothing. An intention is worth as much as a single grain of salt in a vat of herrings. You two could be something. You could have a future. Look at you.

John shakes his head slowly and he's still standing over me like he's in a pulpit.

– I'm looking at you now, he goes, – and I'm gonna

tell you what I see. You got a quick brain, you're smart. You could make yourself a career. Make money. I ain't talking about joining the system, cos it's a mess and it'll be a bigger mess one day if we carry on like this, but I'm talking about playing it. There's a lot of money out there to be made.

– You finished? I ask.

– No I ain't. Cos you need to know if you two carry on like this, you'll end up a bit of dirt on my shoe.

And then John points at Mandy. My hands fold into themselves, bunch up. They make fists.

– I thought you was gonna look after her, he says.

Mandy looks at him. Looks at me. – He does, she says.

– You call this being looked after? You ain't never been looked after ever. Not properly. Don't confuse attention with care. They ain't the same.

– John, I say. – Shut up.

He shrugs. – Home truths hurt the most.

– Ah, I go. – So we're dealing with home truths, are we? Is that what you want then? Home truths?

John Fingers smiles. Puts his fists up as if to fight. – Bring it to me, son. Don't spare me nothing.

I leap to my feet and to stop myself hitting him I walk behind him, circle him. I carry on circling. Round I go. Round and frigging round.

– Come on then, he says. – You got something to say, so say it.

– All right, I go. – You come round here telling me how to live my life. But what about you? What've you ever done? You're on your own, reduced to finding friends outside pubs, buying drinks for strangers to talk to you cos you ain't got a single person in your life. You're a walking bag of coughing phlegm. Look at you. Dressed up like anyone's gonna look. You're an old twat in a bag of old skin. You're no use to no one. Any sex you ever had is over. All you can do is ogle young women and you think they don't know but they all get creeped out by you. Mandy does, she says you ogle cos you can't do nothing. Cos when you get back home you grab hold of your dick but you can't even get a rise out of it.

John Fingers nods and turns to Mandy. – You got anything to say?

Mandy's looking down at the floor. I know what she thinks: she knows she ought to tell him it's a lie and that she don't think like that. She knows she ought to put it right. But this is the thing. She knows, like I know, that there's some stuff in the wooden box on the table. It's waiting for us.

I see her glance at the box. I glance at the box. It's all we can think about. The sooner he goes out, the sooner we can get going. Everything in our life's boiled down to the contents of a wooden box.

Mandy don't say nothing. I don't say nothing.

I see his head drop down into his shoulders, as though the marrow in his bones has dried instantly, as though the cartilage down his spine has been ripped out.

– I thought more of you than that, Gary, he says. – I really did.

– Then more fool frigging you, I go.

I turn my back to him and walk to the kitchen. Hear the front door open and close. When I look back, there's a space where he stood and it's a bloody relief.

Tricks

I get out of bed. My legs is weak and I go through into the kitchen. The sun's creeping in, lighting up the scene. There's plates on the side, there's dirty pans, there's dust in the sink. In the lounge there's bottles on the floor, ashtrays overflowing, stuff on the table: papers, pipe, strips of foil.

I have a piss and go back in the bedroom. My suit's on the floor in the corner. There's dirty mugs and plates. Another ashtray. Foil. The sheets we bought have come untucked and I can see the blue corners of the mattress.

Mandy's lying with her back to me. She ain't got nothing on and I can see the shape of her spine, can see each nodule of bone. At the top of her back, along her shoulders, are pale freckles. She looks like her skin's got thinner, like I can see more of what lies beneath it than I should. There's bones, muscles, and it looks like the skin's been lain over it. Her hip bone sticks up.

I get in the bed next to her. – You awake?

She turns on to her back and looks up at the ceiling. I see her belly's concave like a rock pool and I can't remember the last time we ate.

I light up a fag. Chuck the match on the floor. The

sun's moved up and is coming through the blinds what are broken and the light's shining on the wall and it's so sharp you can see the string of the blind. You can see the slats what are broken. You can see my shadow. The smoke rising up.

– Gary, she says. – We don't do nothing no more. We used to go to places. We used to see things. The view out of a train window. Jobs for Pete. And we used to talk.

– We still talk, I go. – What you reckon we're doing now?

– We're talking but we ain't saying nothing, are we?

– I'll tell you what we need to talk about, I say. – We ain't got no money.

– You looked under the mattress?

– Yeah.

– I put some under the chopping board.

– That went last week.

She sits up, puts her head in her hands. I look at her spine under the skin. She stand up, gets dressed.

– Where you going? I ask.

– I'm gonna go and get some.

– How?

– I'll work it out.

I stay in bed a bit then get up and go and wait in the lounge. I look at the walls. I stand up, sit down. I go to the window, see if I can spot her walking back towards the block. I stand by the glass and look out. Nothing.

Then I hear the door banging shut at the end of the

corridor outside and I hear feet approaching down the hallway. I hear them stop, hear the key feel for the hole, hear the chambers turn, the handle go down. She comes in.

We sit on the settee and she pulls out of her bag what she's got and we take it and the shaking in my hands stops. We take some more. And then when it's done and we're eyes half closed, I ask where she got the money from.

She shrugs. – I sold a necklace I had.

I look sideways at her. I feel cold. – What necklace?

– You wouldn't know. You never seen it.

She's busy with her hands, folding foil, ripping it into tiny pieces, laying them out on her lap. She's doing it too much, looking at it too hard. – Mandy? I go.

– What?

– I never saw you come back in the block. I was looking out the window. You never went out in the street, did you?

– I went the back way.

– You don't never do that.

– I did this time. Stop questioning me, Gary. I got what you wanted, didn't I?

I grab her arm. Stare at her. She looks away.

– Mandy, I go. – You never had no necklace.

I feel the blood in her veins change direction. Feel each tiny hair on her arms rise up. Feel the change in the air. Now, in this moment, I can sense everything again. I can read her. – Look at me, I go.

But she won't. – I ain't done nothing, she says.

And then I know. I know why I never saw her come back in the block. I know where she's been. I pull her arm, pull her round. – You been to Pete's to get this.

She don't say nothing, don't move. It's in the air between us. – It's true, ain't it?

She nods.

– And you never needed no money, did you? You give him somethink else for it.

She don't say nothing. She don't deny it. She looks at the floor.

I stand up. Walk away from her cos the anger's got hold of my bones. My head and veins go black then red. I look at her head. Look away. Go to the wall. Hit out. I split my knuckle. Scream. She screams out: No. There's a dent in the wall and there's blood on it and down my arm. She stands up, comes towards me.

I don't look at her. – Get out, I shout. – Get out before I do that to you.

Desperate Measures

Jolly old tale, ain't it? I almost feel sorry for you having to read it. It was bad enough to live it but now you're living it too. Oh well. Don't whinge. Cos whatever happens next, we got our agreement and we both know it all ends up all bloody right. Let's just get on with it, shall we?

Roll up, roll up. Come and see the Gary show.

We need even more money. I get up from the settee and put on shoes; my feet feel soft in the hard casing like my bones is melting. I pull on a coat and it feels rough on my skin, too heavy.

The day's bright outside and it's like there's a film over my eyes, like I got cataracts. Cars pass on the street and the sound's too close and too loud.

In the shop they watch me, follow me. I go out in the street and people walk round me, stare at me. I realize I'm telling a different story now and it's one they don't wanna listen to; I need to stand straight, need to pull myself together.

The entrance to the tube looks like a mouth and I go into the throat. Jump barriers. Run and get on a train as the doors close. It's rush hour. Push hour. Push and bloody shove you out the way hour. There's people sat and there's people stood. There's people who can't fall down cos they're packed so tight. There's people with their noses in armpits. But as I get on something happens and they make room. The seas part. They stand aside, let me in.

The train stops and starts. Doors open and close. A woman gets on and I see the top edge of her purse in her outside pocket. I keep looking at it. The train swings round a bend and I lose footing, fall against her. She backs away from me and then the train stops. She gets off and I see her get in the next carriage.

The train sets off again and I see a bag on the floor. It's a woman's bag and it's open, and a newspaper's sticking out of it, and next to it I can see a purse. I move a step closer, creep towards it each time the train sways. I crouch down, do up my shoelace. I'm inches from it. But she sees me and reaches down, snatches it up and on to her lap. The train stops and I get off, go down two carriages, get back on.

This time I stand close to a bloke. His arm's stretched up high, hanging on the bar to hold his self steady. His coat's pulled up and the top of his pocket's exposed and inside there's a bit of leather and stitching and some paper. The train goes round a bend and I sway, bump hard into him. I apologize. Sorry, sorry. It's the train, you know what these drivers are like, what these trains are like, what these busy morning commutes are like. He raises his hand to say oh that's all right, don't you worry. And I realize I'm back to the old games, being able to see things on the train that no one else can. It's all still there somewhere tucked inside me. I know the whole carriage, everything what's going on. And I know what to do. Cos the man's relaxed, his body's gone loose. He knows who I am, where I am. He's let me get close to him, and I've broke through the old animal instinct which tells him I shouldn't be so near. I bend down too close to him, pretend to do up my shoelace, then as I stand up, the train's slowing for the station and I reach out my hand and grasp the top of the wallet with thumb and forefinger and pull and it slips out like it's greased in butter. I have it in my hot hands. The train stops and the doors open.

I don't look back. I barge and push my way along the platform. Through the tunnel. Run up the escalator. Don't look back, whatever happens, don't look back.

I'm over the barriers, out into the street and it's daylight and I ain't got a clue where I am. I turn up an alley, lean back against the wall. I'm sweating and my heart's banging a tune in my chest. I feel more than alive. This is stronger than what I done before. It's more raw. The person's there in front of you. You can smell them. They can smell you. It's a live event.

I lift the wallet to my nose. The leather smells of animal and for a second I imagine it coming back to life, unfurling, shedding stitches, lifting its head to the air. I shake my head, pull myself back together. I'm losing it. Don't lose it, all right. Just don't lose it.

The wallet's quality. Fine leather, good stitching. I

open it up and inside there's stamps, receipts, business cards, then, behind all that, in the back of the wallet, a lovely pile of cash.

This way of thieving ain't the business of wood veneers and dovetail joints. There's nothing delicate, no time to appreciate quality. This is smash and grab, dip and run. It's the work of a cornered man. The work of an entrepreneur.

I start to teach myself. I'm a fast learner. The old skills are kicking in and I'm reading people, seeing what others can't. I'm hearing the invisible.

And the first thing I work out is why that man's body went loose. I know it's cos I got close to him, so I work out each person's got this aura round them, the animal self. I have to enter their territory so my aura and theirs mingles. I have to silence their animal. And once I done that they're in my hands. I can do what I want.

There's different ways to do it: I can slowly move closer step by step, or I can do it in one movement and bump into them. Easiest is in a pub then I can put my drink too close to theirs. Move my stool near theirs. Anything to cross the line.

Click click. Lesson in.

I learn new tricks. I get a coat, wear it across one shoulder. When I cross the line into someone's space then the coat becomes the cover and I can do what I want under it. I can lift a purse, a wallet, entire bags. And I don't even have to rush. I walk. I saunter.

In fact, the calmer and slower I am the better the results. Their animal brains've got no reason to be alarmed.

And you know what the truth is? People make it easy for me. And the easier they make it, the more I reckon they deserve what I'm doing. I say to myself, they're asking for it. They're flaunting what they got, and they ought to expect the consequences.

And as I weave my way through people I feel like I'm a fish darting through them all, cleaning up. Tidying, sorting. I've found something I'm good at and the old feelings, they all come back. I got a spring back in my step, I'm back to the cocky self.

Click click. New lesson.

I go into a shop and nick an umbrella, add it to my toolbox. I open it indoors and people draw back, scared of the bad luck. When I close it they're relieved and relax so much they don't notice my dipping and diving and whipping out their money. I use it to hook handles of bags, draw them closer to me. I use it to tap on the floor, distract. I use it for everything except keeping the rain off my head.

I'm out every day looking for easy targets. I see a woman with a purse in the top of her unzipped bag. I follow her in and out of a shop then along the road and we go into the registry office. She sits in the waiting room and her bag's on the floor. I look around the room, read the posters on the wall, then sit down by her. I lean down to do the shoelaces, shuffle my feet a bit closer to her, cross the line into her world. I let my coat slide down, and it lands on top of her bag. I say sorry, sorry, I was just doing up my shoes, and reach down to pick up the coat and under the cover of the fabric I lift the purse out. I don't rush off but leave it a minute, then stand up and look as if I'm searching for the toilets. I shrug like I can't find them and go to the door, leave.

I go round the corner into the next street, then cut through another smaller road what leads to the back of the car park. There's a bin there and I open the purse. Inside there's a photo of a man. I take out the money and cards and chuck the rest in the bin. I count the cash and it's a fair bit. I fold the notes to go in my pocket and it's then I get this realization that we been in the registry office and she must've been there to register a birth or a death. She was too old to have a baby so it must've been a death and it hits me: it was the bloke in the photo. For a second I'm stopped short. Jim the Belly comes back to me, talking of the voice I got inside me, telling me what's right, what's wrong.

This thought comes to me: I'm living off the misery of other people.

But as soon as it lands in my head I know I can't listen to it. I got to ignore it cos otherwise I'll have to stop this. And then what?

And anyway, I tell myself, the truth is if you carry a

bag round like that with it all poking out and show-ing, you're being wilfully stupid. You're asking for it. You tell me how I can be responsible for that.

Click click. Harden up, twat.

It's that same day, that early evening, autumn 1988, and the rain's falling strong enough to dilute the blood, and the leaves are clogging the gutters, and I nip into a pub in Camden and there's a couple there at the bar and her bag's on the floor and I let the coat slip down then take her bag into the toilets and take what she's got before buying them a drink.

And it's while I'm in the loo with them that it occurs to me, Christ, this is complicated. Not just anyone can do it. It involves instinct and our animal selves, and how we got to extend our vision. And I think of the falcon. She don't swivel her head to see a sparrow fly by. She *knows* it's there.

Like I say, it ain't something just any bastard can do. This is something extraordinary. In fact, it's a bit like a ballet. It's a bit like theatre.

You know what it is? It's a fucking art form.

But you know all that already.

You Get Under My Skin

We're a modern couple, the two of us. We got a place to live and we're both earning. We got a double disposable income and no kids.

I'm out all hours working, dipping into the bags and pockets of the morning commuters, the dinner dawdlers, them on the school run. Mandy works evenings. She's bought a school summer dress from the charity shop, puts her hair up, wears white socks. She charges more, ain't never been busier.

Her eyes are paler, her hair longer and thinner. We're both losing weight and the furniture's disappearing. But it's all right. We had too much anyway.

One night I wake up. It's dark and Mandy ain't in the bed. I get up and go in the lounge. I don't see her at first, then as I'm going to the bathroom I catch sight of her feet. She's behind the settee on the floor, back against the wall. She has a tourniquet round her arm, held tight between her teeth. Her eyes are open and the pupils are near gone. And I know from looking at her there's nothing. All of it, all of this, has gone. Everything is in its place.

*

Tiny comes round one night. – You ought to look after yourself, he says.

– I'm all right.

– You ain't, he says. He gets hold of my hands. Then he turns them over, grips them tight, and pushes my sleeves up. He sees the small red marks.

– It's bed bugs, I go.

He shakes his head slow. – You stupid idiot, he goes.

And that's when things started to change. Even back then I knew it but I wouldn't have admitted it. No: it's now I'm saying it. Hindsight, you see, is a beautiful thing.

You know what else is beautiful? Being able to hear the twist and crack of a dead leaf breaking from the stem and falling to the ground. So is being able to hear a piece of grass fold down and the pleating of the skin on an eyelid.

But I couldn't do that no more.

The sun rose and set outside the window. The moon came and went outside the window. Stars died and fell to the ground outside the window.

We didn't see none of it. We drifted in and out of black, in and out of arms.

She was so thin that the few times we fucked, it felt like her pelvis was a china cup.

An Expectant Hush

We are in bed. There's a film of filth on the window, a film of filth on my teeth. It's dark and street light comes through the blinds where the strings are broke and the slats've all slipped down.

Mandy's next to me. The sheet's rucked up under us and my head rests on the bare mattress. She says something but I can't hear.

– What you say? I go.

– I said I think I'm pregnant.

I go quiet. She didn't say that. Not that. Listen harder, twat. Listen to what she says. – I didn't hear you.

– I said I think I'm pregnant.

– You can't be, I go.

– I been sick. And I feel different. And I passed out.

– You can't be. Not with all this going on. And anyway it ain't gonna be mine.

– You're the only one I never used nothing with.

I sit up, turn my back on her and perch on the edge of the bed as though, if I could, I'd fly off, disappear.

– It could be somethink else, I go.

– It ain't, Gary. I got tested at the doctor.

And then my heart slurs and slows. – What they say?

– They say I'm pregnant. They say I have to go back tomorrow to see them, she goes.

And now they know who we are and where we live. They know everything. They say we have to go in. Both of us. They sit us down.

– We need to talk about the effect of the drugs, they say.

We tell them we ain't taking drugs. They nod slowly then repeat themselves. – The effect of the drugs, they say again.

And then the doctor says to Mandy, – Have you considered a termination? Even though it's late and the pregnancy is well progressed, we could do something.

On the way home we go to a park and she sits on a bench. I sit by her. Her teeth are clenched tight enough to shatter the enamel. I feel her shaking through the wood of the bench.

– I ain't getting rid of it, she says.

She touches my hand with hers, holds it. It's the first time we've touched for a long time. I grip it to stop the shaking.

– I could give this baby what I never had, she says.

I look at her. She's staring ahead, got this look on her of stone. This look what says: I made up my mind inside and the outside of me's just copying the inside.

Rubbish flies in the wind and a man walks past. She

waits till he's gone before she speaks. – We could give it a proper start. We could be a family.

– How we gonna do that? I go. – Look at us.

She turns her stone face to look at me. – What?

– How we're living. How it all is.

– It ain't gonna be like that though.

She squeezes my hand tighter. – We can stop the madness. Get clean, start again.

– You and me?

– Yeah. You and me, she says. – You know how we are about each other. Long as we're together we can do it.

– Is that what you want?

She nods. – I just wanna start again. I wanna be like a real person. Normal.

I nod. Say nothing.

She turns to look at me. It's my turn to stare ahead. – There ain't just one way of being, she says. – Just cos we've been like this it don't mean we have to be like this for ever.

I turn and look at her and our eyes see our eyes.

– I want this baby, she goes.

When we get home she goes straight in the kitchen and washes the dust down the sink plughole then cleans the plates. She fills a bin liner with rubbish and I take it down. I clean the bath and she empties every ashtray. She makes beans on toast and we sit at the table to eat.

She talks of getting new sheets.

*

I know what you think.

You think aha, the baby. The son. The one what lives up the road from Gary. This is how he comes into the story. Clever, ain't you?

Craving

I lie in bed and my back's to her. I'm sweating but I ain't talking about a film of sweat and I ain't talking about beads of it. I'm talking about it running off me, soaking down into the sheet. I'm talking about it dripping off my forehead on to my closed eyes, talking about it creeping through the lids, the salt of it stinging.

I sit up and feel on the floor for my jeans. I pull them on, the denim snagging on the sweaty skin, and find a T-shirt. I go out the room, put on shoes. I'm going for a walk. I'm going out into the cool. I'm going to dry off, catch the air. Then I'll go back and she ain't even gonna know I was out.

The streets are near empty. The odd car. The odd person walking home. I stand a while. Breathe it in. I turn and start to walk along the big road, feeling one foot in front of the other. Walk walk. I go faster, so fast I could outwalk my own self. Walk till my body's left behind in a dry husk. I'll be newborn, hatched out wet. I'll be a new me. Every cell changed. Transformed.

I catch up with a woman, older. She's hugging the building, walking quick. She's got a bag over her shoulder, and she's got her hand on it.

I drop back, walk slower. She looks back, has seen me. She goes faster, I track her. She looks back again.

I ain't got time for tricks. I ain't got time for nothing. I speed up and she does. I draw alongside and she stops, tries to turn.

– Give it, I go.

She shakes her head. I see in her eyes and I know what it is she feels. Fear. Made by me. I put out my hand. She steps back. I grab the strap and she holds it. Neither of us says nothing. We pull at the bag and stare at each other. I pull harder. She pulls harder. I grab her lower arm and yank it so I can get the strap down. I yank harder and then feel her arm give. She opens her mouth and lets out a high cry. I see the shock and the look in her eyes and she lets go and I've got the bag. And she's clutching her arm.

And then she looks at me and she finds her voice.

– I hope it makes you happy, she says.

I take the cash to Pete's, exchange it. I use some of it in his place then go back to the flat. I ain't gonna take the rest. The sweats have stopped now and I'm gonna chuck what's left.

She's in the lounge sat on the settee, knees up to her chest, arms round them. She watches me come in and this is the thing: she knows. She knows everything I do and I know everything she does. We've become each other's guards. My heart's beating Morse code and she understands it. My eyes are telling stories and she's listening.

I stand still. She stays sat down. Time passes cos it has to; if it could stop it would. Neither of us says nothing.

And then she puts out her hand. I put my hand in my pocket, pass it over.

Hard Labour

When she pulls off the sheet we can see her whole belly is moving. It's like she's possessed. The muscles go flat, hard. Things move under the skin. She says she's wet between the legs, tells me to call an ambulance.

They take her through the swing doors and up on a high bed. I stay by her side and I don't know what to do and she grips my hand. And then it starts and she bucks and twists. She grips till her hands is white.

Inside the baby headbutts the cervix and shoulders its way down. It's in a hurry this one, gonna have something to say, this one. She screams and they pull her legs apart and tell her it's time to let it out into the world.

The top of a head appears then the shoulder and the midwife grabs and pulls and the whole of it slips out, red and coiled. A boy, it's a boy.

The lights are bright and white bounces off the walls. Mandy raises her head, watches them as they weigh, clean, listen for the first breath. They wrap him in a blanket, pass him to her. She takes him in her arms and folds back the blanket so she can see. We look at him. We see his near-black hair, his eyes blue as the ink on a fiver.

But then the woman holds out her arms. Asks for him. Mandy holds him tight to her. They have a glass crib and there are people in the room, green clothes. The room's full.

– He has to go to be looked after, the woman says.

– I'll look after him, Mandy says.

But the woman takes him from her and he's put in the glass and they wheel him out.

And there's blood everywhere and there's a woman between Mandy's legs and she says they're gonna stitch her up and we're asking where he's gone and they say he needs to be checked and we can see him later.

Mandy's in a wheelchair and I'm pushing her. We go with the midwife up in the lift, along a corridor and we're put in a room what's carpet silent. We wait, the three of us.

And then a doctor comes in, she's got a white coat, badge, all that. She's just a young woman, don't look old enough to know nothing. Another woman comes too.

– What's going on? Mandy goes. – I want to see my baby.

The doctor points at the woman who come in with her. – This is Sharon from Social Services.

Sharon from Social Services smiles. – Hello.

– Where's our son? I ask.

The doctor looks at me. – Your son is upstairs on the high-dependency unit, she says. – If we leave him he could fit. We have to monitor him all the time as we are prescribing something so he can slowly withdraw.

Special care, they call it. It's a room full of glass tanks and his is the corner one. There are two nurses standing by him and the older one watches us as we walk near. The tank's got holes in the side and he's lying there and he's got nothing on, only a nappy. There's tubes into his arm and one up his nose.

He's got his legs crunched up and he's flat on his back. His head to the side, eyes closed. He ain't big and I reckon I could fit him in one hand. Pick him up in one hand.

No one says nothing. The nurses say nothing. I know why. I know what they think, all of them. I know everything.

But this is the thing. They don't know what I think. They think they know us, me and Mandy, but they don't. They don't know nothing.

They don't know that standing here looking at him has turned me upside down. I feel like my heart is at the bottom of my stomach. Like my stomach is in my throat.

I reach out to touch the glass of the incubator, but the nurse reads it as something else. She moves towards me as though I'm a threat which needs stopping. I ain't. I just wanna touch the glass cos it's as though my hand can pass through it and feel his skin the other side.

I turn away, take the handles of Mandy's wheel-chair and we go back through the room, between all the glass tanks.

As we go through the swing door, I look back. I see them all, standing in front of the glass crib. Watching us.

Last Chance Saloon

There's the two of us in the flat. The only thing she's got is the name tag she had on her wrist in the hospital. That and her blood-soaked T-shirt what, she says, still smells of him. We lie side by side in the bed. She's on her back and she's staring at the ceiling.

– What you thinking about? she asks.

– You know what I'm thinking about.

– We're gonna have to fight, Gary. We're gonna have to do this.

– I know.

– And you have to do it with me.

– All right, I go. – You keep saying.

– We need someone to help us.

– I ain't having no do-gooding people coming round here telling us what to do.

– Then they won't let us have him back.

– And you reckon I don't know that? I snap.

She goes silent. Looks up at the ceiling. She gathers thoughts, speaks:

– All this, she says, – all this didn't have to happen. If you hadn't come home that day. I told you. I told you. I bloody told you, Gary. I wanted an ordinary life. A bloody family.

I leap out the bed straight to my feet. It's like my

238

body ain't able to contain it. It's like my skin's split open and it's all falling out. – So it's all my fault. Did I make you do anything? I don't remember making you, forcing it in you. I never made you do nothing, I say.

And the tears start. – I just want him. I just want him.

She's saying it over and over and she's crying and saying it and I can't. I can't stand it. I feel my fists clench and I know what'll happen if I stay there. I ain't in my body no more. I ain't able to hold it in. It's all gone.

I pull on clothes, boots. She gets up on her knees on the bed and she's still crying and she pulls at my back but I shake her off. I could shake anything off. I go out the room and I hear her calling and she's running after me. – Gary. Gary.

But I can't stay. I'm out in the hallway. The door slams. I run down the stairs and out into the street.

I'm walking quick, quicker than anyone can find me. I'm passing through streets. I'm dodging. Ducking. Diving.

Thoughts come: So it's a blame game. So that's what it is. It's whose fault is it we got in this mess? Whose fault is it he ain't with us and he's somewhere else? The blame game and if it's a game there's only gonna be one winner.

Thoughts come: So they think they can ask me to run around doing their bidding. Be here at three. Be there at four. Next there'll be blood tests. Next there'll be making me walk in a straight line before I can look at my son. My son. *Mine*.

Thoughts come: I can't go back to the flat. Can't stand it. Can't stand the sobbing. Not today. Not now.

Another thought comes: If they let me hold him he'd fit in one hand.

That thought ain't allowed nowhere near my head. That's the one thing I ain't allowed to dwell on. So I start to duck and dive, work through the crowd till I see a target, till I see someone who's been stupid enough to put their wallet in an outside pocket, put their purse at the top of an open bag. Then I can go and buy something to stop the thoughts. Yeah, that's it. If a thought comes to you you don't like, don't let it speak. Don't listen. Why would you do that?

With my beautiful hindsight I sometimes think of the two of us in the flat, lying on the mattress on the floor. I think we was like the babes in the wood, lying there under the shade of trees. A blanket of leaves.

We didn't know anything.

The Bottom of a Rock

Tiny takes me in, gives me a spot on his settee. We sit and smoke and he asks me what happened, why I left her and I say pass me the bottle, the smoke, the whatever it is we got.

– But is she all right? he asks.

I nod. – She's better off without me.

And she is. I know she is.

It's that first night I hear the noise. It comes from the front door. I get off the settee, go and open it but there ain't nothing there. I close the door, go back and lie down. It happens again, a light scratching like the claws of a rat on wood.

The next week I hear it again only this time it's coming from the window. It stops and I have a drink, a smoke, and then it starts again, screeching claws on the glass.

And then the next time it's moved and it's by my head and I can't sleep. It's like it's coming from right inside the wall. I make myself close my eyes but then I can hear it in the cushion, scratching in the feathers. I know what it is cos I know everything. She's got them out looking for me. They need to find out where

I am cos they're going to watch me. They need to know exactly what I'm doing.

I get off the settee and see the screen of the telly and it's turned on me and its blank eye's watching me. I pull out the plug, tip it on its front so the screen is looking at the floor then I creep out.

They follow me up the street. Patter feet after mine. Tac tac on the pavement. I keep walking cos if I don't they'll catch me up. I walk streets and parks and it's still dark but there's no moon cos that is the enemy cos if there's a moon they can see me and then they can know what I think.

I walk till the moon's swapped for the sun and they switch off the street lights. I go along Oxford Street and stop outside Marks and Spencer. St Michael, patron saint of me. I push open the doors and walk tall. I walk up the escalator, walk around the shop floor. I stop, finger a jacket. But there's someone behind me and he stops too. I know who it is. I know everything.

I spin round and there's two of them and they cuff me. Call the police. They say stop screaming. But I ain't screaming. Stop doing that.

But I ain't doing nothing.

It's okay. I ain't. I ain't.

The cell's got shit on the walls and the mattress has a stain of blood on it. There's no light and they watch me through the hatch in the door. All I can see is eyes and I can't do nothing without them watching and listening. They know everything. My skin is glass and they see through to my heart and the gush of veins.

Then the cell door opens. – Go on, they say. – Get out.

The streets are bright and I stand under the bridge and feel the train pass over.

I go to the park to sleep on a bench. Only there's no sleep. I stay up till dawn, think of Mandy in the bed in the flat. It's like a different world, like the two of us live in two different worlds now.

They come and tell me I can't stay there. They tell me they got a bed for me. They won't tell anyone where I am, they say. They'll look after me.

The hostel door's set into tall brick walls. Inside's a glass cubicle and a woman inside it. She smiles. Welcome, she says. They show me to a bed to sleep in.

In my new bed I think. I know what it is I should do:

Walk to King's Cross, go to the block, up the stairs and go and see her.

Clean the flat and make the bed and have a hot dinner every Sunday.

Go to the Social Services offices and sit there till they tell me where he is, till I got his address on a piece of paper.

Go to the address on the paper and knock on the door and it'll be answered by a couple and behind them in the hallway I'll see him, our son, and I'll pick him up. I'll carry him back home and Mandy'll be there waiting for him.

But it don't happen cos now we're in two worlds what don't meet and in my world I shuffle along hostel corridors and I'm hot and cold at the same time and when I piss it's brown enough to stain the bowl. And every morning I eat breakfast then we're sent out into the cold light of day to wait on the streets till dusk when we're let back in.

Now, we need a little chat. A little Gary show chat. See, I'm worried you're gonna think that's it, that's where he ends up. But Gary's story ain't ended yet. None of our stories have ended yet. There's one thing you can guarantee in life: you don't know what's gonna happen tomorrow. You don't know what an ending is till you get there. That's the point of it all. That's the great mystery of it all.

Spare Any Change?

I walk London all day. My feet are swollen and the flesh is white and bloated. I get lost and forget where I'm to go and one night I don't go back to the hostel. Then the next night they won't let me in. Then the next I don't try. I spend my days being moved on from library to toilet to bench.

One afternoon I find a doorway cos it's raining. I pull in my legs so they don't get no more wet than they already are and sit on cardboard cos it stops the cold going in the bones. I'm all right here. It's dry and it's warm enough. And I got a bottle with me and that keeps me warm, and keeps Mandy and the boy from my thoughts.

A young bloke comes past, hawks and spits right by me. – Low life, he says. – Scum.

His spit stays on the pavement and I watch till it's dissolved by the rain. People pass but they don't look at me. And if they do they look through me. My eyes might as well be the same colour as the sky behind them.

But then a woman slows down, hesitates. She turns back and looks at me. Not through me. She crouches down beside me and asks if I'm all right. I wanna shrink back into the doorway, press myself backwards right into the building. I wanna be painted to match what's behind me. I can't look at her, can't let her see who I really am.

– I said are you all right? she says. – Do you have somewhere to sleep?

I nod. – A hostel.

– Good. Make sure you get them to find you somewhere to live.

And she opens her purse and takes out a fiver and presses it into my hand.

She squeezes my arm. And I wish she never, cos her touch reminds me of the touch of a woman's hands, reminds me of Mandy's hands, of the glass transparent crib what I touched. I did.

One day I'm watching the street and a lorry parks up opposite, loaded with scaffold gear. The men get out, laughing. They size up the building. Unload boards and tubes, swivels and clips. I watch as they put together the base then the first lift and build up a skeleton on the outside of the building.

In my head I'm with them. In my head I can feel the metal of the tube and the cold clips in my hand. I'm putting up and fastening and I'm running out of clips. I lean out and see Tony's there on the ground. He's getting the clips for me and my arm's outstretched and my palm open and I'm ready to catch. And then he throws one and the clip's rising up, the light glinting off it. It's a golden arc.

★

When they're gone, when the sun's down, when it's dark and no one can see me, I crawl out. I cross the road and hold the scaffolding tube, feel the cold metal. I push to check it's firm. Then my head starts to go and my legs shake and I fall to the floor as though my own skeleton's been whipped out from inside me. I lie on the pavement and feet pass by. Black and brown leather. Heels. Bare feet in sandals. Painted toes.

I slip under the scaffolding, right behind it. I'm inside the metal cage. It's my new skeleton. It's gonna hold me in.

The sun's gone and no one's thought to warm up the moon.

Blue lights bounce off windows and the wet tarmac and paving stones. The car stops next to me. The lights beat on, off, on, off, they're a pulse, a stream of blood.

Men get out: coppers and filth and pigs. They try to move me on but I ain't going nowhere. They crawl under the scaffolding, put an arm under mine, start to pull. I pick up a swivel clip what's been dropped, hit it at the glass window. Again again. Glass shatters down. I kick out. They hold me tighter, pull me. I hang on to the metal tubes. Kick out at shins, heads. They prise my fingers off, one by one.

The cell's dry and warmer than the street. Sweat streams down as I shake with cold. I get on the bed, curl up. Sweat. Puke into the metal bucket they put on the floor. The cell's full of noise. Metal doors, clanging pipes, shouts, cries. I stink more than the mattress.

The door's locked. I'm trapped inside my cell. I'm trapped inside my self.

I am on my knees and don't know how to get back off them.

I don't mean to go and see the woman. It's just I pass her office every day, that's all. One time she stops me and asks me to come in and talk to her. I start to go back to my cell along the landing. I'm scuttling. A crab, something from a seabed.

She puts her hand on my arm. – It's too late, she says. – I know you want to talk to me, so let's just get it done.

She takes my arm, holds it. Grips it. We go back along the landing to her room. She closes the door, points at one of the two chairs. I sit.

– You want to say something? she says.

I nod but when I open my mouth nothing comes out. I look down at the floor and swallow. Truth is, my heart's going faster than any time when I broke in a house or when I dipped a pocket. My tongue's on the mouth roof and my hands are jammed between my thighs to stop them shaking.

– It's all right, she says. – There's no hurry.

So we sit there for a bit. She puts a glass of water down in front of me but I can't pick it up cos it'll spill.

She sits back down, smiles at me. – I can help you, she says.

I nod. Head down.

– You need help, don't you?

I nod again. – Yeah, I say.

Only the word comes out so quiet I wonder if I've said it.

– Yeah, I make myself say. – Yeah, I need help.

When I go for sentencing she's there with me. My solicitor tells the judge that I'm done with all this. She says I'm determined to start my life again, reads out a report by Julia, makes my case for me.

The judge laughs. – The man in front of me, he says, – is not one who is going to make a fresh start in life. The man in front of me is a career criminal and a recidivist.

He sends me down.

Julia don't give in. We'll appeal, she says. We'll rewrite the report. Make it stronger. Try again.

I spend the days waiting to hear. They keep me on watch. I know I got to do this, make myself strong again. It's the only way, I tell myself, to get back to Mandy. And yeah, to get back to him too.

One morning they take me in the van to court. This judge looks at me while she speaks. She says what's gonna happen next. I'll leave the court and be sent by my probation officer to a rehabilitation centre by the sea, where I'll be detoxed and I'll stay till they deem me ready to leave.

One-way Ticket

I have a train ticket, and I have the money for a taxi. In my pocket's a typed piece of paper with an address for the other end. Over my shoulder's a bag with a change of clothes. It's all I got in the world.

I sit by the window, watch London move away from me.

Once the green stuff starts, the trees and fields, I get up, walk up and down all the carriages. In the buffet car there's a row of sandwiches and, next to them, beer, cider, wine, spirits. I open my mouth to ask for coffee but the word whisky comes out. Double.

I pour it on to the ice and hold it up, look at it. I roll the cubes round the cup, and then I drink. Soon as it's in my blood I need more. I need more before I even finished it. I dig in my pocket, get out the rest of the taxi money, buy another. I got a taste. I'm on one.

I carry on down the train, go to the end carriage. There's a woman there, a baby in her arms. I look away. Quick. I don't want that in my head. I keep walking up the train only it ain't walking, more rocking and swaying, banging into people. Sorry, sorry. It's the train. So sorry. And before I know it a purse has jumped from a bag into my hand. It'd be hard for it not to, the number of bags left open on seats, people gazing out at the green shit, people asleep.

The barman only lets me have a few more doubles, says I've reached my limit. The train's at my stop and I get off and it's only after it leaves I remember my bag of stuff.

Next drinks are from the pub by the station but then they say I've had enough and I kick off. Ain't my money as good as anyone else's? They call the filth who drag me outside and cuff me. They find the piece of typed paper in my pocket. Read it. They know the story, know why I'm here. They've seen this played out before.

I'm shoved in the back of the car and driven around the streets. They stop, take me out. The door of a house opens.

This is what I see: a woman silhouetted, the light from the hallway behind her.

This is what the woman sees: cuffed hands; piss-marked jeans; trainers so filthy she don't think they can ever have been white; hair oiled down with grease; livid red scar on a nose that's been broken and fixed, broken and fixed; skin which is alcohol thickened; hunched shoulders; bleeding palms; broken knuckles.

And as she takes me in, she sees one other thing. Inside the jaundiced ring of yellowed eye whites, she sees a tiny piece of blue.

Chapter One

I don't have a clue where or what I am. Or even if I am. My body aches. The bed hurts where it touches my weight. I turn and it hurts; I lie still and it hurts. My bones weigh too much.

There's a body on a chair next to me. Shadow shapes pass through the room. I feel something on my skin and a voice in my ear. – Don't move. It's all right, it's only me.

And so I don't move but I can't anyway. I'm man-handled and turned over. My skin is stretched and pleated into sheets. My lips creak open; spittle stretches. – What you doing?

– What?

I try again. – What you doing?

– I'm just rubbing cream into your skin, Gary.

The hands move over me, two hands, one hand. Cream, no cream. Skin.

I hear the plastic twang of glove on wrist. More hands. I ache. She pulls the sheet off and I grab it, cover up.

She slaps my hand. – Stop that. I have to do it, you've got scabies, love.

She squeezes white slugs of cream from the tube, spreads it over me. Smothers skin and hairs.

And then she sits by me and watches me as I sleep. My eyeballs move under the lids. My chest rises and falls. And even though I am what I am, I know what she thinks: she wonders about my mother, for every man is a child and has a mother. She wonders what she would do if her son came home like this. She hopes that another woman, another mother possibly, would sit by his side, would be there for him when he opened his eyes.

And I do open my eyes to see the blurred world.

She smiles, says good morning. Says oh you are alive. Her dark hair shines under the lights. She checks my skin. She changes my sheets.

A drip takes medicine under my skin, right down into the red and blue tubes which run through my body. My lungs, they tell me, have had enough of the smoke that made my head turn. They're curled up and forlorn.

I close my eyes again. I sleep.

First time I step out through the doors, the light hurts. The sun's too bright, too hot. It's like bleach has been poured on to the world. Passing cars make walls of sound. The air stinks of people and dogs. My legs are weak. I can see too much, hear too much, smell too much. It's the first time I've met life with a clean head since I was sat in the concrete pipe watching the sun rise and fall. I've been altered all that time and now the world looks like it's freshly made. It's too sharp, too much in focus. It hurts.

*

The sea air smells of salt and my lungs breathe it in. The waves keep coming, drag stones along stones. There ain't one cloud. I take off shoes. Take off socks. I put each sock in a shoe as if I'm putting them to bed.

A seagull flies down, stands on the promenade. It looks around, fixes on me. One round eye staring. Sod it. I take off shirt and jeans, carry them down on to the beach. There's air on my skin and I walk to the edge of the water. Step in. The cold bites but I ain't stopping. Water reaches my knees and thighs. Washes between my legs. I go in deeper. Stomach, chest. I walk till the water lifts me from my own feet and suspends me.

When I plunge my head under it feels like my brain's being washed, like there's ice in the folds. Salt water gets in my eyes and mouth. I swim a few strokes then turn and lie on my back. I'm suspended by water, looking up at the sky. I turn my head to one side, see only the horizon line between water and sky. A bird. Nothing else.

I stay in for a long time. I think. And this is what I think: Once I could drown the memories with drink, cloud them with smoke. Not now. Now I have to face what it is I am and what it is I've done.

I have to face what I ran away from.

I have to face what I lost.

I float.

My head is as cold as the water. My eyes as blue as the sea as blue as the sky. My skin is as white as it was at the beginning. It's waterlogged, salt clean, unborn.

Chapter Two

I live in the House of the Bewildered. We talk all day, smoke fags, and try to see the light. We're children again, seeing the world clearly for the first time, learning to crawl and walk before we can run. I can hold a knife and fork, can hold a conversation.

I am civilized. A new Gary.

The House of the Bewildered is in a genteel resort on the south coast of England, what's full of what was once small family hotels and are now bedsits for people who've been shipped in from courts all over the country to clean themselves up. Doorways have rows of bells. Front gardens grow supermarket trolleys.

In time I get told to move on. In time they say I'm ready for independent living. And so I go to Bedsit Land where I'm given a room at the back of a house. It's got doors into a garden, got a kitchenette, a shower.

Day I move in, I go out to do some shopping. I stand looking through a rail of shirts when I have this moment and I see myself like I'm outside me. As though I'm watching me.

I got a hunched back. Concealed hands. I'm still the old furtive me, and it ain't no good. I pull my shoulders up straight and turn my body so it's open to the whole shop. I have to learn to fight the old pattern; I got to fight everything I am so I can be me how I would've been in another life.

I push my hand in my pocket, feel for the metal coins and notes. I take a shirt from the rail and take it to the till. I count the money into the woman's palm, saying the numbers out loud. Every gesture's too big, as though I'm telling myself, this is what I do now. This is what I am.

Back in the bedsit I close the door behind me. I'm on my own. I put my stuff away in the kitchen, in the drawers and cupboards. Then I open the wardrobe to put my clothes away. The door swings open and there's a full-length mirror on the back of it. And there is me.

The hair's cropped short. My nose is flat. My eyeballs are nearly white now. There's a small triangular scar by the left eye and I don't even know where it come from. On one arm there's an unfinished tattoo done by a cellmate, half a bluebird, one wing. On the other the scar from the tattoo the Old Man told me to get rid of.

My skin still looks like I've slept under a tarpaulin for a decade. I know what I look like, hard, someone you ain't gonna mess with. But believe me, though my skin looks thick, it ain't. Cos everything's been taken away and this new me ain't got nothing to protect his self. It's like the skin's been peeled off and I'm left a quivering mass of flesh and veins and brand-new cells.

I'm still half formed.

I turn away from the mirror and look out the double doors. They give on to the garden and I can't see no other houses, no people. Just green. Where it's rained, it's dripping. Beads of water hang from leaves.

There's bars on the doors but this, I realize, ain't no prison. The prison was my life before. This is now freedom.

I know what you're thinking. I know what questions are going round your head. You'll find out in time, all right? Patience pays off. Patience is a virtue.

I ain't forgotten nothing of what happened. And I know what bits of my story are left undone. I ain't dropped a stitch yet and I ain't planning to.

Chapter Three

There's a car I ain't seen before outside Bedsit Land and the side gate's been left open. I look through to the garden and a bloke's on the bench, back to me. He's got short hair and a blue short-sleeved shirt. I know exactly who he is. I watch for a bit while he looks at his watch then up at the sky. He sighs.

– Alan? I go.

His head whips round. He jumps to his feet, drops his car keys in a fluster and then picks them up, drops them again. By the time he's upright, his face is red.

He looks at me, scans me head to toe. I catch the minute adjustment in his eyes and know what's going on in his head. When he looks at me, he sees everything he's ever hidden. The respectable exterior he's worked so hard to build is like heavy wallpaper rolling off a wall. Underneath there's a damp wall with bare plaster. Underneath he's back with me and Sharon. The Old Man's yelling. The neighbours are staring. The garden's full of broken fence and bikes.

I break the moment for him. – Nice car, I go.

He looks surprised. – It's out there on the road.

– I know, I go. – So how d'you find me?

– I made some enquiries. I went to the other place first. They said you'd moved on.

– Yeah, I got a bedsit here.

He nods. – That's good you got your own place. She said you're clean. What does that mean, clean?

I point at the bench. – Shall we sit down?

He nods, relieved. When we sit I can feel him relax. He can look straight ahead and it's less eye contact.

– So what does clean mean? he asks.

I don't say nothing for a bit. Take a breath. Let the feelings subside cos the new Gary ain't gonna be the one what loses control. – How long is it since you seen me, Alan? I ask.

– I did ask. No one knew where you were.

– I know, I go. – Don't worry about that. I wasn't exactly someone you wanted to find. But it's been a long time, ain't it? I don't even know how long it's been.

– Years.

– Years, it would be, yeah. And we are brothers, ain't we?

– Of course we are.

– We're flesh and blood the same. Same mother, same old man. Same sister. We grew up together. We ain't seen each other for years and the first thing you ask me is what does clean mean. You ain't asked me how I am. You ain't given me a chance to ask how you are. How your kids are. Your wife.

He thinks for a bit. He thinks he ain't used to this. He thinks he ain't never heard me talking like this, telling him the way it is.

– No, he says. – No, I haven't, have I?

He thinks for a bit. Says: – Can we start again?

I nod. – Sure.

– Tell me how you ended up here.

– The court sent me. I said I wanted a new start. The judge said it was my last chance to redeem myself.

– And when you're finished, will you go back to London?

I shake my head. – Too many temptations. I needed a new start.

He nods. – I suppose that makes sense.

– So where are you living?

– Cheam, Surrey. It's great for the kids. Good schools, safe area. Not that you'd know all that kind of stuff.

I look away, at the tree in the garden. – No, I go, – I wouldn't know what it's like to be a father.

– No one does till they have their own kids.

– No. Exactly.

He coughs, clears his throat. I'm still looking at the tree.

– Gary, he goes, – d'you know where Sharon is? No one seems to know.

– How am I gonna know? I ask.

– Cos she's leading that kind of life.

– What kind is that?

– Messy. I mean it's one thing to make a mess of your own life, it's another to get her into it.

And then I feel the muscles contract in my body, feel the red wash over my eyeballs.

– I never got her into nothing, I say.

– Really? So it was just a coincidence she happened to arrive in King's Cross where you lived. A coincidence she took whatever it was you were taking. A coincidence she moved in with your friend. You've done a great job. Older brother. Jesus.

I slam my hands down on to the bench so hard my palms sting. I stand up. – Fuck you, I go.

– Nothing's truly changed, has it, Gary? he says. – Same frigging old.

– You pompous cunt, I go. – I don't need your grand charity visit.

And I leave.

I lie down on the bed and do some ceiling study. And then the bell goes. Again. Again.

I take a deep breath to steady my thinking. I know I got to get up and open the door. I have to be the new person, not the old.

I push the handle down and the door swings open and he stands there, his head slightly bowed.

– Please, he goes.

– If you wanna talk to me, I say, – then you got to find a whole new way to do it.

– I know. I will. You have to let me make mistakes, this is all new.

– All right, I go. And then some words come from somewhere so deep that I don't even recognize them, though I know they're mine: – Whatever you thought of me, whatever I did to you, whatever I done to anyone else, whatever terrible mistakes I made, I ain't that person now. I am the man who stands in front of you today. I am a human being and deserve to be spoken to like one.

He swallows. Looks me right in the eye.

– I agree, he says. – I really do.

He hands me a business card. – Call me if you need anything.

All right, all right. I know what I said to him in the garden. I ain't thick, I know.

Just wait and it'll work out. All right?

It's a bastard. You sober up and get clean, you stop dipping from bags and pockets, stop breaking into houses and rifling through knicker drawers, stop delivering drugs, stop lifting from shops, start paying your way and open a bank account and have your own door key, start going for morning bloody walks, changing your pants and socks every day, start telling the truth and you know what happens? People expect a storm of it. They expect you to be turned inside out and all your secrets to tumble out like you're a pocket in a pair of trousers.

Chapter Four

He answers on the second ring: – Gary? Anything wrong?

– If anything was really wrong, I say, – you wouldn't be getting a phone call.

– No. No. Of course.

– Unless I'd overdosed and was in a body bag, but then anyway it wouldn't be me calling you, would it? Cos that'd be what you might call a miracle.

He laughs and I play with his business card, turn it over and over.

– Alan, I go, – there's somethink I wanna do, but I need your help.

As we drive up through the streets, further into the centre of London, as we get nearer to King's Cross, I start to see everything I know.

We cross the river, turn up and head north. My hands are holding on to the leather seat, gripping. I feel like I'm awake but dreaming. Like time's collapsed and at the same time I'm both back then and here now.

He parks up. Switches off the engine. I don't move. – Gary? he says. – You all right?

I let go of the car seat. Make myself speak. – I'm fine.

When I get out of the car I slam the door and it makes an expensive noise; it triggers something in my head and I don't know what I'm doing in a car like that. Is it nicked? No, it can't be cos I'm with Alan and he's putting money in the meter. I'm here with him, now. I am here. Now.

Now. Jesus, get a grip. Harden up and stop this.

He locks the car door and looks at me. – You sure?

I nod. – Yeah. I'm fine.

I walk off and he follows. We find the street and stop halfway down at one of the big houses. The front-door lock's broken and we step over the stack of post and pizza flyers, and walk up the stairs.

I do the special knock, then call out. – Cracker. I got you somethink.

The chain is unthreaded and we hear three bolts undone. Top, bottom, middle. The key turns and the door swings open. Even I'm shocked. He's bone thin and his nose is raw. Wild eyes stare at me.

– It's me, Cracker. Gary. Let us in.

– Who's Gary?

– Me. I used to come round. Come on, let me in.

The table's covered in foil, but it ain't ripped into smoking strips. It's wrapped in it. Legs too. So are the chairs and the floor and the walls and windows. The whole room's silver. The bare bulb is on and it's like standing inside a diamond.

He sees us looking around. – It's the only way to get rid of the signals, he says.

I look at Alan whose eyes are twice the size they was when he parked the car. He don't know where to look, what to think. And so he says the only thing that comes to him. – How did the foil stay on the window?

Cracker sticks out his tongue. – I licked it all, man. It sticks on.

– That's a lot of licking, I go. – You must've got a sore tongue.

I wink at Alan. See the corners of his mouth start to lift. – We're looking for Shaz, I say. – When d'you last see her?

He sits down and puts his head in his hands. He groans. – I don't know, man. Leave me alone.

I step forward. Grab his hair and pull his head up, make him look at me. – Where is she?

– Don't do that, Alan says. – You'll hurt him.

I whip round. – He knows where she is.

I grab Cracker's T-shirt and bunch it up in my hand. Pull him up to standing. Push him across to the wall and back him against it, hard. Air comes out of him.

– Now where is she?

Cracker stares at me. – You broke my nose, he says suddenly like he's just realized who I am.

– I'll break it again if I have to.

– Shaz loved me.

I pull one fist back and let it go into his belly, which is thin and soft at the same time.

He grunts. Folds over. Alan pulls me off him, picks up Cracker from the floor. – Leave him alone, he says to me.

– No, don't leave me, Cracker says. – Gary. Don't ever leave me.

And that's when me and Alan touch eyes and we're in this silver room covered in foil and Cracker's doubled over, asking me not to leave when it was me what was hitting him. It's me starts to laugh first. Alan ain't far behind. And once we start we can't stop. And Alan gets it so bad that he lets go of Cracker and he falls to the floor. That makes us worse. And in that minute it's us again. We're brothers.

When I can speak again I ask where Shaz is.

– Anywhere, he says. – She could be anywhere.

– You fucked her up, I go.

He looks at me. Speaks: – I fucked her.

And then Alan can't help his self. He leaps forward, puts his face so close to Cracker's the spit from his shouting smears his skin. – *Shut up.*

And it works. Cracker stops. Shocked. But Alan's even more shocked. His past self is still there within his adult body. However many years he has spent burying it, layering over it, it's still there. He is still who he was.

He bends down next to Cracker and whispers in his ear. I watch him take something from his pocket and slip it into his hand. Cracker looks at it. He beckons Alan back down, whispers.

Alan stands, nods towards the door and we both go.

Outside he leans back against the wall. – What is it? I ask. – Where is she?

He shakes his head, starts to laugh. – Back home. She's moved back home.

The car engine's running and Alan puts his seat belt on. His body shifts as he prepares to put the car into first gear.

– Alan, I go. – I think I wanna stay round here a bit.

He turns off the engine. – Fine. If that's what you want.

– No, I go. – I mean you can go back home.

He turns to look at me and I see in his eyes what he's thinking, that this is the last time he'll see me, cos soon as he drives off I'll be back in the madness, diving down into the dark and littered doorways.

– It's all right, I go. – I'll be fine.

– You sure?

I nod. – I'm sure. And anyway, you can't police me all my life.

– No, of course, he says. He swallows but it ain't just excess spit going down his throat. It's him trying not to argue the case; it's him swallowing his instinct to not let me go.

– Right, he says. – Right.

I open the car door, get my bag out the boot. He's got out too and he holds his hand out to shake mine but when I take it, I pull him towards me and put my arm round him. For a second he don't do nothing, stands stiff, but then he puts his arm round me too.

– You need any money? he asks.

– I got some. Thanks.

– Call me. Anything you want, just call.

And he steps back into his black car with the polished chrome bits and the hoovered carpets, and he
drives off.

And I am on my own. It's just me and my bag and no
one knows where I am. It's all up to me, what I do,
how I carry myself.

It's near dusk. Street lights are on and a light rain's
starting. I breathe through my nose, take in the
smells. The fumes, the city stink. The plane trees have
been pollarded and the bare trunks and branches look
like clenched fists ready to punch.

I put my bag over my shoulder and start to walk.

The sign for the boxing ring is faded but the lights
are on inside. There's the sound of gloves hitting
punchbags. I can feel it in my arms, the coiled muscles
and the thrust. I can smell the blood. Through the
window I see a young boy, shaved head, sat on the
dirty concrete floor. He's lacing up his boots and
thinking of the bout he's gonna have that night. He's
lost in it, got nothing else going on in his head apart
from playing out his punches and his moves. I'm in
his head, I am him. But then he stands and walks off
and I lose sight of him and I go back to being me
again.

I walk away, along the street. I know where I'm
going towards. It's like there ain't nothing I can do
about it. Like my legs is moving independently of me.

The block of flats is still there. I'm surprised to see

nothing's really changed except the paint on the windows is a bit more flaked. I dunno what I thought would've happened but this ain't it. It's like I thought everything else would change the same as I have.

I go through the archway into the courtyard. There's the same rubbish and dead leaves blown into corners. The same scrawl on the walls. I stand there and look up at the windows of the flat. I need to go through the archway, up the stairs. But like my legs moved on their own before, now they won't move even when my head says so.

I need to go, knock on the door, find out if she's there. And if she ain't there, see if they know where she is. I need to do this. I got to look at the truth now.

I tell myself all the things I done in my life, all the things I ain't been scared of. I've walked into people's houses in the black of night and taken their stuff. Dipped into their pockets in the white of day and taken their wallets. I've laid grown men out on the boxing canvas, watched their blood stream. I've put things in my body what I don't even know what they are. I've made my heart race till it's turning over itself and made my stomach bleed. I've watched a child being born.

But this. I can't do this.

Paddy's pub is round the corner. I look through the clear glass between the etched letters, see a bloke at the bar. Elbow bent. Pint in hand. I know how he feels, the warmth inside his head, the blurring and smoking of his mind. I feel the liquid on my tongue. There's only the glass window between us and I could smash it with my elbow.

It's all raining down on me now. Memory's got hold of me, images climbing up into the front of my brain. I know what they are. You know what they are. My teeth are so gritted together you can hardly get air between them.

There's a half-finished pint on the bench outside. I pick it up, hold it. The liquid sways in the glass and I watch the bubbles rise to the top and burst. I can smell it. Feel the solid smell on my tongue.

I'm wet through. My hair stuck to my head, my clothes drenched.

I look at the drink. Swill it round in the glass till every bubble's been released. All I want is to lose myself. Not to think.

It moves towards my mouth. My mouth moves towards it.

But something in my head happens. Click click. I know if I take a sip of this, I ain't gonna see the bottom of the glass. If I take one sip I ain't never gonna see her again. I ain't never gonna see him again.

I hurl the pint at the pavement. The glass smashes and the drink's spilt. I turn and run through the rain, run till I can't.

Chapter Five

Back in my new life I start to look for work and discover an honest shilling ain't hard to find.

The lorry pulls over to pick me up and Trevor shifts to make way. George is driving. It's his lorry, his set-up. There's the tabloid rag on the dashboard, a packet of open biscuits. On the back there's scaffolding tubes, joints, pins, swivels and boards. George puts the indicator on, checks the traffic. Pulls out.

– I heard you'd be useful, George goes to me. – So you better be.

– Trust me, Trevor goes. – He's got experience.

George splutters. – I'd trust the word of a copper rather than you, Trev.

We drive and I'm sat in the cab and the seat is soft from years of arses and all that bullshit chatting. A blonde walks by and George sounds the horn, says what he'd do to her.

– I ain't sure she'd do it to you, Trevor goes.

– She'd do it to me more than she'd do it to you. If she had to choose. Think of the experience I got. I know my way round a woman better than I know my way round the engine of this lorry.

I half listen, half watch the world waking up. Greengrocers and newsagents opening. Early workers at bus stops. Today, I too have a reason to be up, a purpose. My head ain't full of memories and drifting crap, it ain't full of what I ain't put right. I'm in a new world, the cab of a lorry world.

The first job just wants two lifts and before the engine's turned off I'm out the cab and I'm sizing it up. There's an awkward bay we got to get round and a protruding wall. I work it out and start to unload, get the tubes and base plates ready. Trevor falls in, takes my lead. We get it done quick and the bay window's good as gold.

Back in the cab George's got his hand on the key but he don't start the lorry yet. He turns to me.
– What you doing tomorrow?

That weekend I go down the yard and look through the gear. His tubes are cut different lengths and where they're all in together you don't know what ones you're pulling out. So I get them on the ground and sort them into lengths. Then separate the other gear so the swivels is in one bucket, the clips in another. Then I sort the lorry itself, tidy it up, get metal buckets for the different fittings.

By the second week he asks if I'll drive and when I tell him I ain't got a licence he shrugs cos it's no skin off his back. I tell him I'll apply for one, I'll even do the test. So now it's me picks up the lorry at the yard in the morning; it's me what picks George up.

Each night after work I sit by my open door into the garden and eat then have a smoke. I ain't got no

TV and I often sit there thinking while the light goes. One night the fox comes. I watch him climb over the wall and drop down. He stops and sees me. Our eyes meet. Then he creeps along the back wall and is gone. Next night I leave him some food out. And the next. It becomes a habit.

The wind's blowing off the sea, across the clifftop. It's bending the small trees further, hurling leaves up into the air where they're spun around then dropped. It's hitting the side of the lorry and worming its way through the crack in the window. It's making the smoke from my fag go into curled tendrils.

I turn the window handle right round to stop the wind but it don't make no difference. Trevor's out taking down a job and it's just the two of us. George drags the smoke deep into his lungs. Breathes it out into the cab then sighs. – I ain't getting no younger, he goes.

– It'd be weird if you were, I go.

– Spose, yeah.

He looks out the window. – This job, he says, – it ain't forgiving as you get older. My joints is going and I don't wanna get out of bed come the mornings.

– So what you gonna do?

He picks up the address book what's always on the dashboard, the one what runs the company, and he hands it to me.

– What's that for? I go.

– It's yours, he goes. He slaps his chest. – I just ain't got the heart for it no more, Gary.

I look at the address book. Uncertain, not sure what he's saying.

– I don't need nothing for it right now, he goes. – Run the business and just give me some money as and when you got it.

First day it's all mine I call each of his contacts, go and see them. I offer the builders a bundle if they pass me work. Then I go round the builders' yards, tell them I'll give them a bundle if they pass me work. I talk to anyone and everyone, tell them. And then the phone starts to ring.

When I cost the jobs I don't write nothing down. Everything's in my head. First time I have to remember what I quoted, I ain't got a clue what I'd said, so I tell them to pay me what they reckon it was worth. And they pay twice what I'd ask. So when anyone asks how much they owe me, I say I've left the job book at home. Nine out of ten times they pay more than I'd ever have quoted them for. And anyway, there ain't no job book.

The phone rings one evening. I answer.

– Gary? he goes. – You there?

– Who give you this number? I ask.

He laughs. – Nice thing to say to your father. I saw Alan and he told me what you're up to. He says you're all right. He says you turned yourself round.

– Does he?

– He says you gone into business.

– I wouldn't call it that. I got a lorry on HP. I got some blokes what'll work for the day for cash. I got a bit of gear and an address book. If you call that a business then yeah I got one. But I don't call it that. I call it a way to make money what ain't smashing windows and grabbing whatever I can.

There's a silence while he takes in what I said.

– I need money, son, he says.

I start to laugh.

– Don't laugh, he says.

– All right. Keep your hair on if you got any left.

– I got bills to pay, Gary. The women have spent me up.

– Dad, you know I ain't in London.

– Alan told me you'd made a big move. I don't blame you, son. Air's filthy up here, ain't it? And the traffic's bad. Bet it's all right down there. Sea air. Is that a seagull I can hear in the background?

– No, Dad, I go. – It ain't a frigging seagull. So what exactly are you asking for?

– Thought I'd come and pay you a visit, see how you're getting on for myself.

He's one of the last off the train. His hair's receded but still oiled back, each black strand stuck to his scalp. He's got a padded checked shirt on and a pair of jeans, still rolled up over Doc Martens. – I'm gasping, he goes.

– That all you got to say after all them years? I ask.

– I ain't had one for hours.

He pulls out a roll-up from behind his ear and sticks it in his gob. Lights it.

– I still smoke too, I go.

– I only got this one, Gary. Told you, times is tight.

– So if times are that tight, how you get the train?

He stares at me like we never seen each other before. – I never paid for a bleeding ticket, he says. – Only mugs do that.

He chucks his small bag in the cab and we get in. As I pull out the station, he sees a young bird with a pull-along case and high heels. He sucks air in through his wobbly teeth and says, – Christ, look at her.

– Still? I go.

– Still got an engine under the bonnet, Gary.

He settles on the chair in front of the open door into the garden. I take him tea and pull up the other chair next to him.

I light up a fag and he turns, looks at me. I sigh and hand him one.

– Thanks, son.

– So, I go. – What made you get back in touch?

He sips his tea. – How many you put in this?

– Three.

– Can't hardly taste any sugar. Put another one in.

– You do it.

– You're younger than me. I ache if I get up too much.

I take the mug off him, go and stir in another two spoons. Hand it back. He don't say nothing. – You gonna say thanks? I go.

– You been to etiquette school? That what you been doing down here, is it?

I drink my tea and he finishes his. We look out at the garden. The grass is long and the leaves are starting to blow in through the door. It's taking over.

– Alan says you don't do nothing now, says you don't drink no more. I told him not to be soft.

– He's right. I don't do none of it.

– Jesus. You got to be bored.

– You get used to it. You get to live with yourself all the time.

– Sounds like hell.

– Probably would be for you. You might have to think about some things.

– No need for that, he says. He looks around the room. – So you ain't got no beer in here? Nothing to drink?

– Got a bottle of orange squash somewhere.

– It's like being in a bloody church. You become a vicar?

– No I ain't. And anyway, it ain't about what you do. I don't care what you do. It's just about me, about how I wanna live. And I don't want drink in my house.

We sit, silent. Both look out at the garden. – You get any animals out there? he asks.

– Foxes. Birds.

– What kind of birds?

– Ones with wings and beaks, I go. – So how come you seen Alan?

– He come and found me. Said you'd been out looking for Shaz. He told me I ought to get in touch with you.

– So you only contacted me cos Alan told you to.

– It wasn't just that.

– Oh, good, I say.

– I'm getting older, he goes.

– What and you was thinking it'd been too long since you saw me?

He stares at me. – No. Been starting to think about who was gonna look after me.

I daren't say nothing cos I don't trust what words'd come out. I wait then change the subject.

– You seen Sharon?

– She's with your mother.

– I know. I asked if you'd seen her.

– No, but I know what she looks like.

– Is she all right?

He shrugs. Lights a fag, inhales and examines the lit tip of it. – I spec she's alive, he goes, – otherwise your mother would've organized a wake for her cos imagine the booze we'd bring.

That evening I cook for him and we stay sitting by the doors. I ain't turned the light on and the garden's lit by the upstairs flat.

– Why ain't you got a telly? the Old Man asks. – What's wrong with you?

– Don't want that shit cluttering up my head, I go.

– I love a bit of telly. They teach you everything. Cleaning, holiday homes, antiques.

– They don't know nothing about antiques, I go.

– They do. You ought to go on that programme, where you get some money and you got to buy well and sell it. You'd do all right at that. You could nick a few to add to it. You'd win then.

– I ain't going on telly. And I don't nick no more.

– That's what you say but you know you won't keep to it.

– I will, I go.

He laughs. – Yeah, yeah.

– It was you took me nicking first, I go.

– I never. I wouldn't do that.

– You took me to the factory one night, taught me everything. It was when I found the key to the safe.

He's shaking his head. – I never would've took you nicking.

– You said I was to learn that the moon was my enemy.

– Common sense, ain't it? Never nick on a full moon. How old you say you was?

– Young. Junior school. It was when I had the dog.

– We never had a dog.

– We had a dog I found on the wasteland. Birdy it was called.

– I had a cat once.

– This was a dog. It barked. Ate bones and pissed on lamp posts. That's how I know it was a dog, Dad. There were clues, see.

– They teach you to be clever at that place you been to?

– No. They taught me how to know the truth.

– I dunno what you're talking about.

– I know you don't.

He don't say nothing for a long time.

– What you trying to do? Blame me?

– Who else should I blame?

– You was just born like it. Born no good.

– If only, I say, – life was that simple. We're born a certain way and that's that. Our whole life's mapped out.

He turns and looks at me. – What's wrong with you?

– Nothing. Nothing's wrong. I'm just trying to work out some things.

We don't say nothing for a bit. Then he coughs and I know it ain't cos there's something stuck in his throat. It's an excuse cough. A change the direction of the air in the room cough. He stretches his legs, stands, says he's going for a piss. He's gone a bit then when he comes back he sits down. Stares straight ahead.

He speaks. – My dad used to belt me. Said I was no good. Used to sit in the middle of the room with a stick and he'd hit me when I went past.

– You never said that before.

– Ain't I?

– No.

He does an empty laugh. – I got used to bloodstains on the floor. Didn't do me no harm. Plenty more blood where that came from.

I think about a hundred things to say and decide it's best to say nothing.

The light outside's gone and there's no sign of the fox. A few drops of rain fall.

It's him who breaks the silence. – I remember you had a dog now.

He points at his own chest. – He had a bit of white here.

I release the breath I didn't even know I been holding in; it's from such a deep place it's like I've had it in me since the womb.

– That's right, I go.

– He got really old and stiff, he says, – could hardly walk.

My shoulders sink. – He never got old, I say.

– Must've been old when you got him.

– He was a puppy, I go.

He shakes his head. – Nope. He wasn't never a puppy. What happened to him in the end?

I let out another breath.

– Gary, I said what happened to him?

– You got rid of him. You left him by the roadside. Drove off.

– I wouldn't've done that.

281

I look at him. I expect to feel red rage but I don't. Instead I feel tired. I just feel tired of all this.

– No, Dad, you wouldn't, I go.

He nods, satisfied.

And inside me something shifts. It's like there's something moving up, threatening to break out. It's as though now I'm living like this, now my cells are starting to die off, grow again, now I'm being changed and transformed, now I'm heading towards my whole new life, I got no choice but to attend to it.

Chapter Six

Alan's picked us up and we're driving to London. A family get-together, he says. It's important to do it, for us all to be together, he says. I can't bleeding wait.

The Old Man's in the back and has slept all the way. Alan puts the indicator on and comes off at a junction.

– We ain't in London, I go.

– I know. We're calling in at mine on the way.

– You never said nothing.

– If I did, you might have refused to come.

The house is a new build on an estate. Freshly laid turf. New plants with tags on still. And pillars each side of the front door.

– Doric columns, I say.

Alan looks at me.

– My education might not've been the same as yours, I go, – but I did learn some things.

Before we got time to put the key in the lock the door's opened. She puts her hand out. – I'm Davina, she says. – Welcome.

We go into the lounge and have tea and cake and I'm scared of crumbs on the carpet and the room's airless with the closed windows. The wine rack's empty and I know she done it cos I was coming, as if I'd have no control and would leap across the room, drag the bottles out, pull out the corks with my teeth and down them. Daniel and Laura come in, have tea with us. Laura asks me about the beach where I live and I ask her about school. Daniel's looking at me. He waits till I've ate the cake then asks if I'll go upstairs with him cos he's got something he wants me to see.

His room's tidy, the bed made, chair pushed under the desk. There's schoolbooks and a pot of pens and pencils.

– You always keep it like this? I ask.

– I have to, he goes, – or I don't get pocket money.

– Then you're accepting bribery.

He laughs. – Do you think I've sold out?

– No, I go. – You're all right.

– Uncle Gary, he says, and the words hit behind my knees, strong enough to floor me. I should have seen them coming, heard them before he said them, heard them before he even thought them, but I didn't. – I'm glad you come.

I don't know what to say so I nod.

– Why didn't you come before?

– Cos I was an idiot.

He shrugs. – There are a lot of them about.

– I know, I say. – Too many.

He points at a cabinet with glass doors, trophies on three shelves. – You seen these?

– What are they for?

– Swimming, he goes.

– You must be good.

He shrugs. – I've got big feet. Got to do something
with them.

He reaches his hand in to the shelf and pulls out
one of them. He passes it to me and I feel the weight
of it in my hand. Look at it. But it ain't for swimming.
I turn it over, look. It's a pair of laced-up gloves. Fists
clenched. There's a small plaque engraved, the ink in
the letters fading. But I can still read it, still make out
every letter of my name.

It's like the wind's gone out of me, like I can't
breathe. I sit on the side of the bed.

– You okay?

I nod. But I ain't. I really ain't, and you know it.

He takes the trophy out of my hand and puts it
back. He sits on the floor next to me. – I shouldn't
have shown you it, he goes. – Dad told us you've been
struggling.

– Is that what he said?

He shrugs. – I don't know what he said exactly but
we know you were living rough and that.

– He don't know everything about me.

– No one, he says, – knows everything about anyone else.

I laugh inside, think bloody hell there's no one says
it like a kid does. We're silent for a bit then I take a
breath.

– Daniel, I go.

– Yeah.

– Next week it's my son's birthday.

He don't say nothing for a bit. I know he's rattling it round in his head, trying to make sense of it. He shifts, tips his head to the side. – No one said you have a son.

– No one knows.

– Oh.

A long time passes. I can see him thinking thoughts. I can hear his brain cogs whirring. – So I've got a cousin.

– I spose, yeah.

– Where is he?

– I don't know.

He thinks for a bit. – How can you not know where he is?

I stand up and walk to the window. Outside I can see Alan and the Old Man. The Old Man's smoking and I can see a bald spot on the back of his head and I can see where Alan's hair's thinning.

– Uncle Gary?

Sod me, I think, he's got this thing where he's just gonna ask and ask till he's at the bottom of it.

– He was taken away, I say.

– Who by?

– People who do that. If they say you ain't fit to look after your kids.

– Oh. Where is he now?

– I don't know where he is.

– How can you not know?

I shrug, but it don't stop the inquisition and I think

if he ain't a lawyer when he grows up then I dunno what's wrong with the world.

– Have you got any contact with him? he asks.

I shake my head. – No.

Outside the window the Old Man sits down on the bench in the garden. Alan disappears.

– Well, that's shit, Uncle Gary.

– I know, I go. – You're right. It is shit.

Chapter Seven

Right. Where were we? Ah yes. Back where we started in our favourite game of happy families.

We troop in, the three of us: Alan, me, the Old Man. The flat ain't changed none. It's the same wallpaper in the lounge and purple paint on the windows, probably the same fag ends in the fireplace. There's two chairs by the fire and Mum's in one.

– Gary's here, Alan says.

Mum has to put both hands on the arms of the chair to get up. Her hair's grey at the roots and curlier. Her lip colour's bled into the cracks at each side of her mouth. The hairband's long gone. The black trousers are long long gone. – Gary, she goes, and she stares at me and I know she's wondering if she'd have recognized me in the street. – Hello, son.

– Hello, Mum.

– So good you come. I been wanting to see you.

I walk closer to her chair, can smell the drink, the pear drops stink of it. I put my hands on her upper arms, kiss her on the cheek. She backs away, almost falls. – I'm just kissing you, Mum, I go. – I ain't trying to do you damage.

The Old Man sits in the chair opposite. He takes a can out of his bag.

– So how you been, Mum? I ask.

– Been better, been worse, she goes.

The Old Man offers her a can but she looks sly at me, and tells him she don't want nothing. – You shouldn't be drinking with Gary here.

– It's all right, Mum, I go.

Shaz calls through from the kitchen. – Is that Gary?

I go in to see her. She's putting the kettle on, sorting plates. She's wearing a tight vest and skirt and bare feet. I can see she's put some weight on.

– Bloody hell, she goes. – You look a few years older.

I grin. – Thanks. Shame I can't see how you look under all that warpaint.

– Very funny.

– I am funny. And you know it.

– Yeah yeah, she says. – You're just marvellous.

– So you come back to the nest, then, I go.

– Mum's getting older, said she needs help.

– Yeah?

– I do her shopping and that.

– That's good. So you got away from Cracker? Got away from all the madness?

– Yeah. Had enough.

I open the fridge to get out some milk and there's a magnet on the door, hanging by a corner. The Tower of London. I gave it to Mum all them years ago, lifted it from the tourist shop in Piccadilly.

– They say you've become boring, Shaz says.

– Yeah? Well, it's all right cos I ain't gonna preach to you.

289

– Thank God for that.

She puts everything on the tray and I ask her if she needs a hand.

She stares at me. – What the bloody hell's happened? You've become a human being.

– I'm trying, Shaz. I'm trying.

We sit on the sofa, me and Alan and Shaz. The three of us in a row, birds back perched on the edge of the nest. Mum and the Old Man are on their chairs by the fireplace.

– I'm starving, the Old Man says.

Alan hands out the slices of cake.

– Don't he feed you down by the sea? Mum asks.

– He's eaten everything bar the settee, I go.

– Very funny, the Old Man goes. – What he ain't saying is he's got me working all hours, all weathers. It's brutal.

– It's called a job, Dad.

Mum looks over, smiles. – You got a nice place, love?

I nod. Swallow my cake. – It ain't very big. But it's good, yeah.

– By the sea, Alan says.

– About a ten-minute walk.

– He's getting a job doing Punch and Judy next, Shaz says. – Only he don't need no training cos he's been living a Punch and Judy show all his life, ain't that right, Gary?

– That's not very nice, Mum says. She looks at Alan and changes the subject quick. – How are the kids?

– Good, Alan says. – We called in to see them on the way here. They're doing well at school. Carry on like this and they'll be going off to university.

The Old Man flicks his fag end into the fireplace and it lands on top of all the others. – What'd they wanna do that for?

– Better themselves, Alan goes.

– Bloody lose themselves, the crap they teach there.

– What crap? Alan goes. – Go on. What crap is it they teach?

– You know, that crap, the Old Man says.

– Oh, I see, Alan goes. – And you must know cos you're such a bloody expert on university education, ain't you?

– That shit they talk.

– Oh, shit, is it? Alan goes. – And there's me thinking the reason I can always tell whether someone at work's been to university or not is cos they talk sense. They can reason, can keep to a logical line of thinking. But I'm wrong, aren't I? The reason I know they've gone to university is cos when they open their mouths, shit pours out.

Alan stands up, waves the teapot at the Old Man and tea slops out on Shaz's skirt.

– Oi. Watch it, she shouts out.

– Truth is, Alan goes, – I always wish I'd gone to university. I'd give anything to go.

– Frigging go then, the Old Man says. – And stop bleating about it.

– And how am I gonna do that? Alan goes. – I got a job, mortgage, two kids to educate. I got to pay for them to go.

– Well, it's your stupid fault to buy into the system, the Old Man goes. – I never had them problems.

– Only cos you're a feckless wanker who didn't care what his kids did.

I see the Old Man start to rise from his chair.

I stand up before he does. I stand up in front of all of them. – That's enough, I go. – It's the first time we all been together in years so sit down the pair of you. Dad, you drink your tea and eat that lovely cake. Alan, just leave it.

The Old Man glares at Alan. Alan puts the teapot back down, takes a deep breath and sits. The Old Man sits.

– Good, I say. – Thank you.

I move towards the door.

– Where you going? Mum says.

– He's going to find his cassock, Shaz goes. – He's preparing the next sermon.

I touch her on the shoulder. – Very funny. I'm just going for a piss. All right?

– You go, love, Mum says.

I walk out the room, go down the hallway. The toilet's on the left but I ain't going there. I put my hand on the front-door handle, open it as quiet as if I was coming in on a moonless night, and I leave.

Chapter Eight

I don't think about it. Don't let myself change my mind. I go straight there. King's Cross. I stand in front of the block. My heart's knocking as loud as any knuckle on any door. I tell myself: Man up, son. Just get it over with then we can all go home.

I go through the archway, stand in the courtyard. I look up at the sky, at the windows. I go to the stairway, climb up past the rubbish, past the graffiti. I get to the right floor, walk along the hallway and stop at the door. I lift my hand to ring the bell then drop it. I lift it again. Drop it again. I walk two steps away. Two steps back. I tell myself: Time's passed. I tell myself: It'll be a red herring, a goose chase. She ain't gonna live there and he ain't gonna live there and all this effort, all this emotion'll be a waste of time.

I lift my hand to press the bell and that moment I hear the lock being undone, a bolt sliding back.

I step back, try to press myself into the wall. The door opens.

She comes out backwards. Blue coat. Beret on her head, the same green as her hair used to be. She reverses and I see she's pulling the handles of a pushchair. She shuts the door and double locks it. Speaks to what's in the pushchair. – All right, we're going now.

For a second I think it's him. She's got him in the pushchair and he's safe and he's with her. But even as I think it, I know it can't be. Unless there's a parallel world where time's stopped and he ain't grown up, where he's waited, just born, for me to grow up.

She turns to go along the hallway and I step forward. My mouth's dry so I touch her shoulder. She jumps. Hand to her throat. I see it in her eyes: a strange bloke lurking. A dark corridor.

– It's all right, I go.

And that's when she realizes who I am. – Gary?

– I never meant to scare you, I go. – I'm sorry, Mandy.

She bends down, adjusts the blanket in the pushchair. Looks back up. Looks at me. – What do you want?

I shrug. – I come to find you.

– I can see that.

I point at the pushchair. – You going somewhere? Can we go and talk?

She looks at me. – I don't know what there is to say.

When I get back with the tray of tea and cake, she's sat at the outdoor table under the trees, the baby on her lap. She looks up and sees me looking at her and our eyes meet. She looks away quickly. I put the tray on the table, sit down. She still don't look at me.

Neither of us knows how to begin and we're trapped, the two of us under the trees with the traffic in the distance and the birds who are gathering for the crumbs. The tension between us, the air between us, is solid. We could carve it.

– I haven't got long, she says.

– I know. You said.

She bends down, gets a bottle out of her bag, gives it to the baby.

I open my mouth and the words are blurted out. – You ain't got him, have you?

She looks at me. Her eyes are straight, unflinching. – No. No, Gary, I ain't got him.

I nod. Look down at the grass.

– Is that what you thought? That you'd turn up and he'd be here and it'd all be all right? Did you think you could piss off like that and I'd be able to get him back on my own?

I look up, meet her eyes. – I dunno what I thought.

– Well maybe you should have thought about something before you came blundering back into our lives. It's bloody obvious I ain't got him. Bloody obvious he was taken away. They were never gonna let me have him cos when you went, what you reckon happened to me? You reckon I turned into some perfect housewife?

And then she suddenly takes the bottle from the baby's mouth, half stands, goes to put her in the pushchair. – I don't know why you came to see us, she says. – I don't know why I agreed to come here.

– Please don't go, I say.

– It's not good to be this angry. I don't wanna be.

– Then talk to me. Tell me.

– I don't think I've got anything to say.

– Please. Sit. Please.

I see her hesitate. – Just for a bit, I say, – and if you're still angry, then go.

She thinks, nods, sits back down. I pour her some tea and pass it over. I watch her as she looks at the baby, as she wipes its mouth.

– So where is he? I ask.

She sighs. – They don't tell you. They let me write him a letter once a year. Letter-box contact they call it. I call it torture. I send it off but I don't know where I'm sending it to. I don't know where he is. I don't know if he's ever gonna read them.

– No one got in touch with me.

She splutters out an empty laugh. – You were doing your best not to be around. You weren't on the birth certificate anyway. And even if you was, what you reckon would've happened? You'd have gone oh yeah I need to sort all that out, need to find out how to be a father? Well, you're too late. We were both too late.

And then I hear the crack of a leaf above our heads as the weight of it pulls it away from the stem. It falls down and lands on her shoulder. Another drifts down and rests in the sugar bowl. They're loud in my head, crashing.

– I am sorry, I say.

She shrugs. – You got a lot to say sorry for.

– I know I have.

She looks at me. Direct. – Sorry means nothing. It changes nothing. You need to think before you do something then you don't have to go round saying sorry.

– You think I ain't realized that?

She continues to look at me. Then nods and I can see her change as she realizes I have. It's like there's nowhere for the anger to go and it hisses out.

– At least I'm here, I go.

She nods. – I spose, yeah.

– And I'm clean now. You can see that, can't you?

She looks, again.

– Yeah, I can, actually.

And while we're still looking at each other, I see how her face has filled out, and I realize I ain't never seen her like this, the right weight, clear skin. Looking like she was made to look.

– I always thought, she says, – that you'd come and find me one day. That is if you wasn't dead.

– Did you ever check to see if I was?

She shakes her head. – I decided I'd know if anything happened.

– How?

She shrugs. – Sounds bloody stupid, don't it? I just thought with everything . . .

She tails off, looks down at her baby. I know what she's thinking. I hear the thoughts in her head even though I don't want to. With everything that joins us together. With everything that happened.

The baby cries and pushes the bottle out. She holds her up, over her shoulder.

– You look like you done that for ever, I go.

– Do I?

– Yeah.

– They said I was a natural mother.

And with those words it's real, it's out in the open. We sit a while. She puts the baby in the pushchair, tucks her in.

– I'm not who I was then, I say.

She nods. Thinks a moment. – No. I know. I mean I can see.

– Neither of us is.

– No.

Mandy checks the baby's asleep, as though she could hear what we're saying. When she speaks she looks out at the park ahead of her. She's careful not to look at me.

– When I was pregnant this time they said if I wasn't clean they'd take her away as well. They told me that. I had to be the cleanest person possible. They did blood tests on me, came to see me all the time. They still come and see me. Any time, whatever I'm doing, they can come round. But they know she's all right. They say I done a good job.

– Looks like you have.

But she hardly hears me. – If they'd taken her away, she says, – I wouldn't have survived.

And I know it's true. She puts her head in her hands. Waits. Gathers herself. When she can speak she looks at the grass.

– I thought when I had her it would feel better, that she'd fill the hole the other left.

298

The other. Him. The boy.

She stops. Her voice catches. She waits. Continues.

– But it made it worse cos now I got her, I know what it is we done, Gary. I know what we done.

We sit for a while.

She looks down at the grass. I look at the tree. We're rescued by a bird what comes down and lands on our table. Its feathers are black and speckled. It tips its head this way, that. I break a crumb off the cake and we watch it feed.

– What is it you want, Gary?

I look at her. – I don't know if I want anything.

– Everyone always does. That's what you used to say, ain't it? Everyone wants something.

She takes off her beret. Short red hair. Her skin is clear and my breath's caught in my throat.

– I never forgot you, I say.

Our eyes look at each other. The world's reduced.

– I never forgot you, I say again.

Her voice is quiet. – I know what you said, she says.

I've said too much. She takes a sip of tea. I pick up a crumb of the cake and eat it. Pick up another. Throw it down for the birds.

They scramble for it. Wings flap. Beaks peck.

– I was half-made when we met, she says.

– I don't reckon we're ever finished, I say, – we're never fully made. We just run out of time.

She nods. – Strange this, she goes. – Having this conversation. Us. I mean like this. Not like we were.

– What did we talk about then?

She smiles. Small tight smile. – Did we talk? I don't remember.

– We tried.

She shakes her head. At the stupidity of us. The folly of us.

She looks back at the baby as if to check back into her real world. This daily world of looking after another human being. And before I know it, some words fall out of my mouth.

– You ain't told me who her dad is.

She looks up at me, smiles. – That's the most transparent thing you ever said.

I feel myself go red and on to the back foot. – No, I go. – I was just asking who her dad was.

– I'm not stupid, she says. – I know why you're asking. He left before she was born. Bit of a pattern there, isn't it? When I found out I was pregnant, I said that's it, I'll never open my legs again. The door's shut now.

– Door? I go.

– Yeah. Door. You know what I mean.

I can't stop myself smiling.

– It ain't funny, Gary.

I stop. Lean forward. I cross into her world. I take her hands in mine, feel the cool skin. – I know that, I say. – None of it's funny. Don't ever think I reckon any of it's funny cos I don't. But what choice have we got? We can't stop. We got to carry on.

She don't take her hands away. She lets them stay in mine. She looks down at the ground. Her hair falls over the side of her face.

– Look at me, I go.

She looks up. Eye to eye.

– There's something I got to say, I go. – This ain't over yet. You know when he's eighteen, on his birthday, he'll find out who we are. He'll be able to come and find us.

– What if he doesn't?

I shake my head. – He'll come. He's ours, ain't he? He's got us in him. Think about it. He'll have some of us, what we are. He'll be brought up by other people but however much you try and shape someone, they still got themselves inside.

She bites her bottom lip.

– And when he comes we got to have something to show him. We got to prove we ain't the same people as we were back then.

She listens.

– We got to show we know what we did but we put it right.

– But I'll have missed everything, all his growing up, everything. I can't put that right.

– If you see it that way, I go, – you'll go mad.

– I have been going mad.

– Then you got to think of it differently. You got to realize if we hadn't met, he wouldn't exist.

She nods, nods again. And holds that small crumb of comfort in her mind.

Our hands are still touching. We're looking at each other. I know I could lose myself again. We could lose our selves, but I ain't gonna let that happen. We know where that leads, don't we? And I ain't going back there. I ain't.

– Why did we do it? she asks. – Why did we let that happen?

I look at the leaves what are falling on to the table. I shrug. – Cos some people mess up. Some people ain't been showed how to do things.

She nods. I can hear her thinking, can hear her listening.

– The thing we have to understand, Mandy, I say, – is that we're all born naked to damaged people.

We sit there together for a while, the two of us. Time carries on passing and leaves fall.

It gets cold and Mandy tucks the baby in. Stands. I stand up too.

When we're ready, when we've got everything, we look at each other, nod, then walk off through the trees, out into the open.

And behind us, even though we don't see it, the leaves carry on falling. The sun slips down. The moon rises, and the birds come down out the trees. They land on the table among the plates and cups and they clear up every crumb.

The End

be pushing on or gonna let that happen. We know
where it's not...well it is. And I ain't going back there
I said.

Why me? is it she asks. – Why did we let it
happen

You know the leaves what are falling on to the table

Ladies and Gentlemen, it's time to roll up roll up to
the last bit of the Gary show. But there's no hurry
now. Take your time. Stroll gently by, at your ease.
Cos once you're done with this little bit, we're gonna
be parting company and you're gonna have to say
goodbye to me. If you've stuck it this far, if you've
lived through all this with me, you might find I've
grown on you. In fact, you might even find when
you've read the last page you miss me.

Now you know a lot about me cos you been reading my *memoir*, in fact you know shitloads, like I said
you would. But in all that there's this one thing you
really know (and if you don't know it, it's cos you
ain't been paying attention and you need your nut
nutting), and it's this: I know everything. And because
I'm a person what knows everything, I know what
you think. And I know what you want.

It goes like this: You want me to tell you what happened next. You wanna know: Did you get back with
Mandy? Did it last? Did your son get in touch? Did
you meet him?

Now the thing is, I could just leave you in this state
and not tell you. I could. I could leave all them stitches
dropped, all that hanging in the air.

I could leave you under them trees in the park without even a crumb.

But I ain't that kind of person, am I?

At the beginning of the *me*moir I told you about him getting in my lorry. About him, my son (still ain't easy to use that word) on his eighteenth. And you've worked out, ain't you, that can't have happened.

There's a reason I lied. The thing is, it's all in the story, ain't it? You got to tell the story people'll believe, the one they wanna hear. And the thing is, while I'm telling the story, I'm listening to it too. I wanna believe it's true as well.

So to find out what *did* happen and to answer all your questions, we got to move time along quick through the years of the dull miracles, the years of walking dogs, laying tables, paying for shopping, all in England-by-the-sea. We got to move forward and see me in my flat on the clifftop where if I leave the windows open I can hear the sea from every room.

Let's give you the scene:

The flat's bigger than the one in Bedsit Land. It's got three bedrooms. A lounge-diner. It's got a three-piece suite, a table and chairs, a full fridge, a telly and a bed with a feather-soft mattress and too many pillows.

It's got something else in it too.

It's early morning and the light hits my face, wakes me before the alarm. I turn on to my side and she's there, her back turned to me, her head on the pillow. And though I been waking up beside her for all these years, I don't never take it for granted. The light's shining on the freckles on her shoulder. Her body's thickened up a bit, and she worries about that, worries that I ain't gonna feel the same about her. But she ain't changed how she smells nor how she feels. She ain't changed who she is, and I ain't changed nothing about the way I feel about her. I reach my hand out under the covers, put it round her waist.

– I'm not asleep, Mandy goes. – I've not slept all night.

– I know, I go. – Cos I woke up round three and you wasn't in the bed.

She shifts on to her back, looks up at the ceiling. My hand's rested on her belly. – I got up, she says, – and made some tea. I drank it in the lounge, never even put the light on.

– You should've woke me.

– I didn't like to. You was snoring.

– I don't snore.

– That's what everyone says, she goes. She pushes her hair off her face, rubs her eyes. – Gary?

– What?

– What's he gonna be like?

– We don't know till we see him.

– What if we don't like him?

– It ain't about liking him or not.

– What if he's all educated? What if he speaks posh? What if he's completely different from us?

– We'll deal with it.

She thinks for a minute. – Okay. What'd you do if he was taller than you?

– Look up to him.

– If he was better looking than you?

– That'd be impossible.

– All right. What if he was ugly?

I start to laugh.

– It ain't funny. He might be.

– It bloody is funny, I go. – Is that what kept you up all night? Anyway, you seen a photo of him.

– It wasn't clear. You said that.

– Well, he ain't ever gonna be ugly if he's anything to do with you.

She turns her head to the side, eyeballs me. – Flattery ain't gonna get you nowhere.

– It never does, Mand, and it never did. You have to trust. It'll be all right.

– I'm scared.

– Course you are.

And we stay there for a bit. What I wanna say is so am I. I'm so bleeding scared I don't want the day to happen. I don't wanna go.

I go into the kitchen and get breakfast ready. I can hear Mandy in the bedrooms, can hear her telling them where the clean clothes are, checking they got what they need. And then they all come in the room. Mandy and the two girls. They sit down to eat the food I made for them and I look at them. Mandy's sat in the middle. To her left is the older girl, the taller girl, who was once the baby in the cafe in the park. She's dressed in her secondary school uniform, her white shirt clean, freshly ironed. And the other one, three years younger, our baby, is in a blue sweatshirt. She's got a clean face, Mand's freckles, gappy teeth. And every morning I look at them and I think: We done it, Mand, we done it.

We drop them at their schools and take the dog down the beach, chuck the ball a few times for him. I ring the lads, check they know what they're doing and that they got the right stock on the lorry. Then Mandy and I look at each other. We nod. It's time to go.

We get in the car and I drive. We go a fair way without wanting to say nothing but even if we did have something to say we couldn't cos our tongues is stuck to the roof of our mouths.

I put the radio on but she only leaves it a couple of minutes then turns it off again. She opens the glove pocket, pulls out brown leather gloves. She holds them up. – Who d'you borrow this car off?

I shrug. – One of the lads bought it off of someone. He's gonna sell it.

– Is it clean?

– Looks clean enough.

She stares at me. – You know what I mean. Is it nicked?

– Probably, I go. – But, look, it's got a tax disc. That's somethink legal, ain't it?

She shakes her head. – Gary.

– I know, I know, I go. – But it's the last one, all right?

We're in the car park and I light up a fag, suck smoke down into every nook and cranny of the lungs.

– I've changed my mind, she goes. – I don't want to see him.

– Well change it back cos you got no choice.

I get out the car and slam the door shut then lock it. I'm about to walk away when I hear a banging and I look back, see her face shouting at me behind the glass and realize I've gone and locked her in. I unlock the door, and I'm laughing. She opens the door. – It ain't funny.

But it bloody is and I can't stop. And she tries not to laugh but she starts and we can't stop and we know it's nerves but we don't care.

We find the cafe and we're halfway through the door to go in when she stops. I walk into the back of her. She's rigid and can't move; I put my arm round her and coax her in. We're both looking around the room, seeing if we can see him. There's one old man sat in the window reading a paper. Two women chatting at a table. That's it.

I take her hand in mine and we go and sit down. She's sat where she can see the front door. I'm sat opposite her. We order coffee and wait.

Time stretches and each minute feels like ten. She

watches every person passing. The windows are big and she's got a good view.

And then the waitress comes over and is standing there taking our order and before we know it there's this confusion cos while we been talking to her someone's come in and there's a young man standing behind her and time's gone from being slowed down to being speeded up and he's ordered something and he's somehow sat with us and we ain't even hugged him nor had a big emotional reunion moment. If this was a film Mum was watching she'd be let down, she'd say she was cheated.

He's sat next to Mandy and he looks first at her, then turns and looks at me. First thing he does is laugh and then we all do and we all know why.

He's skinny, muscular, got near-black hair cropped short. He's got pale, freckled skin. And the thing is, he's got these eyes. They sparkle and there's creases round them when he smiles, and there'd be no mistaking him wherever he was in the world cos they're the exact colour of the ink on a freshly printed fiver.

– Well, he goes, – we don't need a DNA test.

And we all sit there a bit, the three of us. We're just looking.

– You got here all right then? Mandy says.

– It's bloody obvious he did, I go.

He smiles. – So, he goes. – Let's get this straight, you two are still together?

– It ain't straightforward, Mandy goes.

– Long story, I go.

– We got back together, Mandy goes.

– I didn't expect that, he says. – Thought I'd have to find you both separately.

– We thought we'd save you the work, I say. He grins.

Mandy starts to ask a question. – Where were you . . .

– Brought up? he says.

She nods, relieved.

– Small town outside London. Kent.

– Were they?

But though she can't even say a complete sentence, he knows what she's saying.

– They were nice people.

He corrects his self. – They *are* nice people. Shame I broke their hearts.

– Were you bad? Mandy asks.

– You don't have to ask, I go. – You can see what he's like from looking.

– You can? he asks.

I look at him sat there. His whole body's moving with energy. He's fiddling with the sugar packets in the bowl. He's tapping his legs.

– Yeah, I go. – I can.

He looks at me. – Like you?

– Like me.

He nods to his self. – When I told them I was coming today, he says, – you know what they said?

Mandy takes in a breath loud enough for the whole cafe to hear. – You told them you were coming?

He nods. – I don't keep secrets. I don't do that.

– What they say? I ask.

– They said, maybe now you can find out who you are and where you come from. Cos the thing is, I ain't from them. They know it and I know it.

– Tell me more about them, Mandy goes.

– They're good people. You know, good. Sent me to a little school. Gave me everything. But when I was out at nights and running around like the little tearaway shit I am, they just scratched their heads till they had bald spots.

As they talk, I try not to listen cos I don't really wanna know about them. Far as I'm concerned they've had him, now he's ours again. I mean I know he ain't. I ain't stupid. I know what this is, how complicated it all is. But the animal inside me knows that right now he's here with me and I don't wanna know about anything else.

And so I do this thing. I sit back in my chair.

I sit back and watch them and as I watch I think and it's like something starts to join up. Something starts to make sense. All that time I reckoned the family was the cage what I was brought up in, the family shaped every bloody bit of me. But you know, in this moment, I realize it really ain't that simple. It ain't a Gary black-and-white thing. It's grey. Cos them parents, they had their dreams of what they could make him like, they wanted him brought up in a gilded cage. But look what they got and look what he's like. Look at him.

I'm sat there watching and thinking all this and they're still talking and I realize we're gonna be here hours. They're gonna go over the stories, his, theirs, ours, hers, mine. We're gonna get our coffees, let them go cold. We're gonna order more.

And anyway, I know already this ain't the end of it. This ain't the only meeting.

Cos this ain't the ending. This is the beginning and cos I know everything, I can see it all now.

This'll all go well today. It'll go to our heads. But there'll be other times, and some of them'll be dark, angry times. Sometimes we'll see him a lot, sometimes not. We'll have to let him come and go when he needs. He'll meet the girls. It'll be bloody brilliant and bloody horrendous. There'll be days when the shit hits the fan and drips down the walls. There'll be days when I wanna hug him so hard I could push the air out his lungs, kill him with love. But whatever happens for now, in this moment, he's here with us.

I sit back in my chair and let it all unfold in front of me. I watch him talk to her. And I watch her looking at him. The look on her face, just seeing him. She looks at every bit of him. His hair, eyes, nose, mouth. She can't fill her eyes enough.

And then he turns to look at me and he sees me watching and he knows what I'm thinking cos he just does and I know he does, and then he smiles and in that second when he smiles at me it's like I've met my self. It's like I'm less lonely than I ever been.

And then I feel my heart swell. My eyes fill with water.

I'm a soft fucker.

And the thing is, all I dreamed of is true: he's a chip off the old block. An apple from the same tree. A fish what swims the same sea. A fox from the same lair. A bird with the same feathers. A pea from the same pod. He's a son from the father.